Charlie Williams is the author of *Deadfolk, Fags and Lager* and *King of the Road*. He lives in Worcester with his wife and children. Find out more at charliewilliams.net.

Deadfolk

'Charlie Williams has come up trumps...the more politically correct among you can read this as social comment, the rest can just enjoy the ride' *Guardian*

'Cross James Ellroy's unblinking eye for vicious gangland enforcement with Bill James's gut-feeling for Britain's meaner streets and you would end up in a trashcan alley somewhere near Mangel...I can't wait for the next instalment' *Western Daily Press*

'Carnage, chaos and a chainsaw called Susan add to his remarkable debut, which marks the appearance of a totally new voice in British fiction' *Buzz*

Fags and Lager

'To create a world with a genuinely dark and disturbing heart is tricky enough; to do this and be funny at the same time is nigh on impossible, but Charlie Williams pulls it off. *Deadfolk* was a fantastic debut and *Fags and Lager* is even better. Royston Blake is a truly original anti-hero, and reading this latest misadventure is like being smashed in the funny bone by a lump hammer' Mark Billingham

Charlie Williams

STAIRWAY
TO
HELL

A complete catalogue record for this book can be
obtained from the British Library on request

The right of Charlie Williams to be identified as the author
of this work has been asserted by him in accordance with
the Copyright, Designs and Patents Act 1988

First published in 2009 by Serpent's Tail,
an imprint of Profile Books Ltd
3A Exmouth House
Pine Street
London EC1R 0JH

website: www.serpentstail.com

ISBN 978 1 84668 689 4

Designed and typeset by folio at Neuadd Bwll, Llanwrtyd Wells

Printed in the UK by CPI Bookmarque, Croydon, CR0 4TD

10 9 8 7 6 5 4 3 2 1

The paper this book is printed on is certified by the © 1996 Forest
Stewardship Council A.C. (FSC). It is ancient-forest friendly.
The printer holds FSC chain of custody TT-COC-002227

Mixed Sources
Product group from well-managed
forests and other controlled sources
www.fsc.org Cert no. TT-COC-002227
© 1996 Forest Stewardship Council

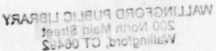

LOCAL MAN WINS PUB IDOL AGAIN

Warehouseman Richard Sutton has won the Pub Idol singing contest for the second year running. Held at The Tap on Frank Street, the talent show saw twenty-three contestants vying for the top prize this year, which was a trophy, a cheque for fifty pounds and some free drink. Sutton clinched the prize with his rendition of 'Silver Lady' by David Soul, beating Marjory Flare's performance of 'China In Your Hand' and Jim Ballock's 'I Want To Sex You Up' into second and third place respectively.

Clutching his trophy, a jubilant Sutton revealed that he had decided to turn professional as a singer. 'To be honest, I've had offers,' he said. 'I like being a man of the people and all that but it's time to put the music first. My fans understand that, and they'll start seeing results straight away. As a full-time singer I'll be able to sing better, sleep properly and get in touch with my song-writing side. And I'm getting stuck into it straight away. I'm recording my first album next week, and the week after I'll be starting as the resident act at the Blue Cairo in Burgmount Street, Warchester. I'll be there Tuesdays, Wednesdays and Sundays.'

1.

I saw the flies when I got within ten feet of him. There had been a lot of them around town in the past couple of days but Martin was surrounded by them. Not close to him, though. None of them were landing on his skin and he had no need to swat them away. They weren't going past him into the Blue Cairo either. His job description required him to keep out undesirable or banned human beings only, but here he seemed to be extending that to the insect world. Which was fine, because I hated flies.

There's nothing worse than one buzzing around your head when you're up on stage, putting on a performance.

I noticed a stranger stood at the bar when I went inside. I always come in the front door at the Cairo, like I do at every other venue. This lets you know what kind of a crowd there is, and also lets the punters see you, which is important. If you hang around a bit and have a drink first, it gives them a chance to come up to you see that you're actually quite a normal person as well as a great performer. People see you chatting with the punters and you become known as a man of the people, which is a good way of building a following.

If you want tips on how to become a successful performer, stick with me.

I'm full of them.

So there was a man by the bar, a stranger, and he had ginger hair. Either it was ginger or the light above the bar was making it look that way, which was just as bad. Hair aside, you could see that he was the ginger type: pale skin and freckles and a chippy look about him, like he knew that people hated him and he liked it no more than he understood it.

He was giving me another type of look as well, one that said he had a problem with me in particular. I was surprised at that. People tend to like me, not have a problem with me. I'm an entertainer, cheering them up and putting some glamour into their dull lives. The only person with a right to have a problem with me, as I saw it, was a rival singer. Someone jealous of my talent and success. And there was no way this gingernut was a singer. Not one in the same league as me, anyway. For a start, no one would let him near a stage with a moustache like that. If there was a polite way of spilling the beans to a man about his moustache, without others thinking bad of you, I'd have spilled them for him right there. Because it really was like that. But I just let my own tash do the talking, making sure he got a good look at it as I went past him towards Delores.

I liked Delores. She always mixed my drink just right and never made any stupid comments about it. Most people don't appreciate sophistication when they see it and, being humans, are liable to mock that which they do not understand, because it scares them. But Delores knew the deal. She knew what I was about, and that I was the real thing and not just a poseur.

So I sipped the Tequila Sunrise and chatted with her for a while. The other good thing about Delores was that you didn't have to try very hard with her, because she just talked shit most of the time. All you had to do was talk shit back to her, or just nod, and you could concentrate on preparing mentally for the performance ahead. But this time it was different, because she said something of interest.

'You should go on that *X Factor*.'

'What's that?'

'You know, that thing on telly.'

'I ain't got a telly. I don't have time for telly, Del.'

'Course you got a telly. Shell watches telly.'

'Yeah, but *I* don't. And it's her telly, not mine. I can't stop her wasting her life watching *Coronation Street*.'

'She watches *The X Factor*.'

'How do you know?'

'We were talking about it when I spoke to her in town the other day. She said she's told you to apply for it, but that you won't.'

'Too fuckin' right I won't.'

'Why not, though? It could be the break you need.'

'I don't need that kind of break. I mean, do you seriously think I'm the sort of person who goes on that shit? I mean, for fuck's sake.'

'It ain't like that. You get some really good ones on it. Last week there was this one doing Madonna, and he was really good.'

'A bloke doing Madonna? That's quite interesting.'

'Yeah. I thought he was really brave. And no one laughed either.'

'What song did he do?'

'I dunno, but it was about a cake.'

'A Madonna song about a cake?'

'Yeah. No, a pie. Yeah.'

'Oh yeah? Do you know what sort of pie?'

'I think it was an apple pie.'

'Right. Sure it wasn't an American pie?'

'Oh yeah, that's it.'

When I said that Del had something of interest to say, none of this was it. I haven't got to it yet. I just wanted you to see the kind of sharp mind I was contending with here. And why I almost didn't catch the full import of her next bit, which went:

'Someone's come to watch you tonight.'

'Oh yeah?' I said, not getting the full import. 'I got news for you, Del: every time I sing here, people come to watch and listen. Not just someone, but *people*. That's the plural of someone. Look around you: they've all come to see me.'

'No but I mean someone in particular. A man. There was two of them but I only spoke to the older one. He was a charming man, I must say.'

I took a sip through the straw and asked her to point him out.

'I can't see him, but he was here just now. He bought a bottle of wine for his table. Not cheap wine. Do you know what he said, Rik?'

'No.'

'You'll never guess.'

'That's right.'

'All right…he said that I could be a supermodel.'

'Oh, right. Did he say anything about me?'

'He did, but first he said I could be a supermodel, and—'

'Who is he?'

'I dunno his name. He said to keep it quiet in case Stan finds out, but he's on the scout.'

'On the scout? Where's he from?'

'I don't think he said, Rik. But I'm sure he mentioned Burninghouse.'

Keep it calm, Rik.

'But Del,' I said, checking myself in the mirror behind her, 'what were his precise words? I mean, I need to know where he's coming from. So I can tailor my act, like.'

'He's coming from Burninghouse, Rik.'

'No, I mean…Look, what exactly is he after? Balladeer? Soul man? Bit of a swing specialist? That type of thing.'

'I'm sure he wants a singer, Rik.'

I drank some of the cocktail, almost biting a chunk of glass off.

'His words, please. Give me his words.'

'I can't remember, Rik. All I know is he said…'

This is where she stopped and looked at the ceiling, pulling on her lower lip. I'd be happy to stand there for a while watching this, but we were talking shop and I don't fuck about when it comes to shop, so:

'Del!'

'All right! I was just trying to get the words straight. He said a lot of other things as well, you see, about—'

'Yeah, all right, just tell me the stuff about me.'

'He said he had a slot to fill, and he'd heard about you and wondered if you'd be the man to fill it.'

'Slot to fill?'

'Yeah. I remember that because he then said that I looked like I had a slot to fill as well, and he knew a man who could fill that as well.'

'I see,' I said, getting started on the business end of the beverage. There was something wrong with it this time, perhaps cheap orange, but I wasn't about to tell Delores that, her being the bringer of such good tidings. I didn't thank her either. Or pay her. I just walked off to my changing room. On the way I saw Ted Regis by the fag machine so I went over and had a word.

'I know,' he said, puffing on a cigar and waggling his bifocals at me. It was only a small cigar but a cigar nonetheless. Ted never smoked cigars, and I did want to ask him about that, but I had more pressing concerns. Most of them ensuing from what he said next:

'It's all down to me.'

'What is?'

'What you're about to ask about. The scout, come here to watch you and assess your viability.'

'Viability for what? Come on, Ted, stop fuckin' about.'

I do admit that I was fighting a smile.

I could smell the big time.

Ted took a deep puff on his cigar, no doubt thinking for a moment that it was one of his usual Silk Cuts. And he did well to hold back the coughing fit, letting the smoke out slow while salt water welled in his eyes.

'The Miramar,' he spat out finally.

2.

I was taking a sip of the Sunrise just then and snorted some of it out of my nose. I placed it on top of the fag machine, slopping a bit over the edge, and coughed long and hard. Ted took the opportunity to do some of his own long and hard coughing, still suffering from the cigar/fag mix-up.

'The fuckin' Miramar?' I wheezed after a while.

'Yeah...I told you I was settin' up a couple of things. One big thing and one little thing. I think you'll agree, Rik, that this thing here is quite a thing.'

He wasn't wrong there. The Miramar, as you probably know, is one of the top venues in Burninghouse. *The* top venue in that town, depending on who you listen to. The other thing about the Miramar was that it was a chain. You get an act going at one Miramar, you can take it elsewhere. You can work it up and down the country, Miramar to Miramar, building up your following and getting famous. Here at the Blue Cairo I was only getting local support. And I wasn't even getting much of that, the Blue Cairo being a bit shit.

'It's just a scout, though, right? It ain't a done deal.'

'It's as good as a done deal, Rik. I spoke to him on the blower yesterday and the groundwork is done. They know what you are, Rik. They've heard your tape and I've worked my salesmanship on him. This is it, the next rung of the ladder. And it's an important rung, Rik. A bloody important rung.'

'Ted, I…I could kiss you! I could give you a kiss right now. On the—'

'There's just one thing,' he said, putting his hand up. He wasn't looking at me now, which didn't bode well for this one thing. 'A little caveat, if you will. Not a major one, though, and I think you'll have no trouble—'

'What?'

'All right, well, the scout from the Miramar is here today because he's got an opening. They've lost an act, see, and you're gonna be replacing him. It's a perfect opening for you, Rik, cos he was a very similar singer to you in many ways. Same vocal range, give or take a few notes top and bottom. And he had great power, just like yourself.'

'What was his name?'

'Hmm, that's a tricky one, Rik. Although I do believe it was Phil Bottomley.'

'Phil Bottomley? Never heard of him. He can't have been that good.'

'Ah, but he went under a stage name, Rik. Like yourself.'

'I don't use a stage name. I use my birth name, Ted. You know that.'

'Yeah, well, that ain't entirely—'

'I'm talking about Phil Bottomley here. What was his stage name?'

'Well, that's just it, Rik. That's where the caveat comes in.'

'You mean I've got to pretend to be him?'

'Heh heh, not at all, Rik. No one would dream of—'

'Just tell me his stage name.'

Ted looked left and right, then leaned in, whispering 'Raljex.'

'Raljex?'

'Yeah. Raljex, the Singing Cyborg, sent back through time to croon us a selection of hits from the year 2049, or summat. Only these hits from 2049, they're all Frank Sinatra numbers, and Dean Martin and that. Plus a few modern ones for the kids, like Ray Shanks, Zak Bremner, Al Guppy...that kind of affair.'

'A novelty act? Are you shitting me, Ted?'

'Ah, but Raljex weren't no normal novelty act. You see, he had a proper voice on him. Some say he had the best singing voice in Burninghouse.'

'So how come he was a singing robot?'

'*Cyborg*, Rik. There's a big difference. While your robot is a plain machine, your cyborg is a synthesis of mechanical and org—'

'I ain't no novelty act, Ted. I'm a serious performer. And I ain't being no singing cyborg for no one. Not even Mr Miramar.'

'Ah, but that's where I come in. See, using my bargaining skills I've managed to work you a bit of leeway. You don't have to be a cyborg, Rik!'

'*But*?'

'What do you mean by that? Who says there's a but?'

'Just fuckin' tell me.'

'There's no but, Rik. Honest. You do not have to be a robot nor anything like that. You get to do your normal routine, with no outfits, embellishments or silly names whatsoever. However—'

'There.'

'What?'

'There's your but.'

'I said however.'

'That means but.'

'No it don't. Are you gonna let me finish or what? Just let me say my piece, eh.'

'Go on.'

'Right, well, the gentleman at the Miramar did ask for one thing. He said that, if at all possible, he'd like to retain the time travel aspect.'

I started walking away.

'Now hold on,' he said, jumping in front of me. 'Just think about this for a minute. You've only got to make a small adjustment here. And it's nothing to do with your songs or anything like that. It's your *spiel*, Rik, your inter-song patter. All you got to do is throw in some stuff about being a traveller from another time. The seventies, perhaps, which is where most of your songs hail from. It'll be a laugh, Rik. And it'll be an *angle*. Even if Mr Miramar weren't here watching, I reckon it's a good idea. We're always talkin' about angles, Rik, ways to make you different, set you apart from the common—'

'*I* ain't. *You* are. I don't need no angles.'

'You need summat, Rik.'

'Oh yeah?'

'Rik, am I your manager?'

'Yeah. So?'

'And do you trust me?'

'What's you on about?'

'Do you? Do you trust me?'

The fact was, I didn't. I couldn't. Ted didn't understand me, I was coming to realise. And that's where he was failing me as a manager. He had a proper singer under his guidance – one who could go global, given the right chances – and he couldn't even see it. All he could see was the chance of making a bit of short-term wedge out of me, never mind my artistic integrity. None of them understood me around here. Hardly any of them, anyway. And the ones who did were right here in the Blue Cairo, waiting for me to take the stage.

I walked away, leaving Ted with his cigar. I didn't have time for this right now. Yusuf was already setting up and I was on in a couple of minutes. There was one thing I cared about and that was my audience. If your audience makes the effort to turn up on time, you've got to show them the same respect.

'Yoose,' I said, leaning over his keyboard. I wanted to let him know the set-list, but when he saw me he dropped the cables he was holding and got his pad out. Talking while he was writing always felt like I was interrupting him, so I stood quiet and looked around at the growing crowd while he scribbled. He poked my arm and showed me the pad.

TELL STAN TO INTROD ME AS CAT

'Cat?' I said.

He scribbled: Y

'What, Caty?'

CAT. Y MEANS YES

'Well…'

MADE UP MY MIND. WANNA BE KNOWN AS CAT

'I dunno about this, Yoose. I mean, you already changed your name to Joe once. You can't keep changing your name like that. The public gets confused. Know what I mean? You got to stick to one name.'

WANNA STICK TO CAT THEN. MADE UP MY MIND

'Well, all right…Just Cat? Not *the* Cat, or…?'

He was shaking his head, mouthing 'Cat', I think.

'Or Yusuf the Cat? Hey, how about that, Joe the Cat? I quite like that, there's a ring to it. Hmmm…'

Yusuf was getting cross now, and he turned his back and went on with his wires. I shouted down my set-list to him, making sure I got a nod in response, then went off to prepare. On the way there I saw Stan, and I relayed Yusuf's request to him.

3.

In the changing room there was a nice big mirror. It didn't have bulbs all around it but there was a lamp either side and the big strip light overhead, so I liked it. I looked myself over. Really, there was nothing to adjust. I didn't have stage clothes nor need a person to check my hair, because I always looked spot on anyway. I'm not bragging there either. You'll come to know me as an objective person, one who can look at himself in a cold light and see exactly what's in front of him. To make it in this game you've got to know your product. And I did. When it came to my product, I was a fucking expert.

But I still say I looked spot on.

Even so, I got out my little pot of hair wax and refined the texture of my moustache. A professional will always observe the rituals, and this was one of mine. The smell of the wax, the feel of it on your lip…it was as important as limbering up your vocal cords, which was the next step.

I started by massaging the Adam's apple, but before I could sing 'doe', the door opened behind me and someone said:

'You're on.'

'Ladies and gentlemen, Mr Rik Suntan!'

I loved this moment. Just after Stan's announced you, just before he hands you the mike. You're not doing your thing yet but you're not waiting any more either. In that moment you're in a different world. The air crackles with potential. All eyes are on you. Anything can happen and it's all down to the man in the spotlight. You could save the world in a moment like that, I swear.

'Hello ladies and gents,' I said, savouring the deep rumble of my own amplified voice. 'This evening I got a confession to make.'

I strutted the front of the stage, working them. All eyes were on me. Ears strained for my next word.

'I'm not who you think I am.'

I had them rapt. Every word I threw at the audience was like chucking a paving slab in a pond, in terms of the impact I was having on the organisms that lived there. I went back to Yusuf and told him: 'Give it a slow but building rhythm, like a drum roll.'

Back on the edge of the stage I said: 'You see me as plain old Rik Suntan, local singing sensation and winner of 'Pub Idol' for two years on the trot. To you I'm all about the voice. I give you today's hits in a new light, showing you how they ought to have been done, putting on the Ritz at a time when most of your chart acts can't even put on a DHSS hostel.'

I gave them a few seconds to appreciate that one.

'But I also bring back for you the best musical moments from yesteryear. I sort the '80s wheat from the '80s chaff, so *you* don't have to. Like a deep sea diver, I plumb the depths of the '60s hit parade and come up with the finest pearls, and not a barnacle in sight. I sift through the rubble of the '70s to bring you only the nuggets, ladies and gents, only the brightest, shiniest lumps of eighteen carat that decade has to offer. And there's a reason for that, friends. There's a reason why Rik Suntan sings the old songs like no other.'

I gestured to Yusuf.

He upped the tempo.

'I'm actually a time traveller. Like Dr Who.'

Forget paving slabs. This was like dropping a JCB in that poor little pond.

From a helicopter.

'Thirty years ago I was on top of the world: a pop superstar with four number one singles to his name and a couple of top-five albums. I toured the world, playing in front of thousands, appearing on national TV. I had it all, ladies and gents, and then…'

Right on cue, Yusuf gave it the big church organ doom chord. If the Blue Cairo had a proper lighting technician, this is where he'd shut them all down except one big one on me. I said:

'And then I fell into the time warp.'

I couldn't believe the stuff I was coming out with. I was running on pure adrenaline, doing what I had to do, dredging up the words from somewhere deep inside. And they were gold, those words, solid gold like those '70s songs. And somewhere in that audience, without a shadow of a doubt, Mr Miramar was lapping them up.

He wanted a replacement for his novelty cyborg act who was nonetheless a great singer? Well here I was: a time lord with a voice to rival Mr Cliff Richard himself.

'Bollocks!' someone shouted. I think it was Jim Taylor. 'You went to Turnmill High. My mate says he was in the same year as you, and he's only twenty-eight himself. So you can't've come from the fuckin' '70s!'

I hadn't thought of that. I hadn't thought of any of it. I was running on a fuel called instinct, pedal to the metal, eyes shut tight and spewing black fumes out of a tailpipe that I didn't understand. I just had to have faith that the answer would come...an answer that would shut Jim Taylor up and make everyone laugh at him. They didn't even have to believe it.

They just had to recognise that I'd dealt with him.

'Nice one,' I said. 'Did you all hear that? The gentleman here questioned how I could be a famous singer from thirty years ago when I am known to have grown up around here, and indeed went to school with his gay lover.'

After about a minute, when the roar of laughter had died down, I went on:

'I'll tell you, ladies and gents. I'll explain all of it to you. But first, a song.'

Yusuf cranked up the rhythm and started laying down some ground rules. This was going to be raunchy, his chopping chords were saying, so you'd better get your mojo out. I prowled the stage, licking my lips, not in a sexy way but to let them know that I had something and, if they were good, they were going to get some of it. I was looking at them all, sending each of them a look that told them what I was all about.

None of them were laughing now.

This was getting serious and they wanted to be a part of it.

'I've had nothing but bad luck...'

I was putting a lot of heart into it, laying my soul bare for the audience to have its way with. I believe that this is the only way to deliver material. I'd given Mr Miramar the gimmick he was after, and now it was time to back it up with substance.

Quality substance.

'*Since the day I saw my cat on the floor...*'

I was singing 'Devil Woman' like a true star. I was the best act the Blue Cairo had ever seen, and I had a feeling it was to be the last they'd hear of me here. Someone like me, you can't hold him back.

'*So I—*'

That was when the bottle hit me.

'*So...er...*'

I barely felt it, but the noise of it pinging off my skull came through the mike, and I winced. The crowd winced as well. I didn't know what had happened, to be honest, and I went on singing for a line or two. But I was in a muddle now and doing the wrong bit, starting from the top again while Yusuf was building up to the big crescendo before the chorus. I turned to give him a glare. But me fucking up was the last thing he'd have been expecting and he was looking down at his keyboard, getting into it.

'*She's just a devil woman...*' I chimed in, although we hadn't got to that bit yet. I stepped around a bit, feeling the glass crunching underfoot. My head did feel strange now and I went to touch it, and it was wet. I searched my brain for the next line but when I went to sing it the mike was dead.

'Ladies and gents, let's have a big hand for Mr Rik Suntan, accompanied by, er...Joe the Lion, the deaf and dumb organ player!'

Stan Curtis was standing next to the amp with his own mike plugged into it. He clapped. Everyone clapped.

I took a bow and stayed bent for a few seconds, watching blood drip to the floor.

I was back in the changing room. There were a couple of other people in there but they were arguing amongst themselves, ignoring me, even though I was the victim in all this and deserving a bit of attention. I didn't give a shit, to be honest. I wasn't listening to them either. I was thinking. Planning.

You're never shot, you know. The war is never over until they've killed you dead. They knock you down but you can get up. You can. Believe me, I know it.

I grew up learning it.

When my head cleared it seemed like there was only one person in the room, and it was Delores.

'What happened to all the others?' I said.

'What others? Rik, have you calmed–?'

'The ones in here just now.'

'Well, there wasn't—'

'Who did this? Don't fuck me about, Del, just tell me straight – who the fuck threw it?'

'The bottle? I dunno, Rik. I never saw it. Are you all right? Stan told me to come and wait with you a bit. He said you might need, um…watching.'

'Watching? Why?'

'I dunno, Rik. Honest I don't.'

'Did anyone see the cunt, though? Martin stopped him, right? Don't tell me he got past Martin on the door.'

'I really dunno, Rik. You need to just calm down, forget about that for a while.'

She came at me with a damp cloth in her hand. She didn't look like she knew what she was doing.

'Don't touch me,' I said. 'Give it here.'

In the mirror I could see the damage, which consisted of a deep cut on my forehead about an inch long, just above the left eye. I started wiping the dried blood off my face. It was lucky the glass hadn't broken on impact, otherwise there would have been more damage.

But there *was* more.

I was remembering it all.

'What about that bloke?' I said, dabbing at the cut.

'I told you, I don't kn—'

'Not that one, the one from the Miramar.'

'You mean the one who said I could be a supermodel, and that I had a slot that he wanted to—?'

'Yeah, him. Is he still here?'

'No, I…I think him and his mate left.'

'Left? When?'

'Well, not long after the…you…'

'And you didn't try and stop him and explain that…that it wasn't my fault? That it was an act of God? Jesus *fuckin'* Christ, Del. Do you know how big a chance that was for me? That was my big fucking opportunity. *Jesus*.'

I stared at myself in the mirror, focusing on the cut. It would scar, no doubt about it. Everything was turning to shit all around me: my hopes and dreams of becoming a famous singer…my face…my ability to remain calm and be positive at all times…

I turned my head sideways slightly, then the other way. Thinking about it, a scar wouldn't be so bad. Scars can add character and charisma to a face, as long as they're not too scary. They say that beauty is not beauty without some kind of flaw to set it off. Well, maybe this was the flaw I'd been waiting for all of my life. Maybe I'd been too perfect before now. Maybe this scar would finally be the making of me.

Yeah, I could see it.

In the mirror I noticed Delores moving towards the door, and I turned around. 'Hey,' I said in my usual calm, upbeat voice. 'Don't slope off. I didn't mean it.'

She stopped with her hand on the door. I got up, went over to her and placed a hand on her shoulder. She turned and faced me, and you could see the innocence in those baby blue eyes of hers. I could also see my own reflection, and I looked pretty good.

I shouldn't have shouted at her, though. I felt bad about that. I went to touch her cheek, letting her know how I felt, but the door opened before I reached her.

It was Stan.

'What's goin' on here?' he said, looking at my hand.

AN INTRODUCTION TO THE STAIRWAY

I F you are familiar with the song 'Stairway to Heaven' you will have heard a bit about The Stairway. But where the song (which features a flawless string arrangement) gets it wrong lyrically is that The Stairway does not actually go to a place called Heaven. Heaven is not an actual place and neither is Hell. They are states of mind, and can be reached by doing good or bad things in ones life or taking mind-altering drugs.

The Stairway itself is a system of cosmic accomplishment, similar to the belt system in martial arts. A student of kung fu ascends his hierarchy of accomplishment by attaining belts of differing hues. Those belts are like the steps on The Stairway.

But while the belts in martial arts are merely external representations of inner accomplishment, the steps of The Stairway are accomplishments in themselves, and bring cosmic power to anyone who ascends them.

4.

Me and Delores had history. And I'm not talking about the couple of times I'd shagged her over the years. I could say that for many of the females in the area, but I wouldn't say I had history with them. History, like the sort that gets taught in school, is about significant events. Things that happen whereby a tide gets turned, or power goes from one side to the other. Or a very important thing first comes to light.

In the case of Delores, she was instrumental in getting my singing career off the ground. I was out one night and trying to chat her up in The Feathers, which used to do karaoke on Wednesday nights in those days. I'd shagged her twice before but she'd come along a bit since then, and was looking really beautiful in a bright red dress that looked marvellous against her dark hair, sunbed skin and blue eyes. Plus she'd discovered her cleavage and was making the most of it. She was in a higher league now and not so easy to get off with, so a bit of effort was in order. Noticing how she was responding to certain karaoke performers, I knew what I had to do.

Sounds like a piece of piss, don't it? A singer of my quality going up there and showing them all how it's done. But it wasn't like that. You've got to understand that until that night I was the only person who'd heard me sing. For me, coming up the way I had, singing was something you hid. I had a gift and I didn't want it pissed on by twats. I was waiting for the right moment to...I just needed the right audience, and then...

All right, I wasn't so sure of myself back then. I totally knew what I had, but still – you're never a hundred per cent sure until you show it to the world. And that night, standing in front of all the pissheads and slags at The Feathers, I showed it to them.

I told Delores I was just off for a slash, then slipped onstage and sang 'The Lady In Red' by Chris de Burgh, dedicating it to her.

I wanted to actually sing it *to* her, looking at her the whole while and using the song to seduce her, but I couldn't find her in the crowd. And after a few seconds I forgot about her anyway. All the faces became one face, and I found that I was trying to seduce the lot of them. And getting somewhere fast. I felt like I was in control like I'd never been before, that I could stroke the audience's hair or blow in its ear and get it to do whatever I wanted. It was all true, what I'd always believed about myself. I came of age on that stage. I went up there Richard Sutton and came down someone different. I was someone special now, set apart from those around me and yet accepted by them for the joy I brought to them. Through my voice I was able to take them to a place they never knew existed, and yet yearned for every moment of their dull lives. Not that anyone told me this. I just sensed it, clear as smoke in the air.

But the smoke cleared when the song ended.

And everyone came back down to earth.

I walked back to my drink. You had to be on the look-out for it, but people were making way for me slightly more than they had done on my way up. I brushed shoulders instead of squeezing past them. More eyes than backs were turned to me.

I didn't see Delores again that night. I think she got off with Derek Bendall, or Roger Clemence. Either way, I never touched her again. She would go on to shack up with someone for a few weeks before getting a job at the Blue Cairo, and finding the security she never knew she craved in the bed of Stan Curtis. But fuck that.

I was out of *her* league now.

'I'm just saying sorry to her,' I said to Stan, straight off the bat. 'I shouted at her just now. You got a problem with that?'

'Well, no, but—'

'I was a bit shook up and I took it out on Delores. I'm sorry, Delores.'

'That's all right,' she said, slipping out under Stan's armpit.

'Did you get him?' I asked Stan. 'The fucker who glassed me?'

'No one glassed no one else here tonight. He merely threw a bottle at you.'

'How's that not glassing?'

'The bottle never broke before it hit the ground, so there was no sharp edges involved,' he said, glancing at my forehead. 'Minimal harm done, I can see. That'll heal in quick time.'

'Bollocks will it. I got a fuckin' scar coming. Did Martin get him? He got him, right? I can't see how some tosser can lob a bottle and then get past Martin.'

'Martin's just one man. He ain't the KGB.'

'KG…? Are you takin' the piss here, Stan? Cos it seems to me like…And what was that bollocks about Joe the Lion? I told you Yusuf wanted to be called…er…'

'Joe the Lion was what you said,' he said, strolling past me and picking up a woman's hairbrush off the dressing table. 'I only done what you asked.'

'I never said Joe the Lion!'

He held up the hairbrush. 'I ain't arguing about it, Rik. I gotta say, Joe the Lion did strike me as a bit odd, but I never questioned it. He wants to rename himself summat odd, that's his lookout. He's a fine keyboard player and that's all I care about. Mind you, Joe the Lion's still better than that foreign name of his.'

'And why'd you have to call him deaf and dumb? For a start, he ain't deaf.'

'Look, my job is to sell drinks, and if I can rustle up a bit of punter interest by promoting a deaf and dumb organist, that's what I'll do. You got any more complaints? Cos, I gotta tell you, I really ain't in the market for them just now.'

I had a lot of complaints but I couldn't be bothered to trot them out for Stan. I hated Stan and I hated the fucking Blue Cairo. But it was steady work and I wasn't about to jeopardise that. Not until I had something better.

'Look, I think you're all right,' said Stan, playing with the tines on the brush. 'I like your music. It's my kind of music, none of this jungle music they play nowadays on the wireless. You sing like they did in the golden age, and I can see you being associated with the "Rat Pack", had you been around back then. Do you know which one you remind me of?'

'A young Dean Martin.'

'Oh, heh heh…Oddly enough, no. More like—'

'OK, Frank Sinatra. People have sometimes said—'

'Sinatra? I shouldn't think so, Rik. No, you remind me of Sammy Davis J—'

'He was black, for fuck's sake.'

'I know that, but you do. You bring to mind Sammy Davis Junior.'

'I ain't a fuckin' black man, Stan.'

'It don't matter. I'm just saying. You should take it as a compliment, because he was a fine performer.'

I looked at him. It was hard to read his face. Rolls of fat covered most of it so he never really expressed much on it other than his being a fat bastard.

'Yeah, all right,' I said. 'Ta.'

Because I could probably see what he meant. Sammy Davis Jr was a funny man as well as a top singer. And out there tonight, doing that time lord stuff and taking the piss out of Jim Taylor, I felt like I'd discovered that side of myself.

'And he had a nice big moustache, like yours,' said Stan. 'Although I'm not sure he had his for the same reason as you.'

I looked at him.

'Are you takin' the piss out of me, Stan?'

'Calm down, Rik. Just an observation. Nothing meant by it harm-wise.'

'You sound like you're takin' the piss out of me, I swear. And I can't have that. Not tonight.'

He let out a lot of air and pursed his lips at me. 'You'd best get over that stuff, Rik,' he said. 'Summat's right there in front of a man's face, he's gonna mention it. Do you see what I'm saying? Lad of your age, he ought to get used to his facial disfigurement by now.'

This was exactly why I hated the Blue Cairo so much. If I didn't have to deal with dickheads like Stan Curtis it wouldn't be so bad. It was a nice little club. I could see myself getting interviewed later in my career, telling the sexy female reporter about my early years playing dumps like this, with twats like

Stan Curtis giving me a hard time. She'd laugh and I'd laugh, and maybe I'd take her up to my hotel room afterwards and show her that the magic never dies. The next day she'd write it all up in a breathless feature article, and people would read it and believe that anyone can become an icon of the entertainment industry: all you got to do is start at the bottom, in places like the Blue Cairo, and endure no end of shit from Stan Curtis.

And I felt sorry for them.

Actually, no, I didn't.

Fuck them.

I smiled at Stan, wondering if he'd be in the ground by the time the article came out.

'I reckon we should call it quits,' he said.

'What?'

'Your...*tenure* here. For the time being, in the current climate, I think we'll have a break.'

'Wha—? What the fuck are you saying, Stan?'

'If you want it plain, I'll put it plain: this was your last night performing here. I don't mean it personal, but—'

'Just because some nutter tried to kill me with a bottle, you want to kick me out?'

'No, of course not. All right, the bottle didn't help you much but it's more than that. It's about the music, Rik. Like I say, I'm a big fan. But others ain't. And they're the ones who buy the drink in here.'

I couldn't believe what I was hearing. After all the weeks I'd been singing there, building up a regular audience, boosting the profile of the club.

'Tastes change,' he said. You could hear every slimy corner of his mouth as he rolled each word around in it. 'What worked for yesterday don't necessarily work for tomorrow. I mean, I ain't saying you won't be singing here again. It's just that, well, we need to jig up the bookings a bit. Inject a bit of youth. I've got a dwindling clientele, Rik. There was only fifteen, twenty in here tonight. It's the youngsters – they're going elsewhere for their sounds. They're into the new stuff, see. They've no time for a moustachioed Cliff Richard tribute act.'

'I told you – I ain't a tribute act. I am inspired by the work of Richard but I don't pretend to be him. And I do other stuff as well. New stuff. I'm always bringing in the latest chart hits.'

'Rik, you've got the balance all wrong. For every recent hit you've got twenty old songs, most of 'em by your man Cliff. That's not the way to court a younger audience.'

'But I'm about more than the songs, Stan. You know that. You saw me out there tonight, all that time travel stuff…I made it all up on the fly. I was able to look at my audience and adapt the—'

'All the same, Rik, I think we'll call it quits for a while. Eh?'

He put a couple of notes on the dresser: a ten and a five.

Then he left.

5.

I looked at my reflection in the mirror, wondering how I was going to make it now. I could feel that sexy reporter coming back, wanting to ask me about the lean years when I had to get by on just chips. We were sat down all cosy in the lobby of the hotel – a posh one, in Burninghouse. Or even Clandon. I was all set to tell her about the flame in my heart that had always kept on burning, no matter how many times they'd knocked me back, when she said:

'Do you get sick of it?'

'What?'

'People staring at you. I mean, it must be a pain sometimes, being as famous as you.'

'Nah, I don't mind it. I love my fans. When they see me, they can't help but stare. It's like they're coming face-to-face with a—'

'But not all of them are friendly, are they?'

'It's all right. I know they got love in their hearts.'

'That one over there looks like he's got hatred.'

'Which one?'

'Over there. By the front desk.'

I had a look and sure enough, the man there was giving me the death stare. Not only that, but it was the gingernut from the bar.

Opening my eyes, it all came clear. *He* was the cunt who'd thrown the bottle. That look in his eyes when I'd first seen him – it was violent intent. I still didn't know what his problem was but I knew it was him.

I got up and went out into the main area. I was fuming – not only had that man injured me but he'd also cost me my big chance at the Miramar, put me out of my current job and humiliated me in front of my fans. The stage was bare and piped music filled the air – one of these teenybopper acts like Zak Bremner and his ilk. If it hadn't been for the gingernut I'd still be up there, making sounds the way they're meant to be made. I had a quick scan but I couldn't see him. I knew I wouldn't see him. He'd come to do a job – a coward's job – and he'd done it and run off.

'Did you see the gingernut?' I shouted at Delores. She was serving Ted. 'Oi, Del!'

'I'm just serving Ted, Rik.'

'I know, but did you see him? The ginger one with the tash?'

'Eh? Who?'

'Stood just there when I came in. It was him who threw the bottle. I'm gonna kill him.'

'Don't say things like that, Rik.'

'I am gonna kill him. He's ruined my career. He's ruined everything, Del. I wanna find him, find out why he did it and then finish him.'

'Rik,' said Ted, 'come on, there's no saying it was him.'

'Eh? *I'm* fuckin' saying it was him. When I came in, he was giving me the death stare. I might have known he'd do summat like this. Fuckin' ginger people...'

'Well, I'm not so sure. It could have been anyone.'

'Yeah? Well, that's not very helpful, Ted. So if you don't mind, I was just askin' Delores here if she—'

'I mean,' he said, not looking at me, 'it could have been someone like Jim Taylor.'

'Jim Taylor? What d'you mean?'

'Forget it.'

'No, come on.'

'Look,' he said, facing me but not looking like he was enjoying it, 'you gotta admit, you weren't kind to him. You openly insulted him, Rik, humiliating him in front of everyone pres—'

'Humiliating him? You mean the gay lover joke?'

'It was a cheap shot, Rik. And in front of his wife as well.'

'Cheap shot bollocks. What about chucking a bottle at a defenceless singer? *I'm* the injured party here, not Jim fuckin' Taylor. Look at my face! And in the full glare of the spotlight as well.'

'Someone like Jim Taylor gets offended easy, Rik. You should know that.' He looked away again and said: 'I know others were offended.'

'Others? Like who?'

'Never mind.'

'Come on – don't turn away. Are you talkin' to me or what?'

'Maybe I am talkin' to you. Maybe I'm talkin' to a man who's messed up his big chance here tonight...a man who ain't got the...the *sense* to...to...'

'Hold on a minute...where the fuck's all this comin' from? It's *me* who got his face cut, and...and who's lost his job, and...'

'Lost yer job?'

'Yeah.'

'You mean Stan sacked you? Flamin' heck, Rik. Can it get any worse? Is there nothin' you won't do in the pursuit of professional failure? Total and utter professional—'

'Yeah? Well *fuck* off. If I'm a failure, so are you, you fuckin'...'

I didn't enjoy getting like that, raising my voice and using bad words in anger at a person. I was someone who liked to remain cool and calm in his dealings. Emotion was for my music, and I didn't want to waste it elsewhere.

'Yeah, all right,' he said, knocking back some of his pint. 'Point took. Fair enough.' And I knew that was that – he'd said his bit and I'd said mine, and the matter was behind us. It was the way Ted worked. 'Look, I said there was two opportunities. A big one and a little one.'

'Oh yeah?' I said. Although I wasn't that interested. Unlike Ted, I couldn't get over disappointment by swigging ale. 'What's the other one, then?'

He made sure Delores was out of earshot and said: 'It's just about...well, it's about David Bowie.'

'David Bowie?'

'Yeah.'

'What, 'ground control to Major Tom' David Bowie?'

'Nah, the other one. How many flamin' David Bowies do you know?'

'So does he wanna do a duet with me or summat?'

Ted had a little chuckle at that. It was a chuckle I could have done without, just then. The full weight of the evening came bearing down on me with that chuckle. Sometimes it happens that way. And someone's got to bear the brunt.

'Yeah, you have yer little chuckle,' I said. 'You know what the real problem here is? It's *you*. You're a *shit* manager. You never even came to see me when I was back there, bleedin'. I could have been *seriously hurt*, Ted. And you should have stopped that Miramar bloke from pissing off. You should have told him that…that…Ah, fuck off!'

I went. I just needed to be out of there now. I wanted to walk under the moon and think about what I was gonna do next. Because, when you looked at it and you were honest with yourself, you could see how it was going to be hard for me now. I had to look at that fire in my heart and decide how strong it was burning. I could feel the lean times coming and I needed to keep warm.

As I walked out the door I noticed Martin there. On a normal day he'd give me no more than a passing glance, and that's if I'm lucky. He didn't like me and I didn't have any feelings whatsoever about him, good or bad. But this time, as I went past him, I felt his cold glare on the side of my head.

I stopped and returned it.

I could see now that it wasn't so much a glare as a gaze. I had a feeling it was because he had something to tell me. About something in particular.

So I asked him.

'Martin,' I said, 'do you happen to know who it was who—?'
'Yeah.'

I hadn't really heard him talk before, and it was a soft voice. Softer than you'd expect from such a big man.

'What, you know who threw the bottle at me?'
'Yeah, I do.'

'Ah…Do you know,' I said, laughing a bit, 'not one of those twats in there saw it. Not one of 'em. Well done, mate. I owe you one. Was it the gingernut? Don't tell me it was Jim—'
'Nah, it was me.'

I thought he was putting me on at first, and then a car went past and the headlights flashed up his eyes, and I saw that he wasn't. There was a twinkle there and a smile, but no jest. If anything, he seemed quite pleased with himself. He was taking the piss.

And I found myself in a situation.

Here was the one who'd lobbed the bottle, thereby…Well, you know all the things that came of it. And they were all the fault of this doorman here, this Martin, all six foot six and eighteen stone of him. No wonder no one had noticed: he'd lobbed it from the door, everyone in front of him and all eyes on me.

'Hey,' he said.

But I was ten yards away now and shifting fast. There's a time and place for throwing punches at a man, and a time and place for arranging summat a bit special. And I knew which one this was.

'Oi, stop!' he was shouting, coming after me.

'Fuck off!' I shouted, swatting a fly out of my ear. 'You fuckin' stay away from me!'

'Don't run off! I gotta tell you about it. There's so much you gotta be told.'

The shouting stopped. I had a look back when I turned the corner and he was stood in the road, holding a hand up.

THE HUMAN SOUL

THE human soul is an interesting item. Most people don't even know they possess one, but they would know it if it wasn't there, because they would die. Sometimes it appears as if people don't have much of a soul, but they do. Everyone has a soul.

The soul is everything a person does by his own volition. It is his personality, his disposition and his assertiveness. A lot of personality traits are down to the way a person is raised, but his soul is at work there as well. Two different souls will respond to the same upbringing in two different ways. And the weaker soul always responds the most.

6.

I gave it one last go with the key, then started knocking. Then I started ringing, because no one was answering. I was ringing and knocking at the same time for a few seconds when I heard something inside. So I stopped.

'You ain't coming in,' she said.

'There's summat wrong with my key, Shell. You'll have to get us a new one tomorrow, right? Actually I ought to have yours, and you—'

'I said you ain't coming in.'

'What? Stop fuckin' about and let us in. I've had a shit night and I just wanna get some kip.'

'Well kip somewhere else. You're not coming here. Not no more.'

'Shell, don't be—'

'Go and look in the cleaner's cupboard downstairs – you've got two bags of your stuff in there. If you want the rest, you'll find it in there tomorrow night.'

'For fuck's sake, Shell! Don't make me knock this door down.'

'Go away, Rik.'

'I will. I'll knock it down, Shell. Shell? Don't test me! Someone like me…You know I'm highly strung. Shell? Shell! Look, I…I got attacked tonight. Onstage. I got glassed in the face. It's really bad. Still bleeding.'

The door started opening. I went to push it wide but she had the chain on.

'Let me see,' she said.

'Shell, I need to come in,' I said, holding my face close to the gap where she could see it. 'You need to see it properly, under a proper light. Plus you'll have to get the stuff from under the sink and patch it up. You can patch anything up, you know, as long as both sides want it. Come on, Shell.'

She was looking at the cut on my forehead. I was staring at her eyes and trying to draw them to mine, like I usually could. I could do it with anyone. It's part of why I was so good onstage. But it wasn't working this time.

'Tell you what, let's have a cup of tea and talk about it, eh? Come on, undo this chain.'

'You might need a stitch in that. Maybe two. Probably none at all, though. I'd go to A&E, just to get it checked.'

Suddenly the door slammed in my face and footsteps clacked away. I went to knock on the door but didn't. I kicked it instead. About ten times. I punched it as well. I stopped short of headbutting it, though.

I didn't want any more scars.

Downstairs I found my gear. She'd put it in bin bags. I didn't mind so much that she'd kicked me out, now I'd calmed down. It was her flat anyway, when you thought about it. But there was no need for bin bags. It showed a basic lack of respect. It was like she was dumping me in the bin, treating me like so much rubbish. And on this night, when I'd already been treated so rough, I didn't need that. They were good bags, though. The ones with chord up the top that you can pull tight.

I only hoped my velvet jacket was in them.

I picked up the bags and went outside. They hardly weighed anything at all. There was a skip down by the corner and I gave serious consideration to chucking them in it. This was a turning point in my life, I felt, and something needed doing to mark it. With no possessions to my name, no place to live and no means of earning a living, I'd just about hit rock bottom. Like in that song by Linsey De Paul and that bloke, 'Rock Bottom'. In the song they talk about being at rock bottom and rubbing it out and starting again. But the basic difference was that there was two of them and only the one of me. So it was more like the one by Whitesnake, 'Here I Go Again', where he finds himself on his own and going down the only road he's ever known. Except Whitesnake were long-haired grebs, and I was a bit more sophisticated than that.

At the corner I stopped and crouched down. This was what I'd do: if my velvet jacket was in one of the bags, I'd keep them. If not, in the skip they'd both go. I started rummaging. I couldn't find the jacket in the first one but I did find my tapes, which I'd forgot about. In the other bag I found the velvet jacket. I got it out and stood up, looking at it. It was purple and a bit worn in one or two places, but it was still special. To be honest with you, I didn't know why it was special. I'd found it in a charity shop, so long ago that I couldn't remember which one. No one wore purple velvet jackets at the time and no one wears them now, nor at any time in between. But still I tried it on. It fit me perfect, and I knew that anyone looking at me just then would agree about that and not be able to take their eyes off me. When I put that jacket on, you see, it was like I found myself in it.

I was thinking about that, and admiring the jacket, when a midget in a pork pie hat jumped out of the shadows and pointed a rifle at me.

'Freeze, motherfucker,' he said.

I wasn't sure what to do. It's not like when a normal-sized person points a gun at you, or even just shakes a fist at you. I don't want to discriminate against midgets or anything, but I found it hard to take this one seriously. Not even when he told me to put the bags down and my hands up. Especially not when he said that.

'I said *freeze*, you harelipped cunt!' he shouted. The pork pie hat was black and too big for him, and it kept tilting forward over his face. Other than that he looked like a normal midget. 'And put the fuckin' bags down!'

'You got two seconds to turn around and fuck off,' I said, swatting a fly away and standing up. I wasn't angry, I just wasn't having that. Not from a midget, a giant nor any other size of person. 'Else I'm gonna pick you up and toss you in that skip.'

It was then that he shot me.

There wasn't much noise. Just a little zip followed by pain, so I remember thinking the rifle must have a silencer. I wheeled backwards, hitting the wall but holding up all right. All the while he was coming forward on those little legs, pointing the gun and threatening more bullets. I put my hands up and tried to placate him, but my voice failed. I was feeling weaker now. My head was getting heavy and my sight was growing dim, like in 'Hotel California' by The Eagles. I think he'd got me in the chest. My heart was going mental, beating like crazy, fighting against the inevitable. I closed my eyes and pictured Shell when she found out. The cops would come to the door and tell her, and she'd break down and start sobbing.

'Fuckin' hell, Egg, what'd you do that for?'

The voice was sort of behind me and above me, and slightly to the left. I almost recognised it but I felt like my life was leaking out of me, and recognising voices wasn't my primary concern.

'Put it away, Egg!' he shouted at the midget. 'For fuck's sake!'

'Fuck him. He ain't the one.'

'He is, Egg. I swear he is!'

'Bollocks is he! He's a fuckin' twat is what he is!'

'Egg!'

The midget was marching off down the street, so fast that he had to hold his hat down. With his other hand he steadied the rifle, which was slung over his little shoulder. It was almost as long as him and I couldn't see how he had handled it with such accuracy, plugging me right in the heart. He turned down an alley and was gone, and I wondered if he'd ever truly been there.

I struggled on to my feet, leaning against the wall and looking around and thinking this is it, this is the last scene I'll ever look at. This clear eyesight, this ability to stand up…it's the body trying to ward off death. But you can't fight him for long.

And do you know what? I didn't care about it. Death didn't scare me one bit. What did scare me was that I hadn't done my job yet. I had a gift to offer the public and they'd only had it in dribs and drabs so far. They'd not had the full article and now they'd miss out on it. And Rik Suntan would die unfulfilled.

After a while my breathing got steadier. There was a phonebox just up the way, on the corner.

THE SOUL AS CURRENCY

THE soul is the currency of The Stairway. In order to make any progress on it, you need human souls. But not just any old souls.

A cider-maker will get nowhere in his work if he uses bad apples. Maggots, bits of straw and rabbit dung are nothing compared to inappropriate apples when it comes to making bad cider. You need apples that are capable of doing great things. Apples that can stand head and shoulders above other apples. The same token applies on The Stairway. But with souls, not apples.

I call such a soul a High Denomination Soul.

7.

'Look, mate,' the male nurse was saying, 'I wasn't taking the piss. Honest. You've got to wait and let the doc see you, in case…'

I pushed past him and headed for the door. He grabbed my arm.

'Seriously, mate, you'd better wait for the doc. Even an air gun pellet can—'

'Fuck off!' I said, yanking my arm away. 'I ain't staying here to get laughed at. How was I to know it was an air gun, eh? And what's wrong with an air gun? I got *shot*, didn't I?'

'That's what I'm saying. Even a little air gun can—'

'What right you got to talk to me like that? At least I ain't a fuckin' nurse. A nurse is a woman's job. What kind of a man does a woman's job? Eh? Answer me that.'

He looked both ways over my shoulder, then pulled the curtain around our cubicle and got me in a headlock, forcing my head into the seat of the chair.

'This feel like a woman, does it?' he said into my ear. 'This feel like the arm of a man who does woman's work, eh?'

I was trying to answer but I couldn't even breathe.

'One of us works hard for a living, looking after twats who call 999 and tell 'em they've been shot in the heart and they can see a bright white light up ahead,' he said. 'The other…well, he is that twat. You understand where I'm coming from, boy? You see why I won't take *that* off *you*?'

'Mmmmf,' I said.

'Nice one.'

He let me up and pushed me down into the seat, smoothing my hair down. 'You all right?' he said, looking into my eyes. 'I said are you all right?'

'Yeah. I'm fine.'

'Good for you. Right, you can leave here now or wait for the doctor. Personally I think you should just fuck off and never darken the door of this A&E department again, but it's your call, boy. Your life, your choices.'

He pulled the curtains back and went away. I waited for about a minute then fucked off. Going past the reception I thought hard about putting in a complaint, but I didn't need that hassle right now. I just needed fresh air and some exercise.

I was getting knackered now. It was early summer but the night air was a bit parky, and I could feel it on my vocal cords. I needed to get out of it before I did some damage. Even without a regular singing gig I had to protect my prize asset.

That was the only reason I went there.

There was loads of other places I could have gone. I had loads of friends who would have been happy to put me up. Honoured, in fact. But, truth be told, it would have come across like a bit of an intrusion. I'd been neglecting the social side of late, you see, concentrating on my work and not bothering with the lads. And it would have come across wrong, me turning up on their doorsteps at this late hour, nursing butterfly stitches to the head and wanting a sofa to kip on. On top of that I couldn't remember where any of them lived. Or if they were still alive. But I knew Ted Regis was alive.

And where he lived.

It was gone midnight but the living room light was on. I tried finding a crack in the curtains to peer through but I couldn't see much, only the flicker of a telly screen. He was probably sitting in there, supping scotch out of the bottle and going over our last exchange when I'd called him a shit manager and told him to fuck off. He was thinking over the things he'd said that had provoked me, and wishing he'd said them different. It had been agonising for him, me storming off like that and not giving him the chance to apologise. But I was here now.

Shivering.

Soon as I rang the bell I remembered about his wife and kids. I'd never seen the little ones. The couple of times I'd been here before, they'd been either upstairs asleep or off staying with their nan or something. I'd met his wife Jeannie though, and I didn't need that kind of complication right now. So much so that I wished I hadn't rung. Too late now though.

Movement in the hall.

Latch turning.

Me calming.

'Ah,' said Ted, in his dressing gown and holding a tumbler of whisky. 'I was just thinking about you. Look, I'm sorry if I provoked you earlier. I been thinking how I could have said things different, but…'

'Forget it,' I said, bustling past. 'You got any food?' I was glad that we were all right about things because now I could relax.

Relaxing around Ted was something I found easy. Not because of his personality, but because he was my manager and it was my right. But he wasn't a manager in the way you know. For you, your manager is your boss. He's the bloke who gives you shit and makes you do hard work that you don't want to do. He's the one who holds you back and keeps you down. When he needs a favour, and you want to keep your job, you'd better put out for him and hold the backchat. I had the other sort of manager.

I was *his* boss.

For ten per cent of my net earnings I employed him to manage my career. I expected him to bring me exciting work that I wanted to do. He was supposed to lift me up and push me forwards. When I needed a favour, and if he wanted to keep his ten per cent, he'd better—

'I'm glad you came, actually,' he said.

We were in the kitchen now. I opened the fridge and said: 'Oh yeah?' He only had cooking stuff in there, like vegetables and mince and stuff. I wanted something I could eat fast. 'You got any bread?'

He thought about it and went: 'How about a hamburger? You want a burger?'

'Oh yeah, nice one. You got frozen ones, then?'

He was coming over now. 'No.'

'Well there's none in here.'

He reached past me and got the mince, taking it to the side where he had a thing that looked like a flat toaster.

'This, Rik,' he said, 'is a George Foreman grill, and I'm gonna make you a burger with it. You got one of these, Rik? They're marvellous.'

'You can make a burger in that?'

'Oh yeah, you can make loads of things in it. Burgers, erm… other things.'

I sat down at the kitchen table while he got on with it. This is what I was talking about just now, expecting a certain service from your manager.

'You know George Foreman, the boxer?' he was saying, moulding mince with his hands. I hoped he'd washed them. 'He created this thing out of nothing. And do you know what it's worth now? Do you?'

I looked at it and shrugged. 'Fifteen quid? Twenty?'

'No, the company. George Foreman Grills Ltd, or whatever. It's worth millions, Rik. Billions, probably. It's made him more money than he ever made from boxing. And we're talking about a heavyweight world champion here…a man who fought Muhammad Ali.'

'Oh yeah? Did he win?'

'Well, no, he lost, but…Look, what I'm saying here is that Foreman reinvented himself as an entrepreneur after his boxing career was over. He found something new inside of himself, and he used it to *achieve*. He's got to be proud of that, Rik. I'd be proud of it.'

I'm not a big eater normally, but I don't think I'd eaten all day and I was getting really hungry. The grill thing was cooking the mince and Ted was going on, and my attention was heading to the stomach and setting up camp there in a big way. I could hear it growling and whining over the sizzling of the burger.

'You ought to be proud of yourself too, Rik,' he said, buttering a bun, 'for what you've achieved.'

'I've achieved fuck all,' I said.

'Oh, but you have. Achievement ain't just about money and acclaim. It's about *art*, Rik. You're an artist, and the heights you hit for your art have been really…well, high. I didn't mention this at the time because of, you know, events taking over, but I thought you were cracking tonight.'

I was listening now. 'Yeah?'

'Damn right you were. Flamin' superb, like no other singer I've ever seen nor heard. Do you know what you did with "Devil Woman"? You made it your own.'

'I did, didn't I?'

'You didn't half. You took it to a place where no one's ever took it before, not even Mr Richard himself. Very few songs have ever been to that place, Rik, because only a handful of singers throughout history have known the way there. Musical navigators, you might call them, pointing the way to transcendence and enlightenment via a simple song. Sinatra's one. Elvis is another. I'd say Mr Richard gets the nod as well, although not on this particular song. He gives a much better account on "Miss You Nights".'

I was nodding. Ted really knew his stuff and it was good to hear him share some of it. Gave me confidence that one such as him was looking after my financial and creative affairs.

'Then there's Phil Collins,' he went on. 'Some of it's a bit middling but you can't argue with "Against All Odds". I mean, you just can't. And there's Bowie, of course.'

'Bowie?'

'Yeah. You know, David Bowie.'

'What is it with you and him? I don't actually rate him that much. I wouldn't call him a…What was it?'

'Well, maybe you'll change that opinion in time. But there's another musical navigator, Rik, and that's you.'

'Me?'

'You're right up there alongside every one of them.'

'What, even…?'

'I can say without a doubt, as a scientifically provable *fact*, that you are a world famous singer of popular music, renowned for your theatrical stage shows and frequent image overhauls.'

He grinned at me, nodding like he'd just given me a present and I was allowed to open it.

'Oh, right,' I said, like I'd unwrapped the present and found a big steaming shit.

'Don't sound so blasé, Rik. I'm saying that you've already *made it*, mate. Forget potential – you're already a superstar.'

We had a problem here, it looked like. Ted had been working hard on my behalf for a couple of years now. And all to no avail. All his managerial efforts on the blower, through the media and face-to-face pitching had brought him not one little bit of avail. And that can put a man under a lot of pressure. Especially a man with a young family and a wife who has to work in a launderette to make ends meet, and who is also flighty. And you know what happens when pressure is applied.

Sooner or later, a thing cracks.

I should have seen this coming. I'd warned him about it when he took me on. Get some other clients, I'd said. I don't want to be the only chicken in your basket. When you get no eggs, who's to blame?

'Ted,' I said. 'I think you need a—'

'Do you trust me?'

'What?'

'Do you?'

'It ain't a matter of trust. It's about…well…'

'Do you?'

'Course I do, Ted. You know I do. But—'

'Then you'll have to accept certain things as a given. I'm your manager, and I feel out every opportunity that comes your way, make sure it's sound before I even tell you about it. And there's some that haven't made it to you, Rik. Let me tell you that now.'

He was back to making the burger now, turning off the George Foreman and getting some mustard from the fridge.

'Yeah?' I said. 'Like what?'

'Well, mainly things like weddings. I couldn't see you doing that, myself. As a serious artist, I had you down for more integrity than that.'

'You were correct.'

'I thought so. And the odd local radio jingle. You'd have had to sing things like:

Bob Gable in the afternoon
He likes a joke and he likes a tune
Call him up and chat when he's on the air
But you must speak clearly and you're not allowed to swear

People would have been hearing you trot that one out every day, Rik, over and over. I didn't see you in that role.'

'Right,' I was nodding. 'I mean no. No fucking way.'

'What else? Erm...'

A gust of wind barged through the open window, stirring up everything that wasn't tied down. A calendar next to the cooker was fluttering, flashing glimpses of the months to come. A magazine fell off the table and landed face-up. It was *Popular Keyboard*. I frowned at it.

'Oh, there was an offer from a travelling theatre company. They were touring a show all over the country, culminating in the West End. Yeah, they wanted you to play Cliff Richard.'

I gave him a look. 'Cliff Richard? In the West End? And you turned it down?'

'They disregarded the '70s material, Rik. I felt I had to make a stand on that one. I know how you feel about '70s Cliff. Sorry if I misread you there.'

'No, you were all right.'

'And it turned out to be the West End of Burnley.'

'Ah. Where's Burnley?'

'Exactly. There was a lot of demand for a Zak Bremner tribute not so long back, and—'

'Ted, you know I don't do tributes.'

'It was more of a general singer with Bremner-heavy set-list.'

'That ain't my kind of material.'

'Like I said, Rik, these are the ones I've turned down. Then there's the David Bowie opportunity. I mentioned that one to you earlier.'

'Oh yeah. Ted, I'm getting the picture. You know the things that just ain't me, and you're rejecting them right off the bat. I trust you.'

Ted placed a couple of bits of lettuce on the burger and began slicing a tomato. 'I accepted that Bowie one, Rik.'

'Eh? But...Ted, I ain't that fussed about David Bowie.'

'You dunno what the opportunity is yet.'

'It don't matter! I ain't being a David Bowie tribute act!'

'No one is suggesting that.'

'Well, what the fuck are they suggesting?'

He was spreading the mayonnaise now. There was a lot going into that burger. 'That you are actually David Bowie himself. The soul of him anyway, exiled in someone else's body for the past twenty-eight years.' Now finished, he put the lid on the bun and placed it on a plate with a few bits of lettuce beside it.

'Oh fuck...' I said, rubbing my face.

I could see tough times ahead for Ted.

They say it gets worse before it gets better.

An Introduction to the Soulshift

THE soulshift is the means by which two souls may be exchanged. Such an operation requires a donor and a host. The donor is the organism whose soul is identified as a High Denomination Soul. The host is the organism whose body is identified as a suitable storage vessel for the High Denomination Soul, until such time as you wish to deploy it. Once the host and donor have been identified, the soulshift is a simple exchange of souls.

8.

The next morning I found out a couple of things about Ted's situation. It involved alcohol, that was one of them. I'd left him downstairs at about one in the morning and gone up to the spare room as per his directions, creeping up the stairs and not wanting to wake the family. And there he still was when I came down a few hours later: fully-clothed, crashed on the sofa with an empty bottle of Bell's beside him, telly on.

I wondered how long he'd been hitting the sauce, and how much of his mental situation was down to it. You can addle your brain with the hard stuff, everyone knows that.

The other thing I found out was about his family. I'd forgot my watch so I crept back upstairs. It was 7 a.m. and about time folks were stirring, this being a school day, so I had to work sharpish and stealthy. One of the doors had a sign saying NATALIE AND SAMANTHAS ROOM GET LOST, which I had a little smirk at. Must be a nightmare living under a roof with three females, and I could see how that might drive a man a bit bonkers perhaps. Then I noticed that the door was ajar, light streaming out of it past undrawn curtains. I had a peak inside.

No kids.

No one in the other rooms either. Which meant one of two things:

1. They fucked off because he went mad or
2. He went mad because they fucked off.

All in all, a chicken and egg scenario. And one I didn't want any part of. I had troubles of my own to sort out. Even worse ones than Ted, when you thought about it. I'd lost my job and been kicked out of my home. At least he still had his home. Even if it was cold and lonely just then.

I stopped in the living room doorway and had a last look at him. He was snoring and spluttering and having a troubled dream, arms and legs jerking. I felt sorry for the poor bloke. All right, so he'd done me no favours career-wise, and his recent lack of sanity had no doubt contributed to me getting the sack last night. But he'd stood by me when no one else had.

Jeannie worked in a laundrette on Faith Street. She frowned when I walked in. She'd never had much time for me. In her book, Ted linking up with me had been the start of his downfall. I was a waste of space. More than that, I was actually quite evil for encouraging a stable family man to join him in my stroll down the path of decadence and ruination.

Looking at her now, with the corners of her mouth plumbing new depths, I realised that there was probably some truth in her opinions. But I wasn't as bad as her. At least I hadn't abandoned my spouse in his time of need.

'You what?' she was shrieking, scaring two old men who

were waiting for their spin cycles to finish. 'You come in here and have the *gall* to pass judgement on *me*? *I* didn't abandon him. You *wrenched* him from me. It was *you* who put all them ideas in his head about—'

'Ted came to me, remember?' I said. 'He already had ideas in his head. You remember that.'

'He wouldn't have had them ideas if it wasn't for you! Ted was...he was steady, dependable. I lost my Ted when he met you.'

'Jeannie, this door's stuck,' one of the codgers was saying. She swatted him away and yanked the door open, then went to the corner and faced it, wrapping a black bin liner round her hand like a boxer preparing for a fight.

'Look,' I said, going nearer. Not too near though, 'I didn't come here for a row.' Because I hadn't. Disagreeing with Jeannie was tantamount to removing part of your eardrum, such was the power and banshee-like quality of her inevitable comeback. 'Some of what you say is true. I accept my role in Ted's current problems, and for that I'm sorry. I'm sorry for the pain I've brought you, Jeannie, and for the disruption caused to your two beautiful daughters, Natalie and Samantha.'

'You stay away from my daughters!' she said, flashing me her irate profile before facing the corner again. 'They've been through enough. We all have.'

'Jeannie, I haven't even gone near your daughters.'

'Well don't even think about them, all right?'

'Eh? Come on, Jeannie,' I said, stepping even closer and putting a hand on her bird-like shoulder. She flinched like I'd touched her with a live cable, then sank into it. I gave her a friendly squeeze. 'I ain't like that, Jeannie. I'm all right. If you knew me, you'd see that I was—'

'I've no time for people like you!' she said, yanking herself away and facing me. 'You're a bad man, Rik Suntan. Only harm can come to anyone who touches you…I mean…anyone you touch, with your strong, firm hands…and stare broodingly at with those big brown—'

'Eh?'

'Oh just get out of here! Go on, I can't have you coming around here!'

She was saying one thing but her body was saying different. It was betraying her, telling the world that she had hidden feelings that wanted out. I stood there with my arms at my sides, looking at her with her body half-turned away, her heart torn. It was like a pop video, the wind blowing in through the air vents and the washing machines going round and round, representing a woman's feelings. The conflict was killing her and I could feel it. I'm sensitive like that. If you're a singer of emotional songs, you have to be.

'I told you before,' I said in a gentle voice, low so nobody could hear but her. Mind you, the two codgers were probably deaf. 'We can't be. I couldn't do that to Ted.'

'Well…if you feel so strongly for him, why don't *you* go and look after him?' Her dark side was winning, beating down the sweet, sensuous feminine nature I'd seen and admired in her before, the side that had told me my bone structure was so perfect that it made up for my facial disfigurement. It was a shame. But it was the usual way of things. For men and women alike.

I really felt in song-writing mode, and I wished I had a pen and paper handy.

'Me and the girls, we've had enough. Do you hear me? Had *enough*.'

'Jeannie,' I said. I knew I was causing her pain just by saying her name, but I couldn't do anything about that. It was my burden.

To kill people softly with my words.

Especially women.

'Jeannie…Jeannie…'

'What?'

'Ted is sick. He's mentally ill, and he needs—'

'I can't have that. If he's going off his rocker, I…I couldn't bear the stigma, Rik. No, I can't help him. I…just…'

A waver.

Compassion?

'All he needs is love,' I said, hoping to drive it home.

'Well…*you* give it him. Me? I'm filin' for divorce. Now fuck off!'

9.

'Ted?'

I didn't have a mobile phone. I'd had one once but I found that it messed with my natural rhythms. As a musician I couldn't have that. You'd be walking along, humming and tapping out a new tune that had been offered up by your muse, and your mobile would go off in your pocket, barging in with a new beat and in a different key entirely. I couldn't have that. Only those who are disconnected from technology can tap into the earth's heartbeat, which is where music comes from. Plus Ted was the only one who ever used to ring it anyway.

'Ted?'

So that's why I was in a phone box. The one up by Gulliver Park. It reeked of urine and most of the glass was smashed. Plus I'd had to buy a phone card to make the call. But it didn't mess with my natural rhythms.

'Ted? Is that Ted or what?'

'Rik!' he finally said. It was good to hear someone who was pleased to talk to me. Even if he was a bit slow off the mark. And a nutter. 'What happened to you this morning? I was gonna rustle up some eggs.'

'Never mind about eggs. I need a word with you.'

'Oh yeah? Well, come round here, mate. There's a couple of people I want you to—'

'No. Somewhere public, like—'

'Somewhere public? What's this? You consider me a danger to you, Rik?'

I was beginning to doubt my own sanity here. Ted sounded all right, didn't he? He didn't sound like a lunatic anyway. Maybe I was the one with the malfunctioning head? Maybe Ted hadn't really said all that David Bowie stuff last night, and I'd just dreamed it? I'd always had powerful dreams, and it's possible I was confusing them with reality.

'Course I don't. I just—'

'Well it sounds like you do. It sounds like I've scared you a bit with that David Bowie malarkey. You think I'm mad, don't you?'

'I don't think you're *mad*, Ted. I just think you're having a little nervous breakdown or summat. It happens to the best of us. Especially when you're not getting the support at home that you need.'

There was no reply for a bit, followed by:

'You've been talking to Jeannie, ain't you?'

'Jeannie? Course I ain't. I can work things out for myself, Ted. And I can see when certain things ain't there. Like the support at home you need.'

'Well, you don't have to—'

'I'm concerned about you, Ted. And I thought you'd be more grateful.'

'I am grateful, very grateful. You're a special person, Rik. Or, should I say, David.'

'Don't fuckin' start that again. Look, can you meet me later or what? I really want you to. And I don't think you're mad, just—'

'Yeah, just having a little mental breakdown.'

'Oh, don't be like—'

'I'll see you at Covelli's for a spot of lunch. All right?'

He hung up. I was glad the conversation was over because the stench of piss was beginning to overwhelm me. I got out fast, crunching glass underfoot and trying to chase down a thought that had just whizzed past my head. I didn't know what the thought was about but I knew it was important, because it was black and yellow and had a siren on top. I had to catch it, and I sat down on the perimeter wall of the park to do just that. But trying gets you nowhere in that scenario. The more you chase, the more elusive the bugger is. It's best to feign nonchalance, so I started picking bits of glass out of the sole of my shoe. It was brown and curved, this particular bit, like it was from a…

10.

'Beer bottle.'

She looked at me blank. That didn't mean anything. Blank was normal for Delores. It had been a long time ago, but I'm pretty sure blank was her look when I'd shagged her as well. And that's no slight on me.

'Last night,' I said. 'The one that I got hit by.'

'Oh yeah,' she said, coming alive like someone had flicked a switch on her. 'Stan says it never smashed.'

'That's right. It was a hard bottle all right, and I took it on the face and didn't even break my stride. Not that I was walking at the time. But I was singing, and I never…What's the phrase?'

We were in the Cairo. It was early – only about ten – but I'd seen her Fiesta parked outside and got her to let me in, saying it was a fucking emergency. And it *was* an emergency, because it was about me getting my job back.

'Miss a beat, yeah,' I said. 'I never missed a beat.'

'No,' Delores said. 'Of course you never. Was it a plastic bottle? Because a glass bottle would kill a man, wouldn't it?'

'It was a glass bottle, Del. A plastic bottle wouldn't have travelled so far through the air, at such a rate of knots and with such accuracy.'

'Well, Stan says he found it and it was plastic.'

'He said what?'

'He said—'

'Does this cut here on my face look like the work of a plastic bottle?'

'Don't ask me, Rik. Stan said that—'

'Look, it don't matter. I just wanna see him. About the bottle issue.'

'He was quite positive that it was made of—'

'This issue ain't about what it was *made* of. It's about... Fuckin' hell, Del. Is he in or what?'

'No, he ain't. He's at the bank.'

'Shit...Look, can I have a drink?'

'We're not open yet. I'm only here to let in the estate agents.'

'Well can you just tell him...Tell him Rik came round, and he's got some information about the bottling incident from last night. You getting this? You wanna write it down?'

'Go on. I'll remember it.'

I didn't know if that was true, but I had to take the risk. It would be better coming from Delores. I felt that she was on my side, even if she'd never shown any particular interest in my music. She knew I was all right and she knew I needed a break. And she could twist Stan around her little finger like it was a pole and he was a fat, ugly pole dancer.

'Tell him I know who threw it. Right? It's one of his employees right here at the Cairo. I've had a confession from him and everything. So really, if Stan thinks about it, it's an industrial incident. Which means that I could sue him for it. Do you see what I mean?'

Her look was, as ever, blank.

'Sue Stan?'

'Yeah. For damages, on account of the injury incurred in the line of…Look, it don't matter. What matters is that I *won't* sue. Course I won't sue. I wouldn't sue Stan, would I? He's your husband. And you're my mate. Ain't you, Del?'

'Well…'

'So of course I wouldn't litigate Stan. So long as he gives me my job back. See what I mean?'

'Well, I think I…'

She was still processing it, bless her. I gave her a minute to catch up. Poor old Delores, getting lumbered with this when she'd only come in to—

'Hang on,' I said. 'Estate agents?'

'What does litigate mean?'

'Never mind that – what's this about you meeting estate agents here?'

'Yeah, I am. They should be here in…Ooh, they're late.'

'What for, though? You and Stan getting a new house?'

'No, Stan wants to sell the Blue Cairo.'

'But…'

'It just came on him last night, when we got home. "I lost one of the finest, most talented individuals I've ever worked with tonight," he said. I always remember exactly what people say, you see. "And do you know what it's made me realise? That my heart ain't in this business no more. It's about people, Del. Not just *any* people, but *certain* people. And when you start losing them people, well…Do you know what I'm gonna do, Delores? I'm gonna sell up the Cairo and go into the used car business." That's exactly what he said.'

'Fuck. What did he say after that?'

'Umm…he said: "Del, have you seen my handcuffs?" I told him yeah, they were in his box. He looked in his box again and went: "Oh yeah, they were under the dog col—"'

'All right, Del…But he definitely said "one of the finest, most talented singers I've ever had the pleasure of working with"?'

'It was "individuals", not "singers".'

'Oh well, same difference.'

'Not really, because—'

'And it's nice to know what he thinks of me. Stuff like that keeps you going, you know?'

'No, he was talking about Yusuf, not you.'

'Oh. Right. He sacked him too?'

'No, Yusuf quit. He said he had a better offer.'

'From who?'

'He wouldn't say.'

'Fuck. Bollocks. Fuckin' hell.'

'What's the matter?'

'What's the matter? I've lost my job, Del. I'm without a job, and I can't get it back cos the place it was in is about to shut up shop. Not only that, but my old employer thinks more of a fuckin' amateur keyboard player than he does of me! I'm a professional, Del. It's hard for me to take.'

'Well, there's always *The X Factor*.'

'What? Oh, don't start that again…'

'I entered you in it.'

'You done what?'

'Auditions are this Friday in Burninghouse. You're gonna be on the telly, Rik!'

'I ain't gonna be on telly cos I ain't going. I already told you – I won't have nothing to do with that shit. It's beneath me.'

'That man from the Miramar don't think it's shit. He says it's "a vital component of the music industry. And anyone blaming it for the degradation of modern culture has got it the wrong way round. Modern culture was already degraded, and *The X Factor* has simply wrapped itself around that." I dunno what he meant by that, though.'

'He said that last night, when he was in here?'

'No, just now. When he rang up about you.'

'He never.'

'He did. He said he was interested in you, and asked how he could reach you. He's been trying Ted's number but nobody's answering. He also mentioned my breasts and how attractive he found them, and how did I feel about older men. He was a bit cheeky actually, Rik. I mean, there's flirting and then there's—'

'Did he leave a number?'

'What? Yes he did. It's...'

She gave me the number. I wanted to kiss her, but it was a bit far to reach across the bar and I might get my clothes snagged on one of the beer levers, which would be an awkward and clumsy moment. But not even awkward and clumsy moments were capable of bothering me, the way I felt just then. I was on the up again, heading for the big time and looking success in the face. Sometimes you've got to hit rock-bottom before you can scale the heights, and that's what had happened here. I still didn't kiss Delores, though. Despite what Mr Miramar had told her, she wasn't actually that fit these days. I think he was just being nice to her, because someone like him would have better taste than that. I mean, he knew a star when he saw one.

I asked Delores if I could use the phone.

'Why? You gonna ring him now? Ooh, I dunno if Stan'll stretch to long distance.'

'What he don't know about can't harm him. And I ain't calling him anyway.'

'Who you calling, then?'

'That's private.'

'Oh.'

'But if you must know, it's the Samaritans.'

11.

Growing a moustache was one of the best things I ever did. Some of the older lads in the home had them, and you could see the effect it had on them and everyone else. It was like they were putting on the mask of a grown-up, hiding the gormless young face behind it and reaping the rewards of respect, confidence and more of a chance with the girls. I didn't have a gormless face, but I had a good reason to cover my top lip.

I started as soon as I could, putting Baby Bio on my bum-fluff and combing the little hairs to make them feel wanted. None of that worked and I shaved it all off in a rage, albeit a very calm and controlled rage, taking care not to slice myself. Within a couple days it was growing back and showing signs of taking itself seriously. Gone were the soft whispy hairs, replaced by thick, hard ones of a rich brown hue. It was like they'd gone down the gym overnight and toughened up. Within a couple of weeks I had a tash. A proper one, like Magnum PI.

And the world saw me differently.

Back in the here and now, I was smoothing down the hairs of that very same tash as I strolled up Commercial Road, whistling a merry tune. I couldn't put my finger on what the tune was or who it was by, although I assumed it was a proper song by a famous person. It had to be, because it really was a nice tune. And then I started wondering if it was a gift.

Sometimes you get that: a fully formed song sent down to you by your muse. It sounds familiar and you know all of it as soon as the first bars hit your inner ear, but it's new. It's never been heard before by anyone but you, and it's all yours. A gift.

Then I caught sight of my reflection in the window of a charity shop, and I realised that it was 'Golden Years'.

By David fucking Bowie.

I stopped whistling straight away. This was bad news. When you find yourself humming or whistling a song you can't stand, it means your head is in the wrong place. It's music's way of telling you that there's something rough coming along and you might not be able to cope with it.

It was half right: something rough was coming along. It was waiting for me only yards down the road, in Covelli's. But it needed doing and I knew I could cope with it. I felt that I couldn't move on with things until I'd sorted Ted out, got him some help and set him straight on a couple of home truths. It was quite possibly going to get ugly in there, because Ted wouldn't enjoy hearing what I had to say. But hear it he would. And then I could leave him be and get on with the real stuff.

Like ringing back this Mr Miramar.

I'd have done that already if I could. That fish needed reeling in and I so desperately wanted to do it without further ado. I had the words in my head and everything. A bucket-load of natural charm was at my disposal. But first things first. The decks had to be cleared. And now was the time.

I pushed the door open and breathed deep the unique, greasy, fly-ridden ambience that was Covelli's at that moment, and straight away I knew I'd made a wrong move. I'd only been in this place three or four times before and each time had been on Ted's beckoning. This was his office in all but name, he'd always said. A place where he felt he could achieve a higher level of concentration, and better tease out the finer threads of his innate business acumen. Which had always been fine by me, if business was on the cards. I wanted Ted to be on the ball, because I trusted him to do right by me. But this was different. Loggerheads would be involved here. I could foresee denial, dismissal and laughing off of serious issues. But it was too late now.

Because he'd seen me.

'Here he is,' I heard him say to his companions. Oh yeah, he had company:

Yusuf
Martin
The fucking midget who'd shot me last night.

'What the fuck are you doing here?' I said. To Yusuf mainly, and also a bit to Martin. But my eyes were locked on the little feller. His shoulders barely reached the table but he had eyes as big as a normal person, and they glared back at me. He got down off the chair as I stepped nearer, which actually made him a bit shorter. By the time I reached the table he was out and ready and in a fighting stance. I found it quite laughable, the prospect of him doing a roundhouse on me, but that's the sort of thing his body language led me to expect. I was all set to deliver him a kick that would break him when I remembered what I was here for.

Whatever you do, don't get him agitated.

I'm talking about Ted there. That's what the Samaritans had advised in respect of him.

Keep his trust or you might lose him for good. Listen to what he's got to say, and don't just laugh at him or tell him it's bollocks.

That wasn't precisely what they'd said, but it was like that. And I hadn't caught all of it anyway. It's hard to concentrate when Delores is letting estate agents in and showing them around. The Blue Cairo was a landmark on the professional history of Rik Suntan, and I dreaded to think what they'd turn it into if the wrong people got hold of it. If I was a couple of steps further along in my career, making a bit of cash, I'd buy the place myself and preserve it as a place of historical interest.

'Look, Ted,' I said, one eye on the midget still, but relaxing my posture, 'I need a word in private.'

'Rik, you're just in time,' he said. 'I'm about to order. You want the ADB? It's on me. Cause for celebration.'

'Oh yeah?' I said, taking in the uncomfortable looks I was getting from Martin and Yusuf. I still couldn't imagine what had led to them being here in this caff with Ted and a psycho midget. Or even sitting at the same table with each other. In all my time at the Cairo I hadn't seen so much as a nod pass between them. And now...

What?

'Ted,' I said. We were up at the counter now, just me and him. 'What the fuck...? I mean, why are they...?'

'Oh, I'm just doing a bit of business with them. Do you want the ADB, Rik?'

'What business? Yeah, all right, the ADB.'

'Four all-day brekkies, love,' he said to the woman there. 'And a mushroom sarnie.'

She didn't seem impressed by that last one, and nor was I.

'Which one of them is having that?' I asked, tossing a look of disgust in their direction. The midget was still staring at me, and I just knew it was him who wanted the mushroom sarnie. Midgets probably have special dietary requirements.

'That's me, I'm afraid,' Ted said, chuckling. 'Part of my new regime. Health food only.'

'Health food?' I was about to tell him a bad diet was the least of his problems when I remembered: this was just another manifestation of his mental illness. 'Ted,' I said instead, 'I really do need to talk to you in private.'

'I don't mind speaking in front of the lads,' he said, fishing coins from his pocket.

'The lads? Ted, they ain't the lads. *I'm* the lads. They ain't even…Look, Ted, why are they here? I thought I was meeting you on your own. We don't need them twats here.'

'No, you've got it all wrong. These are your fellow victims, and we're gonna sort it all out together. It's good that you're here because we can all sit down and iron out the finer details.'

I was speechless. But I knew I had to say something before Ted went back to 'the lads'.

'Look, I did speak to Jeannie,' I blurted. The woman behind the counter was just handing Ted his change and her eyes lit up. I gave her what she wanted: 'I know all about it, Ted. About her and the kids moving out. And her wanting a divorce.'

Ted stood immobile, coins in hand. Looks like I was finally getting through. 'Oh yeah?' he said. 'She all right, is she?'

'Ted, I think it's disgusting, the way she's left you to your own devices at such a time of need. I told her that as well. She should be supporting you and making sure you get the right help. Well, don't you worry. I'm here, and I been doing some homework. I can get you seen, Ted. I know where to go and what to say to them. I'll even go with you, if you like. Although I am a bit busy just now. I'll give you the address, though.'

Ted's eyes moved slowly from the coins to my face. I could see the agitation behind them, and I knew I'd fucked up. What a dickhead. All I'd had to do was listen to him, let him say what he wants to say. Just don't get him pissed off or you'll lose his trust. He was about to say something, probably along the lines of who the fuck did I think I was, snooping around in his business?, when the person behind us went:

'For fuck's sake, would you get a fuckin' shift on? I'm fuckin' starvin' here.'

I turned and said: 'Oh, soz, love,' to the little old lady stood there. Ted was already back at the table and sitting down with 'the lads'. I went and joined him, expecting to get told to fuck off by Ted but you never knew. Maybe he'd forgotten my indiscreet words already, him being a fruitcake and all. And it seems he had, because he acted like I'd never said them.

'All right, gentlemen,' he said, shuffling some papers in front of him. 'Grub on the way, let's get pleasantries over with, shall we? Messrs Yusuf, Martin, Eggy and Rik have been gathered here in relation to a certain proposal that has come into my hands. I've looked into it and found it to be sound in all respects. The proposal, as we all know, is that you should all be sent back through space and time to the mid-'70s or thereabouts, where you shall resume your careers and lives in general as the famous and successful people you once were. Are all parties agreed on that much and keen on going forward?'

Martin and Yusuf were nodding, looking at me like this was all my idea and they thought it was a good one. It was like the whole world was going barmy all around me. Then again, maybe Martin and Yusuf were just helping him in the same way I was.

The midget was staring at me, fists clenched on the table like a couple of walnuts.

'Before I proceed, I think the lads here wanted to say a word of welcome to our newest recruit. Lads, you want to do the honours?'

Martin nodded and looked at Yusuf, who cleared his throat and wrote down on a bit of paper: 'ME AND MY FREINDS WANT TO SAY WE ARE DEEPLY HONURED YOU COMING HERE. AND WE GIVE YOU THIS GIFT AS AN APPRESHATION TOKEN LIKE.'

Martin placed in front of me a CD-shaped thing wrapped up in yellow paper with little pictures of teddy bears and presents on it. I was as charmed as a person could be, given the circumstances. I started opening it.

'No,' said Martin, putting a big hand on the little gift, 'you gotta open it later. It's a surprise. To get you in the mood.' He winked at me.

'Right then, Rik,' Ted was saying, looking at me through his big bifocal lenses. 'I explained the basics to you last night. You were probably a bit bewildered at the time. I knew I was when I first came across this business. And Martin and Eggy here, you should have seen them. Took some convincing, let's just say. But they got there in the end, eh boys?'

Martin nodded hard.

Eggy stared at me.

'But I expect you've come up with a few questions, now you've had time to reflect on it. And now's the time to get some answers. That's what we're all here for, so ask away.'

I wanted some answers all right. But I knew the kind of answers they'd be, and I didn't want to dignify them with a question. So I just asked:

'Look, just tell me how you found out all this.'

'A book,' Martin said. 'That we robbed.'

Ted put his hand up. 'Now now, we don't use the term "robbed" in this instance. Let's say we procured it.'

'I get it,' I said, looking at Martin. 'You happened to 'procure' this book by pure chance when you happened to be doing someone's house over.'

'It wasn't like that,' snapped Ted. 'It was a *mission*. Them two are brave and clever lads. Martin planned it and Eggy carried it out.'

'A midget burglar,' I said. 'Now I seen it all.'

Said midget was halfway over the table already, reaching for my throat. Martin got him by the shoulder, saying:

'We don't call 'em midgets no more. You gotta call 'em dwarves. Or 'little people'. He's a little person.'

The little person took a swipe at me, missing by an inch, and said: 'Yeah, I'm a *bad* little person.'

'Can we just get this back on track?' said Ted. 'Questions pertaining to the matter at hand *only*, please.'

'Right,' I said, nodding to Yusuf. 'Well, what's his part in all this?'

I GOT A NAME, he wrote.

'All right, fuckin' calm down. What's Yoose doing here?'

CAT. MY NAME IS CAT

'All right!'

WELL, I ALREADY FUCKIN TOLD YOU THAT

'I know but I...Hold up, Ted called you Yusuf and you never—'

I KNOW BUT, wrote Yusuf, angling the paper away from Ted. HES A BIT OF A SPANNER

I scratched my head at that.

Ted said: 'Mr Cat is here for the same reason as yourself, Martin and Eggy. You are all featured in *The New Skalanomicon*, and you—'

'The what?'

'The book we, er…procured. You're all in it. The person who wrote it stole loads of souls from sparkling, famous people in the '70s and put them in the dull, obscure ones you find yourselves in now.'

After thinking about that I said: 'Don't call me dull and obscure, you cheeky fucker. I got a following, me.'

'Well, you had more of a following in your old body.'

'And who's supposed to have written this book? Charles Dickens?'

'No, Jimmy Page.'

'And…What?

'Jimmy Page. You know, out of Led Zeppelin.'

'Oh, Ted…' I said, rubbing my forehead. It seemed to give me strength and remind me what I was here for, and how much Ted's mental health had deteriorated. 'Right,' I said, pulling myself together, 'So…Jimmy Page out of Led Zeppelin has written a book – *The New Scally-whatever* – and he's got a special time machine, is it?'

Ted looked at me like I was nuts.

'I'm just trying to get an angle on the technical aspects,' I said. 'I mean, this kind of thing don't happen too often.'

'It did in the '70s,' Martin said. 'Round here.'

'That's right,' said Ted, who seemed to be the brains here, mangled though they were. 'The '70s was a fertile period for this kind of caper. But there's no time machines involved, Rik. I mean, come on…Time machines? Heh heh.'

Martin and Yusuf started laughing as well, followed by the midget, who was clearly a bit slow on the uptake. Not as slow as me, though. Finally I laughed too, remembering how I'm supposed to be going along with all this for Ted's sake.

'Fuckin' time machine…' I said, shaking my head. 'What am I like, eh?'

'No,' said Ted, still chuckling, 'time machines and that – it's all science fiction. None of that kind of thing can ever happen in real life. You'll be coming at us with UFOs next, eh Rik?'

I laughed along with them a bit more, gritting my teeth, then came out with: 'Yeah, what a twat I am. So how did he do it, if you don't mind me asking?'

The midget found that amusing. I wanted to punch his miniature face in, so help me God. I gripped the table leg instead and sought solace in the fact that none of the other three were laughing. Nor even smiling. Then the midget joined in with a po-face of his own.

They all regarded each other for a while, then Ted turned to me, looking like he had some bad news to deliver.

'He used black magic, Rik,' he said. 'In them days, Jimmy Page was like a warlock.'

Experiments in Soulshifting

I perfected the art of soulshifting using scientific methods. Anything worth doing should be done scientifically, and that includes the black arts. The bare-bones theory behind it came into my hands via an ancient document found buried under a cellar, but theory is nothing unless you can put it into practice.

Like any rational person I was at first sceptical. These were the blatherings of a lunatic, surely? But something in the ebb and flow of ritual and theory rang true, and I read on. The words were mesmerising, and before long I was seeing the world as if through a distorted microscope, able to discern hitherto invisible yet impossible entities. I was confused, and believed that I was teetering on the cusp of madness. I had to make a choice: destroy the book and return to the everyday world, or embrace the non-Euclidean perspective preached within the pages of *The Skalanomicon*.

To make up my mind, I decided to put some of the ritual descriptions to the test.

My first experiments were performed on caterpillars and snails. Being slow-moving animals, they were easy to perform the ritual on and there was a plentiful supply of them. But it was difficult to judge the results. Although undoubtedly in possession of souls, it was near impossible to distinguish one snail from the next. Even to a master of the black arts, a snail with a strong soul does not seem much different from one with a weak soul. So I moved on to dogs, which have personalities discernible to humans, and distinguishable souls. Many of the local dogs died during this time but I ironed out nearly all of the technical problems.

After dogs I moved to human subjects. Circumstances around me had changed and there was no time to waste with more experimentation, so I went straight in where it mattered: High Denomination Souls. At the time I had access to many of this type, high-achieving humans whose field of endeavour was mainly music and entertainment. By definition, this type of individual is sophisticated and difficult to trick into submitting to a ritual that would seem deeply strange to them. They were also very high profile and therefore not so easy to take by force. Which is what led me to my secondary line of research: how to negotiate, on a human subject's behalf, diabolical favours.

By now my fate was decided. I was a warlock.

12.

'A warlock?'

'I said *like* a warlock, not necessarily actually one of them,' Ted said. A fly had landed on his ear but he didn't seem bothered by it. 'There's a fair bit of semantical nicety involved here.'

'So…What? Is Jimmy Page a warlock or not?'

'Well, forget what he is or ain't. Cos whatever he was then, he probably ain't now. I mean, this was the '70s. Right, Martin?'

'Right.'

'Right. There was a lot of warlocks going round back then.'

'Look,' I said, 'I'm a bit…'

'Confused,' said Ted. 'Anyone would be, hearing about all this stuff for the first time. I was as well. Remember that, Rik. Before I chanced upon the, erm…Well, before I found out about all this, I didn't even know what a warlock was. I'd grown up thinking a warlock was a lock you put on a war.'

Everyone except Ted had a good look at each other.

'Ted,' I said, representing us all, I think, 'why would someone put a lock on a war?' It was sort of besides the point, I know that. But I could feel this whole getting help for Ted thing slipping away from me and I wanted to stop it.

'To keep it closed,' he said. 'Once the war is over, you don't want it starting again, do you?'

'No, but…'

'Do you mean like a padlock?' said Martin.

'Well, I don't rightly know. Look, all I said was that's what I thought a warlock was when I was growing up. And it's all academic anyway because—'

'Surely,' I said, sliding down the mountain of his madness and reaching out for any toe-hold, 'surely you can't put a lock on a war? A war that's finished can flare up again at any time. All it takes is for the defeated side to get their shit together again, then they can—'

'The Geneva Convention,' said Ted.

This got a bit of silence around the table for a moment or two. Then Martin clapped a couple of times, shaking his head in admiration. 'See?' he said, to me. 'Ted's the man, ain't he? He knows his stuff. Fuckin' hell, The Geneva Convention…There's you checkmated, Rik.'

'What…?' I said, barely able to spit it out. 'How does that checkmate me? I don't even know what the Geneva Convention is!'

'Yeah,' said Ted, 'but you dunno what it *ain't*, neither. Do you?'

'Yeah,' said Martin. 'I mean, er…no.'

I noticed that Yusuf and Eggy were staying out of all this. With Yusuf I knew it was because he had some intelligence on him, although he seemed to be inching down the path towards being fucked in the head. But Eggy was at that place already. He was rotating his shoulders slightly as he sat in his chair, jerking them forward one after the other like he was shifting weight under the table. When you looked at this for a while you got the impression of a classic loon.

I sat back and took in the other three, and I got that same impression from them as well. Yusuf might have had the odd lucid moment but he was actually fully tapped. It was like there was a sanity divide between me and them, and they were on the wrong side of it.

But in actual fact there was no madness threshold of any description between us, only salt, pepper, vinegar and red and brown sauces.

'Tell you what,' Ted went on, 'how about some details, eh? Yusuf, you tell Rik here about some of the details. You know, the rituals and that. It's really interesting.'

Ted beamed at me, nodding hard. I was a bit scared at that point, I don't mind saying. I could empathise with Jeannie and I wanted the fuck out of there.

WELL, wrote Yusuf, FIRST OF ALL JIMMY PAGE GOT SOME OF DAVID BOWIES PISS. IT WAS EASY BECAUSE DAVID USED TO KEEP HIS PISS IN BOTTLES IN THE FRIGE. WITH THE PISS HE

'Hang on…' I said. 'He kept his piss in a fridge?'

YES TO STOP WARLOCKS LIKE PAGE FROM STEALIN IT. AND

'And how'd you know this?'

IN THE BOOK

'In the book you stole?'

NOT THAT ONE. THIS BOOK WAS IN SMITHS

'So…hang on a minute. They're selling warlock books in fuckin' Smiths?'

NO IT WAS JUST A BOOK ABOUT BOWIE. EGGY SWIPED IT

'Look,' said Ted, 'we only had *The New Skalanomicon* for a short while, and I didn't get to read all of it. We've had to piece together all the rest from hither and thither.'

'Thither?'

'Yeah. And hither.'

'Is 'thither' an actual word? No, don't answer that. What I really mean is, erm…Oh yeah, how come you only had the book a short while?'

'It dematerialised.'

'It de…?'

'I had it under lock and key, but he still got it back. Mr Page located it using his warlock skills, and—'

'—dematerialised it. Right.'

'Yeah, then *re*-materialised it back where he had it safe.'

'And where'd you rob it from, eh? Jimmy Page's fuckin' castle, or summat?'

'We ain't meant to say,' said Martin, looking at his tiny neighbour. 'I'll say it was in Warchester, though. In the Tything area.'

'Martin!' hissed Ted.

'For fuck's sake,' I said, leaning back. 'Jimmy Page is a fuckin'…He's a famous rock star, you twats! What's he doing in fuckin'…?'

But I wasn't interested no more. How can a sane person sit there for more than a minute or so and listen to this? It's not so bad if it's just one mentally ill person, but with four it was a nightmare. And not only that, they were all barmy in the same way. It's like there was a very specific brain disease that they'd all caught. And I had a good idea who from.

I stared at the midget. He'd hardly took his gaze off me the whole time, and our eyes locked like a couple of magnets, one of them very small. I could sense his little fists balling even tighter, becoming more like pecans than walnuts. They'd probably sting a bit, if I remembered right from school about when force is applied via a small point of contact. But I couldn't imagine them inflicting much damage. A short little arm like that, he'd get no leverage at all from it. These were the things I was speculating about when he hit me. Blinding fast.

Not once, but multiple times.

By the time I noticed what was going on he was stood on the table, legs planted wide, treating my head like a punch bag. I suppose it did sting, but I was more taken aback than anything else. He must have landed ten of those little hooks by the time I roused myself to action. I reached out with a nice firm jab of my own, capable of sending him across that caff like he'd been fired from a cannon.

But he wasn't there.

And my fist met air.

Martin was holding him above his head. I tried jumping up but Ted got hold of me and held me back. I don't remember much after that, only rage and trying to swing with my free arm while Ted twisted the other, which actually quite hurt. There was blood and shouting and plates of food being thrown, then threats of police and sudden fresh air and more shouting, and when I came to I was alone on a bench in the park, holding a hanky to my nose. It was stuck there with dried blood. My arm still hurt.

I felt depressed.

Sensitive, creative people are prone to depression. We experience the highs and bring them to you in song form, but we get the lows too. Lows so low that you feel like you're underground. It's cold and damp and dark in there and the world outside is muffled and far away. I've actually written a song about this. 'Moles', it's called.

I am like a mole
Digging in my hole
It's very sad in here
I would cry in my beer
If I was in a pub
But there is the rub
Cos I am just a mole
And I'm stuck in this hole

That's just the first verse, which deals with the initial problem. All decent songs take you from one place to another, and this is no exception. The mole comes out of the hole in the end and sees the sun, so he's not in his hole any more. He's actually in a pub beer garden, the gentle breeze ruffling his velvet fur and bringing the fragrance of lager to his little pink nose. But he's not equipped for this world of humans, most of them a bit drunk or getting that way. For a start, he's blind. So he doesn't see it coming when the woman steps on his head with her stiletto heel.

But for a few moments there he transcended his problems and got to his promised land, so it's a song of hope, really.

I took that hope and went home.

13.

'You goin' over or what?' said Elvis, bits of pastie flying from his lips.

'Just gimme a moment. I'm thinkin'.'

'Well stop thinking and fuckin' get on with it. Yer makin' me nervous, hangin' there. And it's fuckin' chilly.'

Elvis lived in the flat next door. Being as I couldn't get into my own flat, Shelley having changed the lock, I had to use his, climbing from his balcony to mine at great risk to myself. Only I hadn't done it yet, because Elvis was still watching.

'Go on in, then,' I told him. 'Don't worry about me.'

He'd been a devil to get past. Elvis was the Neighbourhood Watch representative, and as such wouldn't allow me to hop from his balcony on to Shelley's. 'It's the robber's way round' summed up his firm stance on the matter. So I'd had to promise him that my intention was suicide before he'd let me through his front door. Suicide was fine by him, it seemed, 'as long as it does not compromise the property of any residents on this floor.'

I'd assured him that it wouldn't, and here we now were.

Elvis turned his massive back on me and went to go inside, stopping by the doorway and saying: 'Look, I don't give a fuck if you wanna throw yerself off or what, but don't come knockin' on my window in five minutes, wantin' me to let you in again. I'm sittin' down now and I ain't gettin' up again. Right?'

He turned and started to go through the doorway. It took him a while because his hips didn't fit through frontways and his belly didn't sideways, so he had to twist a bit and do a combination of both. I left him to it and went over on to my balcony.

Luckily Shelley hadn't changed the lock on the door there, and I let myself in using the key I kept hid under a flower pot for occasions such as this one. It was good to be home. I flicked on the telly and crashed on the sofa for a watch. She was off on her nightshift until six the next morning so it didn't matter if I nodded off – I'd still have time to clean myself up and make myself presentable for her. Not that I wasn't always presentable.

She'd cleaned the place up, most likely as a desperate attempt to wash me out of her hair. I couldn't blame her for it. She liked an ordered life, Shelley did, and living with me must have been a challenge for her. But sometimes a person needs a challenge. I brought chaos and excitement into her life, brightening it up with glitz, glamour and sweet sounds. All right, my creative energies rubbed up against her mundane ones and generated a bit of friction at times, but it always worked out in the end. That's the way it was for me and Shell.

She'd be worrying about me now, doing her rounds at the nursing home. Was I safe? Where had I kipped last night? Had I eaten? Yeah, now it was her turn to suffer. Not that I'm a nasty person, but I do know it makes the making up all the sweeter if there's been suffering on both sides. It's like that song by Neil Sedaka, where he goes '*Instead of breaking up I wish that we were making up again.*' That's what Shell would be thinking right now.

But I hadn't come here for that. My primary concern was finding a nice, private environment. A place where I could relax, let the real Rik Suntan come flooding through and forget all the insane bollocks that Ted and his three twats had been spouting. Being around madness wears you down after a while. It's like they're sick and it's contagious, and you just want to steer clear. Especially when you've got a very special phone call to make.

I got myself a cup of tea and went to the phone.

'Samuel J. Marino here. Who can I help and in what way?'

'Are you the Miramar Man?'

'Miramar Man is indeed one of my *noms de plume*, sir, in as much as I do indeed point the rudder in that establishment. But you have me at a disadvantage.'

'I reckon I do. You're one singer down, that's your disadvantage. That's what I'm ringing about, Mr Marino. I'm Rik Suntan, professional vocalist. And if you get me on your team you'll find yourself at an advantage. A distinct advantage, mate. It'll be game, set and match to the Miramar.'

'That's the kind of talk I enjoy hearing, Rik.'

I was loving the patter. This was what I was all about. Apart from singing, of course. I was such a natural wit that I operated on a different level to everyone around me, and you never got to see me at anything near my best most days. But here was an equal, someone I had to raise my game for. And raising it I was, so high that it became pure art form. It made me question why I needed a manager at all. I didn't, really. Especially not a mental one.

'I'm very glad you called back, Mr Suntan. Very much enjoyed your set last night, by the way. I'll say something for you: you can take a bottle.'

'Oh, heh. Erm…what?'

'On the head. The missile that was launched in your direction from the audience. It was a bottle, was it not?'

'Oh yeah…Well, you can't please everyone, can you? I find that the better the music, the stronger the reaction from the audience.'

'You carried the incident quite professionally, I thought. The show must go on and all that. Although it couldn't in this case, and Stan Curtis was quite right to halt it.'

'I could have finished my set, Mr Marino. Stan didn't have to step in. You'd have to kill me to stop me entertaining.'

'Most admirable, Rik. But Stan's an old hand in this game and he knows when to step in. He also knows when his number's up, as you found out. If Stan Curtis has a weakness it's his pride.'

'I'm not following you, Mr Marino.'

'My fault: I do tend towards the cryptic, I admit. Stan Curtis knew he couldn't hold you back any longer, Rik. When he saw me circling, he cut his losses. He'd rather fire an act than see him poached, Rik.'

'Oh,' I said. 'Well, bloody hell. Why didn't I see that?'

'Because you're a gentleman, Rik, and you expect gentlemanly conduct in others. Unfortunately, Stan Curtis is not of the same calibre.'

'Well, I do know my manners.'

'Are you familiar with the current crop of chart acts, Rik? Acts such as Zak Bremner, for instance?'

It was like biting into a big, juicy apple – the best-looking apple you've ever seen – only to find a little maggot waving at you. But I bore it well. And even with a maggot inside, it was still a great apple.

'I'm a big fan of Bremner,' I lied. 'He's one of my inspirations, like.'

'Oh yes? I can't stand him myself. I think he sounds nasal. It's the youngsters who want him and his ilk, and I'm a slave to market forces, Mr Suntan.'

'Oh, right…Erm, well, I can see how he can sound a bit…'

'You don't have to kowtow to me, Mr Suntan. I want someone who can sing the modern hits as well as the classics. It's a business requirement, not an aesthetic one. If you can fill that requirement you will have my full respect and backing, and never mind your taste in music. How does that sound?'

It sounded bloody perfect. Near enough anyway.

And I couldn't believe it.

I mean, was someone winding me up here? I might appear to have unrealistic ambitions in some people's eyes but I'm not thick.

'Good. However, I want you in for an audition. I've heard you sing on your own turf but I need to hear you on mine. We have very particular acoustics in the Miramar. Ever been there?'

'No. But don't worry about that – I'm one of those rare singers who can tell how his voice is coming over in every corner of the building.'

I regretted saying that as soon as it was out. I mean, you want to come across confident – perhaps even cocky – but not like a wanker.

'Good,' he said, 'I like a man who is cocksure and full of beans. We'll have you here tomorrow, after lunch. That all right?'

It wasn't half, and I told him. Then I threw the phone down and punched the air until my shoulder hurt. Then I calmed down and looked out the window for a while, shaking my head slow and trying to pin the smile down. I'd been due a break like this for ages. I drank it down like a parched man and it cooled every part of my being. Suddenly I became aware of a mild tremble that had just been steadied, a quiet headache that was no longer there. I felt great, but I had to keep things in perspective. This was merely one of the bottom rungs on a very long ladder, and it was only what I was due.

14.

I went into the kitchen and put the kettle on. There was half a bottle of Famous Grouse in the cupboard and I didn't half fancy a few celebratory doubles. But that wasn't the way forward. I started running a bath instead. That wasn't the way forward either, but I stank.

While I was getting undressed, I found the present they'd given me in the caff. I didn't recall pocketing it. Maybe someone had stashed it on my person during the ensuing fuss. Either way, I opened it and found a CD inside. It was *The Rise and Fall of Ziggy Stardust and the Spiders from Mars* by David fucking Bowie.

Being open-minded, and boasting some quite eclectic tastes in music, I put it in the stereo.

It was nice to have a bath. I'd run it piping hot and it had taken me over a minute to lower myself into it, but I was in now and enjoying it. I wasn't enjoying the sounds coming from the living room though. I firmly believe that music should bring pleasure and joy, and this brought only misery and sadness. It was like funeral music. I pictured a coffin carried by six bearers, each of them stepping in time to the dirge. Two of the bearers were Ted and Yusuf, and as we moved around the cortege I saw that two others were Cliff Richard and David Bowie, who was looking a bit ragged and tired. The remaining two were Martin and Eggy, and if there's two people who shouldn't be bearing the same coffin, it's them two. Martin was on a rear corner and the midget on the opposite one at the front, the coffin slanting and tilting all over the place between them. Finally it tipped and crashed to the ground, the lid coming off and the bodies of two men with identical suits and haircuts spilling face-down in the dirt.

I opened my eyes, sweat popping from my scalp. The bath was too hot so I put some cold in and tried to relax. The music helped here as well, changing to a more uplifting style towards the end of the song, like a big brother who bullies you for a bit and then lets you have a bite of his Mars Bar.

Just as the second track was starting I heard someone come in the front door. My heart started sinking there and then, and me with it. This was a fucking disaster. Shelley was supposed to be on nightshift, not coming home at nine in the evening or whatever it was. I'd wanted to be ready for her with a bunch of flowers and a nice cup of tea, not sat in her bath, my dirty pants out there in the hall. I lifted myself out of the bath, fast-forwarding a few scenarios in my head. Every one of them involved a big row. A blazing one, most times with actual fire coming out of her mouth and nostrils. None of them featured an axe through the bathroom door, though.

Which is what I got.

It was an unusual axe: red all over, even the metal bit. I looked at it, struggling as it was to get back through the hole it had just made, and I got to thinking. The colour red is meant to be a warning. Get out of my way or I'll hurt you, it proclaimed. Plus it was an axe, which brought along its own set of alarm bells. But I still found it hard to rouse myself from my soak. I was thinking about that, and wondering if the two warnings might perhaps cancel each other out, when the axe came down again, making another hole.

I got out that time.

'Shell!' I shouted.

I was getting annoyed now. She had a temper on her but this was going too far. It was the pants in the hall that had tipped the balance, I just knew it. Strange how she happened to have an axe on her, though.

'Shell?' I said again. I stood naked and dripping, facing the door.

The axe came down again, knocking the two holes into one and letting me get a glimpse beyond. It wasn't Shelley on the other side of it. It was a man.

Wearing a boiler suit and balaclava.

We had a moment of eye contact before he moved his head away from the hole. I watched, expecting other holes to join those first two but getting none. I could hear a clock ticking somewhere and a tap dripping. They were almost in sync but not quite.

Snapping myself out of that, I started thinking in terms of what I was going to do. There was one window but it only opened a few inches. And there was a six-storey drop the other side of it anyway. There wasn't much to defend myself with either. In the toothbrush mug I found a disposable razor that Shelley used to do her armpits and stuff, and I grabbed that and faced the door, holding the plastic razor out like it might make him think twice. But I couldn't see anyone through the hole now and it had gone quiet.

While I was watching and waiting, clutching the razor, I found that the image of the basin and stuff around it was still there in my head, like a photograph. Sometimes that happens, I find, when there's something important you're meant to see that you didn't get first time. I looked at that image without taking my eyes off the door, but didn't see anything odd. So maybe it's your mind's way of making you go back, rather than an actual photograph that you can examine at leisure.

Either way, I turned and had a look at the real thing. All the usual stuff was there: bit of soap, little brush for getting the dirt from under your nails, toothbrush mug. Shelley's pink brush was in it and my blue one wasn't, which was no surprise. But there was another one there instead. A red one. I picked it up.

It wasn't mine.

Above that red toothbrush, in the mirror, I saw the balaclava reappear at the hole in the door. He took it off and revealed himself to be Gingernut, the one from the Cairo last night who'd been giving me unpleasant looks.

He looked unpleasant right now.

'I'm a reasonable man,' he said, 'so I'm gonna give you a chance. Get the fuck out of here, right now, and I'll let you go unharmed. But if you come back here ever again, or if I ever hear of you coming within ten feet of me or Shelley, I swear I'll fuckin'—'

I ran at him. I didn't care. The red toothbrush was his, wasn't it? He'd moved in on my woman while I was out there trying to build something for the both of us. He'd poisoned her against me, making her doubt the dream that she'd once believed in. Not only all that, but he'd had the front to turn up at my place of work and sneer at me.

Quite wisely he stood back from the door. If I was him I'd have done the same. An axe is no good at close quarters and you need a bit of room to swing it. Not that I'd ever swung one. And it didn't help me anyway, knowing what he'd be doing. I could feel myself splitting into two people: the one who was aware of what was going on and able to analyse it; and the one who didn't give a shit so long as he destroyed the thing in front of him.

As predicted, he swung the axe at me when I came out the door. The cheek of him, trying to kill a man in his own home. Looking at it now, I can see how he had no choice. I must have been quite intimidating, the jilted boyfriend out for revenge, naked and holding a toothbrush.

His toothbrush. A red one.

His toothbrush in my...

By accident or design – I don't know – I kind of fell under the axe as it traced a big horizontal arc at roughly stomach height. I hit the carpet and the axe hit the wall, knocking a big lump of plaster out of it and ruining the wallpaper that Shelley had put up not a couple of months ago. Meanwhile I grabbed his legs. I had no plan other than to right the wrongs that had been inflicted upon me. One part of me didn't even want to do that, but it was the other part which had control.

Gingernut planted a knee in my face, knocking me on to my back.

It was an undignified situation, me sprawled naked on my back and him stood over me, axe raised to finish me off. It pains me to recall the depths to which I sank in those moments, knowing as I do the heights I'm capable of. But I hadn't actually sunk that deep yet. I was headed for way deeper.

He brought the axe down.

For a man who owned an axe he wasn't very good with it. The sharp bit hit the floor between arm and ribs, about an inch from the armpit. While he tried to pull it out, leaning over me to get a grip, I jabbed the toothbrush in his face. I had to do something. I didn't mean to kill him.

Not like that anyway.

In the background David Bowie sang about a star man wanting to come and meet us, but he thought he'd blow our minds.

NEGOTIATING WITH
THE DEVIL

THE devil is a tricky customer. I summoned him on a blustery Monday afternoon in May. He came up from the cellar. Not because that way lies hell (which is not a real place anyway) but because that is where I had summoned him to. This was my way of telling him from the off that he was dealing with a worthy opponent. He was not very pleased about it and let me know his displeasure by urinating a jet of orange piss on the ceiling, simultaneously staring at me and singing drunkenly in Latin. But I knew he was not drunk. The Devil is a master salesman and will employ any tactic to get the better of you.

The Devil is also an extremely rude individual, and will try to stir up your bile by insulting you, your wife and your mother if he cannot instil a false sense of security in you. I weathered that storm as well, and set up some music on the record player while he spat his filth at my back. Everyone knows that the Devil is a keen follower of music, and I had chosen some fiddle pieces especially for him, that instrument being his favoured one, so I had read from an old source. But the fiddle music caused a furious reaction in him, and he defecated voluminously upon the floor and caused the record player to combust. I was prepared for this also. I had read that the Devil moves with the times, and had taken the precaution of procuring another record player and another genre of music. So it happened that I put on some Rolling Stones.

Outraged at my forethought, yet unable to resist the stimulus, he began strutting like a massive, cloven-hoofed cockerel. The momentum built until he could stand it no longer, and broke into a spontaneous and free dance, hopping around on his short, bowed legs while masturbating furiously and screaming obscenities at me. Anyone can beat the Devil once, I had also read.

I had the souls of musicians, I told him. I could deliver to him the souls of the finest purveyors of music known to this modern age. They will all come to you as Robert Johnson did, freely and of their own volition.

He laughed at me. No music man worth a pint of his venomous urine would come to a foul-smelling backwater such as this.

Name your musicians, I told him, shuffling away from the gelatinous urine that still dripped from the ceiling. Draw up your list and I promise to deliver at least one name on it. He laughed long and hard. Having once harked the Devil's mirth, your remaining years of sanity will be barren of merriment. But this was nothing to me. My work meant more. I faced him down and awaited his list.

A rolled-up parchment oozed forth from the ceiling, seemingly born from the orange viscous piss, and fluttered to the ground. I did not even pick it up, such was my misplaced confidence. He asked me what I wished for in return.

Only his assurance, I told him, that he would do with them the same deal as with Johnson, Cromwell and Faust. And that he do it anonymously. He can take the spoils when the time comes, but I want each victim to believe that the deal is being done with me and not the Devil. And I wanted that assurance in writing.

A second parchment came forth.

I picked up this contract and read it several times. It was watertight and there were no tricks. One clause I approved of was that he had given me a very long lead time. I asked him why he had chosen thirty-seven years. His reply was that I had put him in a bad mood, and the number thirty-seven is the most ignominious of numbers.

Then we each signed – me with a Bic biro, him with a sharpened finger – and had a glass of cider together to seal the deal. The Devil's mood seemed to lighten and he even told me some jokes. With each Satanic guffaw I was reminded that I would never again share in mortal humour. After that he vanished in a cloud of loathsome fart gas.

I picked up his list of names from the floor and squinted at them. But there was only one name, and it was my own.

As I have said, the Devil is a tricky customer.

15.

There was a light on upstairs at Ted's house. You could see his shadow in the yellow curtain as he scribbled away at his desk up there. Or maybe he was wanking. Either way, he was about to be interrupted.

I rang the bell.

Within a couple of seconds I heard his feet clobbering the staircase and the door was open. Anyone would have thought this was the middle of the day and he'd been expecting company. But he couldn't have been expecting me. The way it had gone with him yesterday, in the caff, I hadn't wanted to see him for a few days yet. I'd tried to help him and I'd failed. If he was mentally ill, he'd have to sort himself out. But now the ball was on my foot. I needed his assistance.

Mentally ill or not.

'Ted,' I said.

He took one glance at me and bustled me inside, looking both ways up the dark street before easing the door shut.

'All right,' he said. He was wearing pyjamas and a grubby dressing gown. 'What's happened?'

I sat down and put my arm on the table, noticing how much it was shaking. 'How'd you know summat's happened?'

'Because there's no other reason why you would come here at this hour. Plus you've got blood all over your face.'

'Oh fuck...' I said, looking at my reflection in the kitchen window. I couldn't see much but I could see enough, and I turned on the taps in the sink. Waiting for the hot one to stop running cold, I watched the water swirl around and go down the plug hole. Then I puked my guts.

'Don't worry,' he said behind me. I think he'd said it a few times. I was sitting on the lino now, wiping my mouth. He had a hot flannel and he was wiping my face. I grabbed it off him and did it myself. 'Don't worry,' he said again.

'I ain't worrying.' I tried to tongue a bit of puke out of the corner of my mouth but my tongue didn't reach it. I used my finger instead. 'I just couldn't help being sick there. Soz about the—'

'I said don't worry. How long have you been walking around like that?'

'Like what?'

'With your jacket on inside out.'

'Oh...I dunno. A while.'

'How'd you get here? You walked up Bath Road?'

'Well, no. I went the back way. Clandon Road, then I cut through the—'

'Good man. And have you been anywhere else?'

'Just...Look, what's with the fuckin' questions? I just came here to...erm...'

'You killed a feller, didn't you?'

I puked again. I wasn't even feeling sick now, just wrong.

I didn't want to be inside myself, knowing what I'd been up to. Not that I regretted that Gingernut was dead. He was a vindictive little cunt and he'd been shagging my woman. Plus he'd attacked me, so it was self-defence really. I just wished someone else could have done the deed. I wanted to get his blood off my face and the pictures out of my brain. But I couldn't. So I puked.

And when I couldn't puke any more I retched. In between retches I told Ted the score.

'They won't see it that way,' he said.

'Who won't?'

'The law. They'll take one look at the situation and see a jealous man putting one over on his love rival.'

I wanted to ask him more questions about that, and explain a bit more about the background, but some undigested food turned up in a corner of my guts and was sent up for duty. After that I couldn't stop gagging. I was lying on my front, pulling my knees up and kissing lino for a long while. Soon enough the lino disappeared and I was chewing air, and my body wasn't touching anything at all. I think this was me passed out, but I didn't know it at the time. All I knew was that I was a ball, floating in space, doing slow, gentle somersaults through the black void, spun casually by an indifferent god who was likely to get bored very quickly and swat me into oblivion. I wanted him to do it, at that moment. I felt that there was more chance of getting what I wanted in oblivion. It couldn't be harder than this world anyway. There's no music on Planet Oblivion but there's no failing either.

I woke up and I was on Planet Oblivion. I was naked, lying on hard, wet ground and being rained down upon. The rain was hot and didn't feel too bad and there was a scent of pine in the air very much like Lynx shower gel. I got my eyes open a fraction and closed them again. Nothing but mist and water and darkness here.

I felt a song coming on and reached blindly for a pen and paper, finding only what felt like a flannel and some soap.

I felt white light hit my eyelids, then:

'Do you want me to fix it?'

It echoed through the wet air like a foghorn at midnight. I knew it was the indifferent god, fucking me around, probably, before the final flick on to the planet proper, where my body would be dashed to nothing and I'd become vapour.

'Do you want me to fix it?' That foghorn again.

'Do it,' I croaked.

'I will, but you gotta promise to do summat for me in return.'

'Yeah.'

'You gotta promise to be on our side.'

'Yeah. Do it.'

'Do you promise?'

'Yeah.'

'Right. Oh, you still got a bit of puke in your hair, there.'

Darkness again.

'Flick me,' I said.

But I knew I was alone. The rain hammered my back. I started spinning again. Maybe I wasn't alone? Maybe there was someone else there, attached to me via a long piece of cable coming out of my belly button? Nah – that was just a feeling I sometimes got. And it meant nothing.

When I came to I was in a bed. The same one I'd kipped in the night before. I was wearing clean pyjamas and I gloried in a pine fresh fragrance. The curtains were drawn, although I could see it was light outside. A new day, and I wasn't on Planet Oblivion. I was back on the same old shit-brown earth, where you had things like murder and police and jail. And music.

The kind of music that you had to face.

Shelley would be home by now, trudging up the stairs after her nightshift. She'd open the door and head straight for the kitchen after a cup of tea, but she'd notice something big on the hall carpet, half-hidden in shadow, and she'd stop. He's drunk, she might think. That ginger-haired cunt, he's gone out and got bladdered and passed out before he can even reach the sofa. Words would flare up inside her, ready for her to spit out and him to suck up. Then she'd come close, and notice that he didn't look right. He wasn't moving. He had a toothbrush rammed four inches up his nostril.

I sat up, expecting more puke. But it wasn't coming. And not just because my guts were empty. I'd done it now. It couldn't be changed. The dice had been rolled and come up one and six. Sixteen years – that seemed about right for murder.

I reached for the luke-warm mug of tea that was on the bedside. You've got to enjoy life's pleasures while you can. I was halfway down it, and enjoying it quite a lot, when the door opened and in came Ted. He looked preoccupied and dog-tired, and I got no more than a glance from him. He went straight to the window and lifted a curtain, saying:

'It's all sorted.'

'Ta for the tea,' I said. 'Bit cool, but hey. And ta for, you know, giving us a place to…What's all sorted?'

'The body. Everything. It's all tidied up.'

'What is?'

He let go of the curtain and came over to me. I thought he was going to hit me. Not that I was afraid of that – Ted was not known for his physical prowess. But I probably flinched anyway.

103

And he didn't even hit me – he just got my empty mug off the bedside.

'Rik, get a grip,' he said. 'We've done our bit, now you've gotta do yours. And that means waking up and getting wise to the situation. You killed a man, Rik.' He stood in the middle of the floor and looked at me. 'And we've got rid of the body for you.'

He went back to the window.

'What're you looking out there for?'

'Coppers. In case we got followed.'

'Oh fuck...'

'It's all sorted, Rik,' he said, noting my despondency. 'You're in the clear, long as you keep a cool head. The police might question you at some point, but as far as they're concerned there's no crime right now. The man with the er...toothbrush, he's just gone missing. No evidence to suggest otherwise. We've cleaned the carpet and everything. Eggy's a cleaner, you see. Your woman won't even know we've been there. She'll know *you've* been there, though. We didn't try and hide that. But you just gotta work out your story. You never saw the dead bloke.'

'But...' I said. I'd been wanting to say that for ages, only I couldn't work out what words to follow it up with. So I just let it float on its own.

'Ain't you got nothing to say, Rik?' said Ted. 'Besides 'but'? I mean, anyone'd think you're not grateful. We've saved your skin.'

'Well, yeah...I mean thanks and all, but—'

'Don't thank me – thank Martin and Eggy. It's them who did the graft. I just directed 'em.'

'Yeah, I will thank them...But...'

'Good, cos they're downstairs.'

'What? Now?'

'Yeah. I'm making all-day breakfast.'

'But...Ted, you don't *make* all-day breakfast. You go to the caff and buy one.'

'There's nothing stopping me from makin' it.'

I looked at my watch. 'Plus it's eight o'clock.'

'Yeah.'

'How can you have all-day breakfast at eight o'clock?'

'You can have ADB any time.'

'Yeah, but if it's breakfast time it's just breakfast.'

Ted picked up the empty mug and said:

'Ah, but is it? Is everything as it appears to the naked eye? Or does the truth lurk beneath the surface?'

I couldn't believe I was having an argument about food. What had he said about the body of Gingernut? It's all tidied up? And Shelley...what did I have to do there? Make up some sort of a story?

Ted went out the door, leaning back in to say:

'Your togs are over the back of that chair. You'll find they've been washed and dried. I'll do you two eggs.'

SOULSHIFTING: A GUIDE

THE practicalities of soulshifting are simple and almost incidental, although they must be followed to the letter. Once the desired soul is selected, a suitable host organism of the same species must be found. In snails and caterpillars this presented no problem, as the soul of these organisms is weak and therefore easy to manipulate. But the adult human soul is in most cases too powerful to take against its will, hence the idea of a disguised Faustian pact to induce compliance in the donor organism. The larval human, on the other hand, possesses a soul which is undeveloped and therefore easy to overpower, thereby providing the ideal host for the shifted soul.

In choosing a suitable host organism, the special talent of the donor should be borne in mind. If the host is able to exploit this talent, the soul will be fulfilled in its new body and therefore of less value as currency on The Stairway. In order to retain value until such a time as you need to deploy your stored souls, always select a host with a physical flaw that will prevent that talent from being exploited. For example, the soul of a peerless marksman will forever remain unfulfilled in the body of a blind man.

I located a ready supply of larval humans in the maternal ward of the local infirmary. After procuring the accoutrements of a hospital porter, I encountered no obstacles in gaining access to this supply.

To perform the ritual, you need:

1. A urine sample from both donor and host. Be sure that the urine is undiluted and from the correct organism
2. The magic words (see Appendix A)
3. A third organism, of the same species as host and donor, for blood sacrifice
4. A piece of bark from the rowan tree. This will be used to brand the host organism

The ritual must take place while the donor is engaged in the act of exploiting his talent. Warm blood from the fresh sacrifice must be incorporated with urine from host and donor (the urine samples should not come into contact with each other before mingling with the blood). Throughout, the magic words must be repeated over and over. After a successful exchange of souls, a lock of hair should be taken from the infant host and kept in a secure place.

Clearly, such steps require little mental effort to arrange and execute. What must, however, be taken into consideration are the consequences of the ritual. To perform a soulshift is to tinker with the cosmic order of things. While there is much to be gained by the careful warlock, there is much to be lost by the organisms involved and those close to them. A necromancer should always remember that he is himself a child of the cosmos, and too much change in his environment can be dangerous for him. By the same token, if he seizes control of his environment his power will know no bounds.

16.

The smell of bacon pulled me downstairs. Without that I would have hopped out the bedroom window, across the conservatory roof and over the fence. It was great that Ted had helped out and given me shelter but I just needed some space now. I needed to process events and get my head straight on how things stood. But more than that, I was hungry.

Ted was at the cooker, turning over some eggs. Martin was sat at the table, drinking tea with his huge back to me, two or three flies taking up residence on it. Eggy was stood on a plastic crate, fiddling with the George Foreman grill on the side. He saw me and pulled himself as tall as he went. His eyes looked massive and seemed to issue a challenge to me. But it wasn't like yesterday. He wasn't asking for a fight.

'Cheers,' I said. 'Ted told me what you boys did, and, er... Well, just cheers. That's all I can say.'

Martin got up and held my arm, saying: 'You all right, mate?

You sit down here. Bit of grub and you'll feel better. Go easy on yourself. Don't worry about us.'

I let him sit me down. Ted plonked tea in front of me. Eggy and Martin were sat opposite now and staring at me, like they had been yesterday. But it was different now. A certain barrier between us had gone.

'And don't worry about the favour,' said Ted. 'We done it because we're your mates, right? And we're fans. Ain't we, Egg?'

The midget made some sort of gesture. He was a long way from liking me and, although I wasn't sure why, I felt like I had to make an effort to win him over.

'It was a big favour you did for me,' I said, looking at Eggy. 'And you didn't have to do it. I mean, it couldn't have been easy for you.'

His look changed a bit in reaction to what I'd said. A smile was playing on his lips, and I thought I had him won. Then he said what was on his mind:

'Are you saying I'm small? That what yer saying?'

'No, no, I—'

'You fuckin' are. You're saying I'm so small it's like I ain't even here. You're saying I ain't got no physical presence at all, ain't you?'

'No, I'm just—'

'Egg!' said Martin. 'Leave it.'

'Don't you tell me to leave it!'

'I will tell you to leave it! Rik here is in the fold now. You gotta support him, like we agreed. Right? I said *right*?'

Scowling, Eggy said: 'Right. I suppose.'

Smiling like a patient infant school teacher, Ted said: 'You boys tuck in. And don't worry about me – I had my mushroom sarnie earlier.' He put some plates in front of us and went back to the cooker.

Me and the other two tucked in. My plate had three sausages, two eggs, three bits of bacon and some beans. Eggy and Martin seemed to have twice as much as me. I was a bit irked at that.

'Look,' Martin said, leaning in and whispering so Ted wouldn't hear, 'I realise how Ted probably scared you off a bit last time. Anyone'd find it a bit disconcerting, discovering that they're actually David Bowie. We've all been through it and it was the same for us. Course, it weren't David Bowie in our cases. Eggy here is—'

'Don't,' said the little one, sticking a fork in Martin's arm.

'Ow! You fucker!'

'Don't tell him too much just yet. In case Ted's wrong about him.'

'Ted ain't wrong! What's it gonna take for you to have some faith, Egg?'

'A bit more proof than I've seen so far.'

Martin thought about it, licking his lips, then asked me: 'What sort of dream do you have?'

'Eh? When?'

'Always. What's the dream you have over and over, ever since you can remember? And tell the truth. You won't get nowhere if you don't tell the truth.'

I did tell him the truth. But not because I was afraid of getting nowhere. I was on the back foot and couldn't think up any lies. Martin and Eggy were staring goggle-eyed at me and the truth is what came out.

'I'm on a stage,' I said, picking a bit of sausage skin from between my teeth, 'in front of thousands. They're all screaming for me. There's girls in there, really fit ones. But blokes as well, also screaming for me. My face and hair feels funny, and when I touch it some stuff like paint comes away in my hand. But it's like I ain't in myself. I'm standing by my side, watching myself touching my hair and all that and feeling it at the same time. I'm two people, and—'

'Then what happens?'

'Well, then the music starts. And I feel like…I feel like we're both…'

'Go on.' I don't know who was asking the questions.

'Well, I feel like Jesus.'

I felt like Jesus here as well, in Ted's kitchen. Martin and Eggy were gawping at me still but it was wonderment in their eyes, like I'd just walked on water. Or turned bread into fish, or whatever it was Jesus did.

'Have a kipper,' said Ted, dishing them out.

'Er…ta,' said Martin, rousing as if from a stupor. 'Well, I think that we can conclusively say that Rik here is one of us.'

It went quiet. I looked around for Ted but he seemed to have disappeared. It was just me and the odd brothers, and I was starting to feel uncomfortable. I said:

'This is all really interesting, but can you just tell me in what way I'm David Bowie? And how did I…you know. I mean, I could have sworn I was Rik Suntan.'

'Rik Suntan is who you are on paper,' Martin said. 'And Rik Suntan is who you was born. But—'

'Actually, I wasn't,' I said.

'What?'

'Born Rik Suntan. I was born Richard Sutton. Rik Suntan is like a stage name. But do you see what I'm doing there? I'm hardly changing it at all. Only two letters, really.'

I couldn't believe I was telling them these things.

'Oh, right,' said Martin. 'Well, that's quite interesting. See, there's you trying to become someone else. Because you know in your soul that you ain't you.'

'For fuck's fuckin' sake, Mart!' said Eggy, spitting a couple of beans out. 'Shall I just explain it for him? We'll be here all fucking week, else.'

'I was just laying the ground—'

'What it is, right,' said Eggy, putting down his knife and fork and picking up one of his three sausages, 'is that here's Dave Bowie, going about his daily life, singing and stuff.'

He moved the sausage around like it was dancing, then picked up a couple more and did the same with them.

'It's *David* Bowie, not Dave.'

'Shut up, Mart. And there's these three other fellers, and they're famous and talented as well, like *Dave* Bowie. Then there's these four babies. You see these beans, all cosy and snug over here? That's us as babies. Me, you, Martin here and Yusuf. We've only just been born.'

'It's the maternity ward.'

'Shut up, Mart. And it's the local hospital here in Warchester. And this whole table here, it's the mid-'70s. It's the world as it was thirty-odd year ago. People are wearing flares and that, right?'

Martin only had a waffle left on his plate, which he forked and went to put in his mouth. But Eggy grabbed it off the fork mid-air, saying:

'Now, this here is Jim Page. He's a bit different, Mr Page. He's talented and that, like them others, but he's also a warlock. And by that I don't mean he's a lock that you put on a war, right? I mean he does magic and that. Black magic.'

'It's *Jimmy* Page, not—'

'Mart, just shut it. Right? What *Jim* Page decides to do, using his black magic skills, is give himself some more special talents. He wants to be a super-warlock or summat. Do you see what I mean? So he has a look around, looking for people who've got some nice talents that he'd like to have. Look at him go, waffling around the place…'

Ted was still nowhere in sight. I was getting worried, because I reckoned these two needed supervising. Not that supervision by another head case was ideal, but it seemed safer.

'Ooh look,' said Eggy, dancing his waffle on to my plate, 'he's having a look over here as well. But he won't find his talents there. It's *here* that he finds 'em – Dave Bowie and the lads over here. Only they ain't together like this. They're dotted around the world. And they don't even know each other. Not personally anyway, although they've probably heard of each other. Anyway, so what Jimmy Waffle over here does, right, is he steals their souls off of 'em.'

Eggy got a knife and started cutting open the sausages, scooping a bit out of each one.

I said: 'I'm dying for a—'

'And when he's got their souls he tries to put them inside him, like so.' He put four lumps of sausage meat in the holes of the waffle. '*But...*'

He turned the waffle over and tipped out the bits of sausage.

'The souls won't stick, see? They won't stay in him because he's *bad*. The souls don't like him and they won't stay in him. I mean, he's a good guitarist and all but they don't fancy sharing him, or summat. I dunno. So they fly around for a bit, looking for a new home. They can't go back where they came from because...erm...'

'The magic,' said Martin. 'It's a separate ritual to get the soul back where it came from.'

'Fuckin' shut up, Mart. So these souls look for new homes. Homes that are easy to get into because they're very young and weak. And guess where they end up? That's right – in *us*.'

He took a knife to the beans and tried forcing the 'souls' inside. Things were getting messy on the table now.

'There,' he said, putting down the knife. Straight away a fly landed on it. 'Oh, and on entering the babies, these souls here kick out the one already there and it flies through the air and enters the body of one of these sausages back here, where the original souls came from. So it's like a straight swap, soul for soul. Do you see what I mean, Rik?'

'Yeah. Look, I really gotta go for a piss. My bladder's...'

I got up and left the kitchen. But instead of going to the bog I opened the front door and pegged it. Only to run into Ted at the end of the garden path.

'You all right, Rik?' he said, looking straight into my eyes. 'You look like you've seen a warlock.'

I looked back into his eyes, expecting to see something mad. Mania, or whatever they call it. But there was nothing like that there. He looked like the same Ted he had ever been. That's what I found confusing about all this. They were saying mad stuff but coming across normal on all other fronts.

'Ted,' I said, 'I can't handle all this. It's too...I mean, I need to go off and get my head straight, and—'

'That's fine, Rik. I think you're right – go away and get some rest. Saying that, you're a bit stuck on where to go, ain't you?'

'Don't worry about that. I'll find...well, don't worry.'

'You sure?'

'Yeah. Positive.'

'And you understand all that now, about Jimmy Page and the black magic rituals? Honestly, when Eggy told me to leave it to him, I wasn't sure how he'd—'

'Oh yeah, he explained it fine. I got it crystal clear. I was a bean, and David Bowie was a sausage, and the great waffle Jimmy Page came along and switched our souls.'

'Heh heh, that bloody Eggy. But you do see it, though, don't you? You accept it as fact, and take it into your heart as a true thing?'

I really needed to get away now. 'Yeah.'

'Good. Because I wouldn't have done this big favour here for someone who wasn't on our side. If I thought you were taking the piss behind our backs, and just saying the right things to keep me sweet, I'd drop that toothbrush of yours in an envelope and send it to the police. It's got prints all over it, you know, and I suspect they're yours. I need everyone singing off the same hymn sheet, Rik. It's a tight ship here and there's no space for loose cannons. Do you hear what I'm saying, Rik?'

'Yeah. Course.'

'Good lad. We'll see you at eight o'clock, then.'

'Eh? Where? What for?'

'The Dead Dog. To support Eggy.'

'Support…? Ted, I ain't—'

'You are, Rik.' He went inside.

17.

Hunger pangs were needling at my guts. I hadn't touched that fry-up at Ted's. I knew that things would seem a lot better after I'd had something to eat so I bought a Milky Way, a bag of mini poppadums and a can of Coke from the paper shop at the bottom of Clandon Road. I walked through town, holding off the urge until I found the right place to sit down and eat them properly. It seemed important at that time. Especially since I couldn't go home. Not until I had my head and my story straight anyway.

I found the right spot on a bench behind the bingo hall on Foregate Street. A bit of traffic was going past but I didn't mind that. What mattered was eating my breakfast and gathering my thoughts. I was going to have to be brave here and face some unpleasant realities, and I needed to be in a peaceful location. This was it.

I sat down and started on the mini poppadums. They made me think of 'Papa Don't Preach' by Madonna. Although I wasn't a fan of hers, I'd always admired Madonna as the model professional. The way she'd gone from humble beginnings to the top of the music world was an inspiration to singers the world over. Especially ones like me who aspired to global superstardom. Looking at her example, you could see that the only way to make it was to be ruthless. You had to be prepared to do anything for success, no matter what sacrifices it entailed. If you weren't up for doing the worst thing imaginable in exchange for a toehold on the next rung of the ladder, you might as well pack it in now.

Well, I was up for it. I'd proved that, right there in the flat last night. Gingernut had been standing in my way and I'd killed him. I'd struck him down like a domino, using only a toothbrush. A man who can do that is a man who cannot be stopped.

I ripped open the Milky Way and started nibbling the chocolate coating off, like I always did. It started out brown and ended up white, like Michael Jackson. He was another example to all up-and-comers. Even strange people can conquer the world of entertainment. I wasn't strange like him, but I felt strange. Now I had blood on my hands I felt out of step with the world, different to every other person and unable to rejoin the herd. In a way, that could be the making of me. A member of the herd doesn't achieve massive success and global fame. It's only a special person who can do that, one who has conversations with chimpanzees or kills people. That was me. Half of it anyway.

But I'd have a chat with a chimpanzee if it got me up a rung, no problem.

(I draw the line at feeling him up, though.)

I finished the Milky Way and moved on to the Coke, which put me in mind of that song from the advert, where she's singing about first times and first kisses and electricity flowing. It's a great song, and perfectly evokes the emotions associated with opening a can of Coke for the very first time and having a sip. It's a masterclass in balladry, and it always made me want to have a crack at writing a song of my own when I heard it.

I was hearing it now, in my head.

When the Coke was gone I was left alone on the bench with only a very loud burp for company, and that didn't stay long. Although I'd worked through my issues and found hidden gold in my problems, I was still feeling a bit out of sorts. But I knew what to do.

I got my notebook and pen out and wrote a song.

I called it 'Toothbrushes'…

There in the bathroom
Like a long red mushroom
Or a long red broom
In the darkening gloom

There on the stair
In his underwear
I imagined him there
With his ginger hair

There on my sheet
With two backs and four feet
A sight not at all sweet
I did sadly meet

Red like a rose
A toothbrush I chose
Which I superimposed
Up his nose

Charlie Williams

> *But it wasn't my fault*
> *And it gave me a jolt*
> *Made my head somersault*
> *And my stomach revolt*

That's just the first few verses for you. The tune for it was a bit like 'Moonlight Shadow' by Mike Oldfield, but slower. And the chorus just went 'Toothbrush, toothbrush, I killed him with a toothbrush.' I was happy with it. It was one of the best songs I'd ever composed, being born of raw experience and strong emotion. I'd looked into the abyss and walked away from it, and here was my account. Shame I couldn't record it though, because I'd probably get locked up for murder if I did.

All in all it took me an hour to write, and when I put the notebook away and got up off the bench, stretching my stiff legs, I felt a lot better about my future. And I only had three hours to prepare for my meeting with Sam Marino.

Problems Encountered

WHAT had started out as an experiment in the occult had turned into a campaign of vital importance, my soul being at stake. My punitive contract with the devil was intact and watertight and I was left with a simple choice: to present myself to the Devil at the allotted hour (summer solstice, 2009).

Or to face him in battle.

The instinct for self-preservation left me with only one option. History was against me. Despite claims to the contrary, no one had ever fought the Devil and won. I was but a novice necromancer, he was Beelzebub, Lord of the Flies and god of the Underworld. It was David and Goliath all over again, but this time I possessed no catapult. There was only one way to stand any chance against the Devil, and that was to compete on equal terms with him. Which meant I had to somehow lay my hands upon more cosmic power than any one person had ever held in their hand. And that meant only one thing.

The Stairway.

18.

HGV was Warchester's only proper record shop. When I was a kid there used to be four, plus the big shops like Smiths and Woollocks that sold records. It was as if a big monster had come to town and sucked all the music out, leaving only the bare minimum that a human needs for survival. I don't know why that sucking monster would do such a thing, but no one else seemed bothered about it. One record shop seemed about right for the town.

I went in it.

I was after Zak Bremner, the one who Sam Marino wanted me to cover. I wasn't a fan at all, him being more of a boyish heart-throb catering to young females than a serious artist, but I knew I could do him. I could do him a lot better than he could do himself once I had the songs down, but for now I just had to know a couple of them. There he was in the chart section – number six in the hit parade with his album *Zakology*. It was a terrible title for a long-player, if you asked me. For a start it looked like you should pronounce it 'Zake-ology'. And it didn't mean anything. No matter how big he is, an artist should stand for something at any given time. With a title like this, the artist was telling the world that he stood only for himself. And that's a wanker in my book.

Checking that no one was looking, I took the CD off the shelf. Not so I could shoplift it, just so no one would see me with a Zak Bremner item. Singing his songs in a professional capacity was one thing, being mistaken for one of his fans was another. And I'd never been much cop at shoplifting anyway. I think it's because I stand out so much. People just can't help staring at me, so I always used to get seen when I thought I was pocketing something on the sly. A professional thief, I would have thought, needs to blend with the shadows.

Gaz was on the desk. I was glad of that because I could explain to him why I was purchasing this particular item. If it had been Sheryl, no amount of explanation would have sufficed. In her eyes I would have been a Bremner fan from thereon in. Or a Zakologist, or whatever.

'You do Sheryl an injustice,' Gaz was saying. 'She ain't as clueless as all that.'

'She knows nothing about proper music, Gary. All the CDs I normally buy, she just makes a face at them. And we're talking about the *greats* here, sometimes.'

'She knows the greats. You cannot work in a record shop and not know the greats.'

'Yeah but she don't *know* them, does she? She wouldn't be able to divide Cliff's career into distinct eras, would she?'

'No, I suppose not. But then, nor would I.'

I looked at Gaz to see if he was winding me up. I've no doubt that he was. I'd known him for a long time and his musical knowledge was second to none, except mine. To be honest, I'd always felt sorry for the guy. Like myself, he'd set off down the path towards being a professional musician, in his case more of a guitarist playing the loud kind of music I don't favour. But we were kindred spirits nonetheless, tastes aside, and it had hurt me in the heart to see him take a full-time job at HGV after they let him out of jail. It was like being at war and seeing your buddy get his head blown off in the trenches. You've got two choices when that happens:

1. Realise you might fail and start doubting yourself
2. Get your head down and work even harder towards the dream

You know the one I went for. But I didn't blame Gaz for giving up. He didn't have a chance. With his withered arm, setting the world alight via his guitar-playing was always going to be a stretch. So he set it alight via other means, torching a series of abandoned buildings. But he'd done his time and he was on the straight and narrow now, sad though it sometimes was to see.

'Mind you,' he said, folding his long, dyed-black hair over a chalk-white ear with his good hand, 'I have noticed a couple of gaping holes in her knowledge recently. Believe it or not,' he said, leaning close across the counter, 'she thought The Beatles were spelt with three Es.'

'No shit?'

'Gospel. She was restocking over there and she shouted, "Gaz, this is spelt wrong." I was shocked.'

'I would have been,' I said, working something out on my fingers.

'And it's not an isolated thing. She thought we'd spelt Jimi Hendrix wrong as well. I mean, come on.'

'Yeah, come on.' I gave up and went: 'How many Es are in it, then?'

'Heh, good one. But I mean, it ain't like these are obscure acts, know what I mean?' He was warming to it now. I could tell because his spots were going redder. I was starting to wish I'd never mentioned Sheryl and her shortcomings. On all other fronts she was a good girl. 'These are icons, Rik. The gods of rock 'n roll, if you will. *And* they played here in Warchester.'

'Who did?'

'The Beatles. And Hendrix. Didn't you know?'

'Well, I—'

'Down at the Gaumont, opposite where the Odeon is.'

'You mean the bingo hall?'

'Yeah, but it wasn't a bingo hall then. It was a big venue. That's what's missing from this town now – a proper venue. Without one of those, no acts will come…and you're out of the loop, musically speaking. But back then it was different. We're talking the sixties and seventies here. All the acts used to come and play Warchester – The Beatles, like I said, The Rolling Stones, your man Cliff Richard…'

'No shit?' To be honest, I thought it was shit. No way would Cliff have played in a town like Warchester. Especially not in the old-fashioned period that Gary was harkening back to. In my memory of things, no one ever came to Warchester. Not even people who weren't famous. That had changed a bit in recent times, what with the motorway, but even now we didn't get anyone worth paying to see. That's the gap that I'd tried and failed to fill. But I was out of it now and bound for Burninghouse. I explained this to Gary. All except the last bit.

'Ah, that's interesting,' he said, acting like he was a wise old man and I was a callow youth. 'Interesting that you should fall for the popular perception of our town as a backwater of no consequence. See, the problem with people these days, as I sees it, is that they're too quick to accept the status quo. And if that status quo gets changed for the worse, one or two voices pipe up in protest but no one supports them, and them voices soon go quiet. That's what happened when the Gaumont closed, I should imagine. And it's what's happing now with the shit that passes for music these days. Look at that fuckin' *X Factor* and the message it sends out. All you need's a pretty face and the ability to hold a fuckin' tune, and we'll do the rest. And do you know what? That message is true. Because it's become the status quo. And no one gives a shit.'

His acne was fierce now. Any more excitement and I could see some of them popping.

'Gaz,' I said, 'just calm down, mate. No need to go overboard, eh?'

'No? Well thanks for letting me know. That'll be five pounds, please.'

'Oh, right,' I said, fishing my wallet out. I wasn't even sure if there was five pounds in it. Gary sometimes let me take a CD home overnight, tape it and then bring it back. I did have a fiver, as it happened, but I didn't hand it over just yet. 'Gary,' I said, 'look, I only said that cos—'

'No offence taken.'

'Good, because—'

'If you don't want to hear the things I know, I'd rather die than force them on you.'

'Nah, I do wanna hear them. I find it really interesting, Gaz.' I was keeping him sweet, trying to find a way to pitch a certain question I had, which was: 'Gaz, do you know much about black magic?'

He gave me a look this time that I recognised. It was the

same one I must have given Ted when he'd broached the subject with me.

'Rik,' he said, 'I'm a *music* historian, not a…a…I dunno, a…'

'It's music I'm asking about. What I'm asking is, do you know anything about famous musicians getting up to that sort of thing?'

He held his weak jaw and looked down, lank hair falling over his face like a cheap curtain. Then he started shaking it. 'Nah,' he said, 'I can't think of any examples of that.'

'Oh, well, it ain't import—'

'Except Jimmy Page, of course. And David Bowie. In the mid-'70s.'

'You what?'

'Page and Bowie. I didn't mention them at first cos it's common knowledge among the cogno…Ah, but I'm forgetting – you didn't even know about the Gaumont.' He swatted a couple of flies out of his face. 'These fuckin' things! They're everywhere at the moment.'

'But what about Page and Bowie? What did they get up to?'

'Well, everyone knows about Bowie and his bottles of piss, and…Oh, sorry, let me start again: Bowie used to keep bottles of piss in his fridge.'

'What sort of piss?'

'What sort of a question is that?'

'Yeah but I mean…whose piss?'

'His own, of course. His idea was that he had to stash away all of his bodily discharges to stop bad people from using them in black magic rituals. Notably Jimmy Page, who was a well-known practitioner of the black arts. But what Bowie didn't realise was that—'

'And what did Jimmy Page do?'

'Look, I don't really like talking about all this stuff. You wanna hear it, you'll have to go to the Lamb and Flag. Up on The Tything.'

'The Lamb and Flag? That's a pub, Gaz.'

'I know. And it's where certain members of Led Zeppelin are rumoured to have performed their magic rituals.'

'Eh? What?'

'That'll be five pounds, please,' he said again, holding out his hand.

'What?'

He was pointing over my shoulder with his eyes. I looked and saw that his concern was Mr Whitchurch, the no-nonsense manager of HGV, standing by the STAFF ONLY door and watching us over his reading glasses.

'Oh,' I said to Gaz, handing over the fiver.

Mr Whitchurch grunted and went back through his door.

'The Lamb and Flag?' I said.

'Just go up there one evening and ask for Randy. He'll set you straight on the rumours, if he's in the mood to. And a few other things. Now if you don't mind, there's a queue forming here.'

I looked behind again and an old lady was there, giving me the evil eye. I could have sworn it was the one from the caff yesterday. Although she didn't swear at me this time.

I walked away. Behind me I heard her saying: 'Have you got that one from *The X Factor*?'

APPENDIX B: CASE STUDY 1 (18 SEPTEMBER 1970)

SPECIMEN was a blisteringly innovative rock guitarist and vocalist from overseas with a habit of indulging in pyromaniac tendencies onstage. His urine was the first I had procured. He had performed locally some years earlier, and his fame had since rocketed to global proportions. By chance, I met an individual who had attended that concert in his capacity as a low-ranking employee at the venue and claimed to have recouped some of the artist's urine. Further questioned about this, he revealed himself to be something of a urine fetishist. My interest was piqued, and I purchased the urine along with that of one other artist and High Denomination Soul possessor who had appeared on the same bill (see Case Study 2). The fetishist was to become my dedicated handler in all subsequent urinary dealings (see section entitled 'Urine' for further discussion of the urine handler role).

A suitable host was selected at the maternity ward: an infant with a withered arm. Never would this boy play the guitar, or indeed any other stringed instrument, to a high standard. The ritual went without mishap. The carcass of the blood sacrifice (a drunken student) was disposed of in the hospital incinerator, and the infant host appeared stable.

But my experiment had failed. The next day's newspapers reported news of the guitarist's sudden death, apparently due to choking upon his own vomit. Although I was now in possession of a High Denomination Soul and the fate of the donor was of no material interest to me, I was nonetheless concerned. If each famous performer died when I shifted their soul, a pattern would emerge and people would investigate. It was vital that my operations remained covert, so I went back to snails and dogs to find out where I had failed.

My instincts told me that it was the three-year staleness of the donor's urine that had caused the mishap. But experiments on progressively aged urine bore no fruit on this front. However, I discovered that the donor's chances of survival increased in proportion with the host's proximity to the scene of the ritual. Indeed, to ensure the continued health of the donor the blood and urine mixing must take place within two feet of the infant host.

19.

I had a little personal CD player that I'd found at a jumble sale once, and I slotted home the Bremner as the train pulled away. It was a ninety minute trip, which was long enough to get the gist of the album and concentrate on learning a couple of tracks. The songs turned out to be dire, which came as no surprise. But I detected a bit of promise in the boy's voice, which was clearly trying to do something beyond the scope of the material. I looked at the sleeve notes and found that none of the songs were written by him. Nothing wrong with that as such, but an artist will get nowhere unless he's got good material. Take Cliff Richard – most of his ones were third-party efforts. Same with Elvis, Engelbert Humperdinck and David Soul.

By the time I reached Burninghouse I felt well-prepared. I could converse at length about Zak Bremner if required, pointing out one or two of his strengths and weaknesses, and sing two songs word for word. The songs I'd chosen were 'Quite Pretty' and 'Memory of Your Chin'. Not because I liked them the best but because they were the first two. It was like swatting up for an exam. And that's what it was, really. I was approaching the gates of Big Time City…but I couldn't get in unless I passed the test.

The audition was still an hour away, so I thought I'd take my time locating the Miramar and have a snoop around town. It had been years since I'd been up here, and I found that things had changed quite a bit. You still came right out of the station into a big shopping centre, but it had all been renovated now and everything was sparkling and no longer smelling like old cabbages. I had a look in one or two clothes shops with a view to finding something for the audition, but I only had ten pounds and all I could get for that were pants and sunglasses. Cursing my poor shoplifting skills, I bought some shades and moved on. Outside the shop I put the shades on so I could start getting used to them, and I liked what I saw when I caught sight of my reflection in a window. It was only a minor bit of accessorising but it made a lot of difference. As well as enhancing my look enough to clinch the Miramar job, I could see it becoming the cornerstone of a whole new image.

I went round a corner and found a record shop. It was another branch of HGV, but you wouldn't know it from the outside. I'd never seen a record shop so big. I went in.

There were a lot of people here for a Wednesday afternoon. They must have been skiving off work or school or something because I couldn't imagine how so many of them could be pros, like me, who visited a record shop in the same way a restaurateur visits the market. Then I noticed that they were all traipsing in the same direction, heading for the escalator that went up. I found it strange that they all moved so slowly yet with such apparent purpose, and I found myself traipsing along with them.

Where the escalator came out on the first floor I found out the reason for the slowness. There was a queue up here about two hundred deep, snaking around the Easy Listening and Classical sections and right through Rock and Pop. Something was going on at the front but I couldn't quite see what. All I made out was people popping behind a curtain for half a minute or so then wandering off with a bag and a big smile. The pace of it was quite brisk, so I stayed in line and slapped the headphones on. I could always bail out if I ran out of time. And I was just a bit curious. There was a buzz in the air that told me something special was going on here. I wanted to know what could generate that buzz, besides all the flies in here.

I gave up on the CD after a couple more tracks. I knew everything I needed to know about Zak Bremner and it wasn't that interesting. And besides, I'd just shuffled past the letter B and seen The Beatles and Bowie, and it had cast me back the two or so hours since I'd been talking to Gaz. It felt weird – not only that I was in another HGV here that dwarfed the poxy one we had in Warchester, but also to remember the things he'd said. I couldn't imagine Gaz believing in stuff like that, but there he was telling it to me...Jimmy Page and David Bowie, going at it with spells and incantations and the like.

Rumours, he'd said.

But where do rumours come from? Who's to say some stuff hadn't gone on, back then in the '70s when order and logic didn't have such a tight grip on civilisation? And wasn't it a bit coincidental that it had gone on right there in the Lamb and Flag – within bottle-throwing distance of Warchester Infirmary?

'No bodily signings, sir.'

There was a strange man in front of me, wearing orange-rimmed glasses and with his ratty hair gelled up in all directions. I tried to ignore him.

'And please do not enter into long conversations. Sir? I need your attention, sir.'

'What?'

'For the signing. There are rules, sir. Failure to accept the rules will mean ejection from the *store*, sir, and not just the queue.'

'Oh,' I said, looking past him at the security guard down by the curtain. He had a shaven head that seemed about five times too small for his body, which didn't bode well for anyone who wanted to reason with him. 'So this is a signing, is it?'

'Of course it's a signing. What do you think this is? The checkout queue?'

He found that amusing, along with some girls behind me. Dickheads. If they only knew who I was, and the profile I had back in –

'So, really, there's no point in taking up space in the queue, sir, if you're not—'

'Who says I ain't?'

'Well, what have you got for Zak to sign?'

'Zak?'

That was another amusing one. 'Obviously—'

'Zak Bremner, you mean?'

Hilarious now. And not just orange specs and the three bitches behind. I had an audience here, front and back, all loving it. But it didn't bother me. I loved an audience. Even a tough one like this. You saw me at the Blue Cairo and the way I'd dealt with Jim Taylor. I'm a man who can think on his feet and adapt to any occasion, audience-wise.

'Hold on a minute…' I said, fishing inside my jacket. 'There,' I said, pulling out my *Zakology* case. 'That's for him to sign.'

His amusement wavered only a tiny bit, him saying: 'That's *Zakology*, sir, an album which is nearly a year old now. Zak is here promoting his *new* album, *Bremnology*. He's really not interested in signing older—'

'Not where I come from,' I said. 'Where I come from, this here album is at number six in the charts. Are you sayin' that Zak don't care about my town?'

'No, *Zakology* is at six in the charts *nationally*, sir. A new Zak release always boosts the back catalogue. If you had taken the trouble to look at the number one spot, in whatever backwoods town you come from, you would have seen *Bremnology*. Unless, of course, it had sold out, which is quite possible. So you see, sir, you really have no place in this queue. Now, if you don't mind, true Zak fans are waiting to see their hero. Perhaps if you removed your...ahem...*Orbisonian* sunglasses you would see that you are becoming an obstacle in their path.'

He stood aside and waved his arm. Behind him stood the baldy security man, hands joined in front of him, lip curling. A little way beyond that a cameraman was getting footage of the fans and coming our way.

'All right, but you'll have to lead me away,' I said, holding my arms out in front of me. 'Or you could ask them to have a look around for my stick. I've lost it.'

'Your stick?' he said.

'Yeah. My white stick.'

'You mean, erm...?'

The cameraman had clocked the situation and was coming over, adjusting his lens. I noticed he was with a female reporter and a man holding a fat microphone on a pole with 'BIG CITY NEWS' on it.

'Look,' I said, loudly, 'I know when I'm not wanted. If Zak Bremner and HGV Records don't want blind people hanging around, then I'll go.'

'Well, I didn't exactly say—'

'It's fine, really. Just lead me away. Oh, and tell Zak I'm very sorry I didn't see that he had a new album. I'm blind, you see, so I didn't notice it there in the number one spot. Tell him I won't bother him again, but I'll always buy his records because, even if he don't like disabled people like me, I still like him. I always will.'

The reporter was coming straight for me, saying to the cameraman: 'Ooh, this looks juicy…'

Just as the fat microphone came looming in, orange specs grabbed my wrist and shouted:

'Zak Bremner is a proud supporter of all differently abled people, whether they are fans or not! He embraces their diversity and…erm…'

He pulled my arm and led me up to the front, offering the reporter a cheesy smile as we went past and saying: 'Zak has asked to see his very special fan!'

We were moving a bit fast for a blind man so I made sure to stumble into some of the fans, knocking them over. One of them was a fat teenager and I think he fell on top of a little girl. Orange specs tried to pull me the other way and I went into a display of *Bremnologys*, knocking them all over and collapsing on the pile. My shades fell off and I lay on my back, rolling around in the CDs and making my eyes look all funny. I knew the camera was on me and I wanted it to look good. I think I even shouted 'Help!' once or twice.

I wasn't sure how all of this looked, but I knew it was a performance.

Like I said – I can turn it on.

A woman came along and helped orange specs get me on my feet again and my shades back on. She was wearing orange specs too. Getting an arm each, they led me with great care to the curtain, pulling it aside to reveal a skinny bloke sat there behind a table, chatting to a girl and her mum. He had shades on like me but they were mirror ones. 'Oh, I just use lacquer,' I heard him say, patting down the sides of his ridiculous hair. All three of them looked up at me, and before I knew it the females were gone and I was in their place, looking at Zak Bremner through my dark glasses and blind eyes.

Something came over me.

I don't know how I knew, but this was one of those moments. You're in the right place at the right time and you've got to do something. It's like you've been sent here. You just feel it.

'Zak,' Orange specs was saying, 'I'd like to present, er…Well, he's one of your favourite type of fans, Zak – the *disabled* ones. What's your name, sir?'

Straight off the bat I said: 'Blind Rik.'

'Blind…really?'

'No, Blind Rik. Not Blind Really.'

'Blind Rik,' said Zak, nodding. 'That's not a bad name. That's a cool name, Blind Rik. Yeah.'

'Right, well…' Orange specs was saying, moving away. 'Zak, I'll leave you with Blind Rik.'

Zak was looking past me and I knew it was at the camera. 'Yeah, I love meeting blind people,' he said. 'So, erm, what d'you think of the album cover? It's a good one, yeah? I designed it myself. The record company drew it up properly and stuff but I basically came up with it. Do you like drawing, Blind Rik?'

In his mirror shades I saw the cameraman get dragged out and the curtain swing to.

'Zak,' I said.

I didn't have much time.

'Zak, I've been sent to you from another time. From the mid-'70s. It was a time when the musical landscape was much richer, a place where creativity blossomed and gave forth fruits rich with melody, nuance and meaning.'

I don't know where this was coming from.

I was as surprised as you by it.

Zak was quite surprised too, going by his hanging jaw.

'You are the special one,' I said. 'The *special* one. But your seed is wasted upon these, er…shit songs they're feeding you. What you need is a special song. For the special one. That's what I've been sent here to give you. Here…'

I found my notebook in its usual pocket and leafed through it, selecting a song for him. I knew I wouldn't get anything at all from this and that I was giving away a part of my soul in exchange for nothing, but I was going with the moment. It was a giving moment for me, and a receiving one for Zak Bremner.

I ripped out a page and handed it to him, saying: 'The tune is a bit like "Moonlight Shadow" by Mike Oldfield, but slower. And the chorus just goes 'Toothbrush, toothbrush, I killed him with a toothbrush'.'

I felt that I wasn't making myself clear, so I quickly ran through the whole song for him, demonstrating where the emphasis had to be, and the tricky bit halfway through the last verse where you jump an octave.

'Take this song,' I said. 'Take it and make it your own, Zak. It's a gift from the past, from a time when songs were songs and singers were stars.'

He did take it, and looked at it. I could tell he was a bit shell-shocked. 'How did you write this if you're blind?'

Barely missing a beat, I said: 'Sometimes I can see. Only when the muse takes me. She gives me enough vision to jot the song down, so I don't forget it, then I'm blind again.'

'But how can you read it again if you—'

'I must go, Zak,' I said, getting up. 'Remember what I said. And don't lose that song.'

I went out the other way and headed for a fire escape. Not that I'd done anything wrong. I just felt a need for a mysterious exit.

My head was spinning as I trotted down those stairs. I really felt like I'd achieved something here, even though I plainly hadn't in any practical sense. Zak had achieved something though. He'd been visited by the ghost of music past, as far as he was concerned, and if he knew what was best for him he'd take what he'd been given and go on to great things. And it was me who'd done it for him. I'd mixed in famous company and lorded over it, told it what to do.

I was thinking about that as I wandered through the shopping centre, looking for the exit. I had fifteen minutes to get to the Miramar and I couldn't remember any of the Bremner lyrics. But I didn't feel I needed them now. I was flying high, capable of anything. I could sing 'Toothbrushes' and claim it as the new, unreleased Bremner. That's the idea I was toying with as I sailed through the exit on to Old Street, and was grabbed by a man in a peaked cap and posh suit who bustled me into the back of a limousine that smelt faintly of piss.

Urine

URINE acts like a passport in the great and grand cosmos, and will uniquely identify one organism alone. A mixture of urines from disparate organisms is not potent enough to work magic and can be fatal to the organisms involved. In the soulshift, urine represents the flow of a soul from A to B.

The reverse, from B to A, is represented by faeces. While a stream carries a man downstream, the land will allow him to walk back to where he started. But a warlock should never need that knowledge, because he should never regret his actions enough to undo them.

As talent increases, so the presence of green in the urine of the organism increases. In a mildly talented organism the green is barely discernible, but that of a true High Denomination Soul is shockingly apparent. It also glistens slightly, as if gently carbonated.

The role of the urine handler became an important one after my disastrous attempt to gain the Devil's assistance. Originally I had been thinking of tricking the prospective donor into submitting to the ritual of his or her own free will, but then I realised that I could do it without their knowledge. If I could get the urine of a High Denomination Soul, I could steal his soul. But I had no means of procuring that urine, being naturally reluctant to dirty my hands in that pursuit myself. The urine handler was the solution.

In person he was a man of lowly status but with access to latrines frequented by the great and good of the music world. In return for cosmic favours he would deliver to me the passed water of whichever High Denomination Soul came within range of him, using a contraption fitted to the pan of a toilet. As a part-time hospital porter he was also in a position to obtain the urine of the infant hosts. I always performed the rituals in the presence of the infant host, but the urine was acquired beforehand to avoid complications.

Another necromancer might have different requirements of his urine handler, but there is one characteristic that is important above all others:

Trustworthiness.

Human souls are at stake. A careless error, indiscretion or betrayal could result in dire consequences throughout the cosmos. It is impossible for the warlock to mistake the urine of a High Denomination Soul due to its green hue and glistening quality, but the urine of the host could be from anyone.

20.

When I say bustled, my forced entrance into the limousine was not a violent one. Far from it. The chauffeur – as he turned out to be – had a firm grip but it was a respectful one, like he was protecting me from some danger I didn't yet know about. By the time I'd processed what was going on the door was shut, he was back up front and the limo was gliding through traffic like a shark through crowded waters.

'Mr Marino,' he said in answer to my question. 'He wait for you.'

'Oh,' I said. To be honest I was a bit surprised. Not that I'd been expecting to get hijacked into a limousine by anyone, but as soon as it had started happening I'd thought it was one of Zak Bremner's people. I thought he'd read the song, listened to it in his head and phoned for his man to get me before I got away…because my lyrics were pure gold and he wanted to sign me as his exclusive songwriter.

But I was a singer more than a songwriter, and I wasn't

going to be in anyone's shadow. Mind you, it was an interesting proposition and I'd have to think about it.

'Mr Marino, eh?' I said, 'How do you know who I am, though? I mean, grabbing me like that. You might have had the wrong person.'

'I hold up the sign. He say 'SUNTAN'. You come to me. That is how it work.'

'A sign?'

'Yes.'

I didn't remember seeing that, but I supposed he must be right. It's hard to disagree with anything when your buttocks are being massaged by some expensive leather upholstery, your soul being soothed by a quality audio system (playing 'Since We've Been Together' by Al Green) and a drinks cabinet being popped out of nowhere.

'You help self,' he said, giving me a friendly wink in the rearview. 'Enjoy ride.' I think he was foreign.

I was enjoying it. I mixed myself a Sunrise and sat back, watching the pedestrians outside. Traffic was murder in this part of town and we spent a lot of time waiting at lights, but that's the bit I enjoyed the most. People couldn't stop staring, you see. One glance at a stretch limo and they've got to know who's inside, because you can bank on it that it's someone special. Some of them even came right up to the glass and peered in. I raised my glass and drank to them, but they couldn't see me. I was on one side and they were on the other. I really felt like it's where I belonged.

'Hang on,' I said, 'this ain't the way to the Miramar.'

'No, you not go to Miramar. Mr Marino want you at private residence.'

'Oh yeah? Why's that? I mean, I thought he wanted to see how my voice came across with the Miramar acoustics?'

'I just take order, Mr Suntan,' he said, turning a sharp right and almost clipping the heel of a young mum pushing a pram. I turned and watched her shouting after us, hate on her face and a foul word on her young lips. She got smaller and smaller until she was gone. It was nice being in a car like this. Nothing outside seemed to matter much. Another sharp right and we were dipping down into an underground car park. There was a bit of gravity involved and I had to juggle my drink a little, but I didn't spill any. Before I knew it the engine was off and the door opened next to me.

'I ain't finished,' I said, showing him the Sunrise. I was only halfway down the orange part.

'You go in now. You get more drink in residence, if Mr Marino allow. Is possible he want you sobriety.'

'I'm always sobriety.'

'Yes,' he said, snatching the glass in one swift move.

I thought that was a bit rude, considering I was Mr Marino's guest. But it was his car, I suppose. To be honest, I wasn't ready to get out of it. I was just getting used to it and I wanted another few rides around the block. Or a couple of trips up and down the length of the country. Anything really. I got out.

He led me to a lift and tapped a code on some buttons beside it. It opened and I found myself inside, alone. It was a surprise to turn and see the doors shut behind me, but at the same time it all made sense. The lift started going up. I could feel the hand of fate under it, pushing me up nice and gentle. Fate had led me to Zak Bremner for one reason and now he was taking me to Mr Marino for another. Or maybe they were the same reason. Whatever, I was in no doubt that the pieces were falling into place for me now, and that these were essential steps along the path to me becoming a famous singer.

And even if they weren't, I was having an interesting afternoon. It was good to get out of Warchester now and then. Especially when you got to hang around in plush environs like this. The lift stopped and the doors opened, and it was only then that I learned what the word 'plush' really meant.

I stepped on to the shag-pile carpet and remained there for maybe five minutes, surveying the splendour of Mr Marino's residence, before a middle-aged man walked past wearing only a nappy and a pair of earphones.

'Good afternoon, Rik,' he said, then disappeared behind a wall.

The nappy was making me think twice about this. I don't mind eccentrics – they're quite common in show business – but a nappy was going beyond that. I had a look behind but the lift had gone, and I couldn't see a button to summon it back. And besides, it was only a nappy. Wasn't like he was wearing a necklace of human skulls.

This was the big time now.

You had to take people as they came.

Bat an eyelid and you're back out in the cold.

I followed him around the corner and found him at a bar, putting the finishing touches to a Sunrise. 'Mikhail phoned up your preference, beverage-wise,' he said, handing it over.

I took it and had a sip. Perfect. 'Mick who?'

'Mikhail.'

'Oh. Right.'

When he next spoke I realised that I'd been staring at his nappy close-range: 'You're concerned by this? No doubt you consider it a nappy. Well, it is. An *intelligent* nappy. I am wearing the most futuristic, state-of-the-art nappy known to mankind. It senses when waste has been passed and neutralises the ambient air accordingly, giving no one cause to suspect.

Really, if I wore trousers over these you need never know of my incontinence. But I choose to display them, sometimes. A garment so practical and revolutionary needs to be showcased. Don't you think, Rik?'

'I do think,' I said. 'But really, it don't bother me. Personally, I think people should be allowed to walk around the streets in nappies. I mean, without trousers over them, normally.'

'They are, Rik.'

'Hmm…I suppose you're right.'

'I am. I know the law, Rik,' he said, strolling away from the bar with a tall glass of what looked like milk. 'But I also understand public perception and its ability to take away a man's power at the drop of a hat. I choose not to wear a nappy in front of the world, but I don't deny what I am. I am many things, Rik. An incontinent man, a businessman, an aesthete, a mover, a shaker…'

'Blimey. And on top of all that you run the Miramar.'

'A hobby, Rik. A highly profitable one but a hobby nonetheless. But don't worry – the Miramar is as professional and legitimate an enterprise as you will find. Come aboard now and you'll go far.' He stopped in front of a huge aquarium. Behind his head a small octopus was gently flapping about. 'I'm talking about your career, Rik.'

I'd been watching the octopus and wondering if it wasn't a squid. I knew there was a difference between the two but I couldn't remember what, and it might be just down to size. This one really was quite small – like a man's fist clutching a few inner-tubes. Anyway, when Marino mentioned my career I looked at him instead.

'Oh, right,' I said. 'Talking about that, you'll never guess who was in that shopping centre back there. Zak Bremner himself. Is that a coincidence or what?'

'No coincidence,' he said, moving away from the aquarium towards a huge leather sofa which he sat on. 'Mr Bremner is in town for four consecutive nights at the NIC. Such is his pulling power in this city, he could block-book that venue for a month and still sell out every night. His popularity is unrivalled all over the nation, but especially in this city, his home town. He is a phenomenon, Mr Suntan. And one I intend to exploit.'

I was sat opposite him on an armchair that was unlike any armchair I'd come across. It had started vibrating when I sat in it and I found that quite alarming, but after a couple of seconds I kicked back and enjoyed the experience. This was the kind of thing I deserved. I said: 'Yeah?'

'Yes. If you're in agreement, that is. What I had in mind, as I hinted at across telephone wires yesterday, is a male vocalist with a unique style...one who can take that Bremner material and interpret it in new and intriguing ways. That's going to pull the crowds, Rik. His songs are the sound of this city. People can simply not get enough of them. And when word gets around that there is a new voice putting a fresh spin on them – and doing it with *respect* – we'll be on to a winner. How do you fancy that, Rik?'

'I fancy it very much, Mr Marino. Like I said, I know all about Zak Bremner. I find that he has a certain swooping movement in his songs, both vocally and thematically. It's a good match between vocalist and material but I feel there could be summat more interesting behind it. I can see a way to introduce a subtly different angle on those songs, one which still swoops in the Bremner fashion but also hints at fun, sex and madness.'

'Madness, eh?'

'Oh yeah. I believe that any good song has elements of insanity. Take your typical song set-up – a man who's driven off the rails by a woman he either can't have or can't handle. What's happening to him? He's going nuts. You can't see it but you can feel it. And that madness – it's what makes the song fly. It ain't the only way to spin a song, but I think it's the way to spin the Bremner songbook. Especially 'Memory of Your Chin'.'

He seemed to be thinking about that. I'd impressed him, I knew. The thought came to me that I might have gone too far with it, intimidating him with too much analysis when he just wanted a common or garden singer. But if I had, fuck it. You know me, and common or garden I ain't. I'd be better off without that job. But he said:

'How do you feel about the commute?'

'The what?'

'You'd be up here three nights a week. I'd pay you three a week to make it worth your while, rising to five if things work out...but would you be all right about the travel? Let's face it, Warchester's a bit of a trek.'

'Three?' I said. 'What, quid?'

'Ha! I like that. I like a man who can banter a crowd. No, I mean three hundred, Rik. And well you know it.'

'Well, yeah, I did.'

I didn't. Three hundred a week? Rising to half a fucking grand? I only got fifteen a night at the Cairo, one night a week. Fucking *hell*.

'You know, I started out in your town. Many moons ago.'

'You came from Warchester?' I was giggling a bit. The thought was a bit hilarious. Or maybe it was the three hundred, rising to five. 'No shit?'

'Well, a bit of shit but not much. I wasn't raised there but I washed up there as a young man, and found myself in a job with limited status but a great deal of power, if you knew how to tap it. It's that job that got me where I am today, Rik.'

He was by the window now, looking out over the conurbation

of Burninghouse. It was the widest window I've ever seen, and I hadn't noticed it before. It was like he'd just conjured it up to illustrate where he was today.

'Of course,' he said, 'I could help you find a place here in Burninghouse if you'd rather relocate. Personally, I'd prefer that option if I was a man of your age and in your position. You have no ties, I take it?'

'Ties? No…none at all.'

'That's what I thought. A man like you has no need of ties. There's a fortune to be sought out there, Rik, and you can't do it with baggage. And I'm not just talking about the pursuit of money and success. There are things out there that you can't see. You hear whispers of them but you don't know if they're real or not. That's what I devoted my life to, Rik – the hunt for those things. And I found them.'

I could take driving lessons. Actually, no, for five hundred a week I could have my own driver, like Mick. Maybe Sam would let me know where he got his limo.

'Do you have a question, Rik?'

A question. I liked that. Not questions, but just one of them. A question. Actually I didn't like it that much, but I did admire it. I could see that this man knew how to do business. He had his own style and used it well.

'You said you was a businessman, and that the Miramar is like a hobby. What line of business are you in, then?'

He thought about that one for a bit. Not like he was stuck for an answer, more like he was relishing it before letting it go.

'Rik, have you perchance read George du Maurier's 1894 novel *Trilby*?'

'Erm, I ain't sure.'

'In that novel the character known as Svengali controls a singer's voice via hypnotism. I do not use hypnotism, Rik. I

Charlie Williams

facilitate. I provide the optimum environment and opportunities for a singer to grow, prosper and become famous. And, yes, from this I profit financially. If that is a svengali, so be it.'

'Famous?'

'Yes. Fame is something I have managed to avoid in my life. But, alas, for clients it is a necessity.'

'So, you're saying…you make your clients famous?'

'If they work out at the Miramar, then yes. But many fall by the wayside, Rik. Many are crushed 'neath the wheels of the lumbering juggernaut that is the music business. They do not become famous. They become…detritus.'

He laughed, the laugh turning into a long, rattling fit of coughing, and by the time he'd finished I couldn't be bothered to ask him what he meant by that statement on the subject of detritus. And who cared anyway?

I was set for growth, prosperity and fame.

Fame.

This was the break I'd been after for ages, the one I'd grafted my arse off for and deserved more than any other person currently operating in the singing industry. I was about to thank Mr Marino for giving me this chance when he said, holding out a pen and gesturing towards a bit of paper on the table:

'Sign here.'

'Sign? I ain't signing nothing without—'

'I'm a businessman, Mr Suntan. If you're interested, sign. Otherwise—'

'Hold on…I…I'd just prefer to, you know, think about it for, erm…'

Three hundred.

'I had you down as a man of good instinct, Mr Suntan. Perhaps I misjudged you.'

'No, you didn't! I just…Can I go over the small print first?'

Rising to five.

'If you choose to, Mr Suntan. But I have laid out my terms already, including working times and rates of pay. There's really nothing else to—'

I grabbed the pen and signed my life away.

And it felt good.

'I want you at 6 p.m. tomorrow for sound checks. And don't say thank you. As I said, I'm a businessman, and I don't do favours. Understand?'

Slightly taken aback, I went: 'I got you, Mr Marino. And thanks.'

Post-Soulshift Behaviour

POST soulshift, neither donor nor host retain any memory of the act. Furthermore, as I write this, no host nor donor has ever discovered by other means the alien nature of the soul within them.

This is not to say that the behaviour of both parties should not change drastically. Each now possesses a new soul and therefore a different personality. In the host, this can lead to frustrated attempts to take advantage of the talent that they were never born with, and a subsequent descent into depression. This depression should be monitored, and measures taken to prevent suicide attempts and subsequent loss of the High Denomination Soul.

The course of the donor's life post-soulshift is of no consequence.

21.

I had to find my own way back. And I didn't mind that anyway. I'd loved the limo but it was better on foot now, the sun going down and a mellow ambience in the air. The rush hour hadn't started and those not working were milling around, chatting in coffee bars and doing a bit of shopping. There were a lot of women around, nice ones. I could see that working in my favour. I knew my strengths and onstage sexual charisma was one of them. All in all, I was happy to make Burninghouse my new home for the time being, while I proved myself worthy. After that I'd probably move to Clandon. If furthering your career is your angle, there's no better place than the big one down south. But Burninghouse wasn't far off, these days. And any step up the stairway was a step towards the top.

I noticed a coffee shop called Café Tempo and liked the sound of it. It had a musical connotation and I felt that it was calling me, so I went in and bought myself a cappuccino and some sort of biscuit, which I took outside to an *al fresco* table.

I sat and sipped the coffee and nibbled the biscuit, which was basically a gingerbread man but in the shape of an alarm clock. I'd never seen a biscuit quite like it and it seemed a shame to eat it, but I did. My mind and body started relaxing and I was soon thinking things out. What sort of flat I'd have here…how the more urban environment would affect my creativity…how to build on that new image I'd started with the shades…maybe getting an aquarium and some squid. Lots of decisions to be made, all of them about exciting things. And the only thing that tore my attention from them was a screech of brakes in the road, about ten yards from where I was sat.

I looked up in time to see the back wheels of a cab roll over a little dog. The driver nearly came to a stop but thought better of it and put his foot down, leaving the dog twitching in a growing pool of blood. It was a little thing with curly white fur, and I think it was a poodle. A fat woman was standing over it, screaming some foreign words after the cab. The lead was still attached to the dog's collar and she picked it up, trying to get him on his feet. But he was dead. She shouted after the cab one more time then walked off, leaving the poor little bugger in the road.

It seemed wrong to just leave him there. Cars were going around him and pedestrians carrying on their way, glancing at the dog and grimacing. I put down my drink and went over to it, drawing a couple of beeps and waving them off. I felt confident that I was doing the right thing here, proving myself to be a man of common decency and not just a star with an exorbitant salary. Any luck and someone would recognise me when I started performing at the Miramar and link the two events up, and from thereon in I'd be known as a friend to all animals, all-round hero and able to do no wrong. As I reached the dog I had a strong feeling that this whole event had taken place for my benefit alone.

The puddle of blood wasn't that big after all, a small animal like this only containing so much. It had a pink collar on, so I guessed it was a she. You wouldn't be able to tell otherwise because her hind-quarters were crushed. I crouched down for a closer look. It was quite alarming, the way she was so still. Something had gone from her body and it was more than just life. Her soul, that was it. The little thing used to be home to a yappy little soul and now it had fled. But where to?

I mean, where *do* souls go? Bodies rot and go back to the ground, but where does a dog's soul go? Or a person's? Does it rot and go back to the air? That didn't seem right to me. I picked the dog up, wondering if her soul wasn't living on in some way, perhaps looking for a new home right there and then as I placed her old one in the gutter.

But never mind all that for now. Here was a dead dog and I'd just ate a clock.

It was eight o'clock when I reached the Dead Dog, a pub so named in honour of a time in the late '60s when half the dogs in Warchester dropped dead of unknown causes. I was knackered from having to stand up on a crowded train nearly all the way back from Burninghouse, and then running most of the way from the station to out here, but Ted didn't look very appreciative when I saw him striding up from the entrance. I wasn't very happy with him either. I'd been doing some thinking on the way back.

Before he could get his gripe in, I said:

'What was all that bollocks about the Singing Cyborg?'

'Eh?'

'The Miramar. You said they were after a novelty act.'

'What? Oh…I just wanted to simplify things for you. Listen, there's been some—'

'Simplify things? How?'

'I dunno…The feller contacted me, but I didn't want to tell you about it. I knew what else we had planned, see. But at the same time I thought it was only fair to give you a chance. So—'

'But you jeopardised my big opportunity, Ted! The Miramar weren't interested in singing cyborgs or time-travelling whatevers. A manager is meant to look after his client's interests, not—'

'I know, I made all that up. It was a sort of a compromise: I tell you about the Miramar opportunity, but I angle it so you're running with a handicap. If you could still impress the Miramar man, even though you came across weird, maybe you had a hope in the normal world, and maybe I shouldn't…Look, it's all moot anyway. Compared to what we got going on here with the Jimmy Page business, the Miramar is small fry. You got a chance here of going back in time and becoming David Bowie *at his height*, Rik. That's your rightful place in history and we're gonna get you there. But never mind that, summat's—'

'I just wish you'd been straight with me, that's all.'

'Right, well I'll be straight with you now – Yusuf's dead.'

22.

'What?' I said. But I'd heard it.

And so had a couple of teenage girls and boys coming around the corner just then. They stopped and watched us, grinning and having a good whisper at our expense.

'Come on,' said Ted.

We went inside, the familiar sight and sound of a couple of hundred flies greeting me. It was years since I'd been in here. Used to be a popular haunt for the under-aged end of the market when I was one of them myself. It was a bit out of the way but you were guaranteed no questions asked age-wise, as long as you could see over the bar. There was still a lot of that going on, judging by the bum fluff and acne scattered all over, but there was a more mature crowd as well, most of them sporting flat noses and clustered around a ramshackle boxing ring in the middle of the floor. Inside the ring a couple of overweight fortyish blokes were trying to slug it out, although neither could lift their arms very high and it was all they could do to suck some air into their lungs. A big effort saw one of them swing a right hook at nose-height, but he missed and went down himself. The crowd started baying like goons. I hadn't really heard goons baying before but I was sure this was what they sounded like.

Ted had got himself swallowed up into a wall of sweaty backs and tattoos at the bar, and when he came out again, holding two pints, I said:

'You know I don't drink that stuff, Ted.'

'Bloody hell! Won't you shut up about your bloody Tequila Sunrises! I asked if I can have one and they called me a poof, all right? You want a Tequila Sunrise or Sunset or Shit-storm or whatever kind of tequila cocktail you want, *you* go and ask.'

'I'm only saying.'

'Yeah, and Yusuf's dead.'

'Fuck's sake, Ted. You say that like it's my fault.'

'Well, that ain't what I'm saying. But ain't you even interested in how he's dead? This is Yusuf, for God's sake. *Yusuf.*'

'Course I'm interested. But look at it from my angle – you've dragged me out here to this shit-hole, I've found out about you jeopardising my career and now you give me a pint of... eeurgh...what *is* that?'

'It's bitter, Rik. Like the pill that Yusuf had to swallow when he saw that artic bearing down on him. He never had a chance, Rik. Out of nowhere it came, this truck, and he—'

'Yusuf got run over?'

'Yeah, and—'

'When?'

'What d'you mean, when? What does it matter? He's dead, and no amount of asking 'when?' is gonna—'

'Was it this afternoon, about five?'

'Was it...? Well, yeah, by all accounts it was.'

'Well fuck me,' I swore. 'Do you know what? I saw a poodle get run over and killed at more or less *exactly* the same moment.'

Ted just looked at me. I thought he was as amazed as me, but it turned out he wasn't.

'A poodle?' he said, spilling some of his beer. 'A flamin' *poodle*? I'm talking about Yusuf – a *human being*, and…and our *friend* – and you're saying…What are you saying?'

'I'm just saying it's a coincidence, that's all. When you mentioned it about Yusuf, it seemed relevant to—'

'Look, could you just shut up about flamin' poodles? I've got some things I need to say to you…about Yusuf and about Jimmy P—'

'Ladies and gentlemen…' The voice came blaring out of the PA like a combine harvester over the horizon, obliterating every conversation in its path. 'Dead Dog Promotions in association with Ted Regis Management is proud to present tonight's main event – a ten-round contest for the Warchester and District featherweight title, featuring the champion: Mohammed Nazir of Cyril Road, and the challenger: Egbert McLaren of…erm, no fixed abode.'

I used the pause to look at Ted and say:

'Ted Regis Management? The fuck's this?'

'It's the first step,' he said, not taking his glistening eyes off the announcer, 'Eggy's going back!'

'Back where?'

'Where? To 1977, of course. To the moment when his soul was took from his true self – George Foreman!'

'George Foreman?'

'Yes!'

'You mean, the grill maker?'

'No! I mean the feller who fought Ali! All right, he also made some grills, but—'

'In the red corner – weighing in at one hundred twenty-six pounds bang on, with a height of five foot seven inches and a reach of sixty-five inches – the champion, Mohammed "the Ring Stinger" Nazir!'

The crowd went nuts. And by that I mean they all jumped up and down and started nutting each other. They seemed happy and I think most of it was accidental, but you couldn't be sure. And there was some blood. Making its way through all this, to the accompaniment of 'Eye of the Tiger' blaring through the PA, you could see a flag with a bulldog on it. When it reached the ring a skinny Asian bloke in frilly shorts jumped in and started punching the air and skipping around. His gloves seemed like lollipops on the end of his skinny arms.

While all that was going on I was saying:

'You mean...the midget is George Foreman? I mean, his soul...'

'Yeah!'

'But how...? I mean, why would—?'

'We ain't sure, Rik. But we think Jimmy Page was interested in boxing at the time, and—'

'In the blue corner – weighing in at one twenty-five pounds, with a height of four foot two inches and a reach of twenty-nine inches – introducing the challenger, Egbert 'the Egg Man' McLaren!'

'Eye of the Tiger' started up again, but this time there was no general nutting of each other in the crowd. They were baying again in that goon-like way, though. There was no flag either, just Martin's big head and wooden face surging through, towering above everyone and attracting about fifty flies. Some of the crowd had a go at him when he went past. He tried to fight them off but went down once or twice, coming up with a bloody nose and looking paler each time. When he got ringside he bent down and came up holding Eggy, who he chucked into the ring before going down again.

You should have seen Eggy.

It was a strange sight. If the other lad's arms were like lollipops, Eggy's were like chicken drumsticks with meatballs on the end. His shorts came all the way up to his armpits and were held up with a belt that had EGG MAN emblazoned across it. I only got one good glimpse of him, though, as he didn't come above the ropes.

'What the fuck is this for, though?' I shouted at Ted.

'It's part of the ritual, Rik. "The ritual must take place while the donor is engaged in the act of exploiting his talent," the book said. I jotted that bit down before it—'

'So is he meant to turn into George Foreman or what?'

'I dunno, Rik. I'm as interested as you. But I'll tell you summat – I ain't half excited. It's like…this is the reason why I became a manager. Not to make money, but to…well, do magic and stuff.'

'Right. And is that all? He's just got to win this fight?'

'No, he's got to *lose* this fight. We think. Way we see it, the thing that defines George Foreman, as he was back then, was getting beat by Muhammad Ali.'

'This ain't Muhammad Ali.'

'No, but his name's Mohammed, which is close enough. And anyway, it's the gesture that counts. Rituals are all about symbolism, Rik. And there's more to the ritual. Afterwards, we've gotta—'

'Ladies and gentlemen – let's get ready to rumble!'

The nutting goons started jumping up and down again. Some of them at the back were quite close to us, and one took a hairy elbow to the face and went down, crashing into Ted's flank and sending him down too. The goon was up and back into the mosh before I could chastise him for his clumsiness. Actually it was all quite amusing for the neutral observer. I helped Ted up.

'Me glasses!' he was shouting. 'Where's me...?'

I picked them up and handed them to him.

He said: 'Where's the lenses?'

I shrugged, feeling glass crunch underfoot.

The bell went ding ding and the fighters were off. Or is that horse racing?

'You'll have to tell me what's happening.'

'Eh? I can't even see most of the—'

'I have to know! Timing is of the essence, Rik. Don't let me down!'

'All right!'

I climbed up on the table. I could see Eggy properly now. He didn't half look odd, all pale and dumpy next to his lanky, brown-skinned opponent. I shouted down:

'They're sort of circling each other. Not much is...Oh, that's wossname coming in with a—'

'Mohammed.'

'Yeah, he tried to punch Eggy, but Eggy—'

'He's got good defence.'

'Yeah, he does seem to...Ooh, Mohammed's trying to punch him again. He's really swinging 'em in, trying to...But no, Eggy's bouncing and swerving around like a...a...'

'A chicken.'

'Yeah, he is actually moving like a chicken, and—'

'That's good. All part of the plan. Low centre of gravity.'

'Mohammed's taking a step back now, trying to work out a new way of...Hold up, Eggy's doing summat...He's crouching down low, like a...'

'Tiger.'

'Yeah, a very strange tiger but...Fuckin' hell! Did you see that?'

'No I bloody did not!'

'Oh yeah...He sort of jumped up in the air and hit Mohammed under the chin. Woo-hoo! How'd he do that? Mohammed's fucked now! He's against the ropes. Ooh, the ref's stepping in and—'

'Ah, bollocks.'

'What? Eggy's doing brilliant here!'

'He's meant to lose. By knock-out.'

'Oh yeah. Well, it's still on the cards. The ref's waved him on and Mohammed's regrouping now, getting his guard up and... What the fuck was that?'

'What happened?'

'Eggy just put his head down and *rammed* him in the nuts. The ref's telling him off.'

'Bloody hell! I told him to forget the goat. It's all going egg-shaped.'

'Ha, that's not a bad one!'

'It ain't meant to be funny!'

'All right, calm down. The action's on again, Eggy's...What's he doing? He seems to be hovering a couple of inches above the canvas, floating like a...'

'A flamin' butterfly! It's the other feller who's meant to be doing that!'

'Mohammed's keeping clear of him for the moment. He's got his guard up and he's backing off. Eggy's pursuing him around the ring, but no, Mohammed's back-heeling it like a Lotus in reverse, sliding off the ropes and wanting none of it. Hey, I'm good at this, ain't I? I could get a job—'

'The action, Rik!'

'Right...Er...Eggy's got him cornered. There's nowhere for

Mohammed to go. Eggy's going in for the kill! He leaps up, like a salmon, and hits Mohammed on the fist with his...face?'

'And?'

'Well, he's gone down. Eggy's gone down. The ref's stood over him. Ten, nine, eight...'

'Go on Eggy my son! You can do it!'

'...three, two one. He's out!'

'You beauty!'

APPENDIX F: CASE STUDY 3 (17 MARCH 1977)

SPECIMEN was a boxer, and the only soul I shifted whose field of accomplishment was sports. But his fame was equal to most of the musicians I had soulshifted and his talent was equivalent. As ever his sample came to me via my urine handler, who had now taken to the road in a bid to procure the urine of better and more varied High Denomination Souls on my behalf. This one had been picked up in central Africa, where the donor had been engaged in a fight.

One notable variation this time was that the donor was to be overseas at the time of the ritual. I wanted to test my theory that spatial considerations were irrelevant when dealing with the cosmos, and here was my opportunity.

The host organism was selected: a dwarf infant. My researches showed that no dwarves had ever achieved any significant success in boxing and so I was confident that the displaced soul would remain unfulfilled.

The ritual went without mishap. A local tramp

was used as the blood sacrifice, and I disposed of his remains in the usual manner. Upon completion of the ritual the host infant started behaving aggressively in his cot, suggesting that the soul of the surly boxer was within him. It was more difficult to gauge success on the other end, however, the donor being on a different continent. No communication with the donor being possible, I had to use the international media for my information, and confirmation of a successful soulshift did not come for some months.

The donor seems to have experienced an adverse reaction post-soulshift. In most cases, the infant host's soul is accepted quietly into the adult donor without much outward change in the short term, but the boxer appears to have sunk into some kind of spiritual despair in the immediate aftermath of the soulshift, rather like a patient's body rejecting a transplanted organ. This despair turned out to be temporary, and the donor soon stabilised and absorbed his new personality, albeit with a great deal of impact on his life, including temporary retirement from boxing and declaring himself a born-again Christian. It is both unknowable and immaterial whether his spiritual crisis was due to the long-distance nature of the soulshift or the strength of character of the new soul entering his body.

23.

There was a chill in the air as we went out the back door of the Dead Dog, and it reflected the mood of everyone present. Not to say that there weren't some positive vibes. Ted was trying to hold it together with his big smiles and warm hugs, although that stuff lost some of its lustre when it became apparent, after he'd walked into a couple of lamp posts, that he didn't know who he was smiling at.

Martin just ignored him, preoccupied with a nose that wouldn't stop bleeding. He'd fallen foul of the nutting goons. Or gooning nuts.

Eggy was raging about nothing in particular, roaring and punching walls and making noises like a wild boar with haemorrhoids. If you paid close attention to his gruntings you could discern two dominant themes:

1. Having to throw the fight
2. His mate Yusuf being dead

There were no specific words coherent enough to back that up but it was the impression I got.

Personally I was harbouring thoughts of jumping ship. I'd done what Ted had asked: turn up at the Dead Dog at eight o'clock and support the midget in his determined failure to win the local title. It was time for me to fuck off now, leaving this madness behind before I got into any more shit. I'm not a bad man and I did intend on seeing Shelley before I went, explaining why I had to go and picking up a few more things while I was there, since I seemed to have lost my two bin bags. And I'd probably go to Yusuf's funeral, as long as I was in the mood for that kind of thing on the day. But apart from those two I was free to go. I just wanted Ted to confirm it, him holding some quite dangerous cards over me.

'This is shit! Fuckin' bollocks!' Eggy was blurting, finally locating the ability to shape words in his mouth. He took a swing at a fly that was heading for his nose, calling to mind the way he'd ended the fight just now. 'I should've won that! I should've fucked the fuckin' ritual and won the local featherweight title for Yusuf!'

'Look,' said Ted, putting his hands on the midget's head.

Eggy swung with a clenched little fist that stopped an inch short of Ted's knackers. But such self-restraint comes at a price, and in Eggy's case it was a massive roar as he wheeled away, head tilted up at the moon.

'Eggy,' Ted was saying, addressing a nearby dustbin, 'you got to calm down, mate. Think of the ritual. You've done the hard part! Not exactly in the spirit of a prime George Foreman but you did what you had to do, and now there's nothing in our path. Nothing! You can go back to the '70s! You can be reunited with that big black body!'

'Yeah, but Yusuf can't, can he? Yusuf can't go nowhere now.

All that effort and he gets squished under a fuckin' lorry. Life ain't fair!'

He ran up and laid into the dustbin that Ted had been talking to. The lid flew off and hit Martin in the face, even though he was stood way back, tending his nose.

'Ooyah!' he said, staggering back.

'Who's that?' said Ted. 'What's happenin'?'

'Look,' I said. Because someone had to step in here. They all forgot their concerns for the moment and looked at me, and I wished I'd done a quiet runner instead, 'Yusuf's dead and you're all fucked off about it. Well, I am too. He was my keyboard player, and I'd never known a finer one. Now, I dunno none of the details of how he went, but it sounds to me like an accident. He got caught crossing the road – doing summat that we all do everyday. Seems to me like it was just his time. Life is a long roll of the dice, and you never know when it's gonna end. Or what number it lands on.'

They all looked from one to the other. Except Ted, who looked from a tree to a moped parked behind me. Eggy said: 'Who the fuck asked you?'

'No, he's right,' said Martin, holding his bloody hanky to both his nose and his forehead now. You could only see one of his eyes. 'Yusuf went the way he was always gonna. It's fate, and you can't argue with that.'

'You know what?' said Ted, fighting manfully to put on a strong front. 'I'm inclined to agree with you there. I mean, you only had to look at some of his lyrics to see he wasn't that happy in this world.'

'What lyrics?' I said. 'And will someone tell me who he was meant to be?'

Ted took a deep breath, smiled and announced: 'Yusuf was Cat Stevens, Rik. And he was very proud of that fact.'

'Oh, I see,' I said, thinking about that. 'You know, I can't picture any of his songs just now.'

'He did some good ones,' said Martin. 'That one that goes *Morning has bro-ken, like the first*—'

'That's a good one,' said Ted. 'My mam used to sing it.'

I said: 'Bit boring, though, ennit?'

'A bit, yeah.'

'Martin!' said Ted. 'That's Yusuf you're talking about there!'

'Yeah, but it weren't much of a foot-tapper, was it?'

'Well, no, not if you look at it like—'

'And do you know what? I hate to say this, but I don't reckon Yusuf was that bothered about it. I don't think he was a fan of his own material.'

'Martin!'

'I'm just saying it like it is. When you told him he was Cat Stevens, I reckon he was a bit disappointed. I think he'd've preferred to be David Bowie.'

'Yeah, well David Bowie's taken,' I blurted, drawing some surprised looks. 'I mean, erm…'

'Shut yer fuckin' traps!' Eggy shouted, face screwed up and tears in his eyes. A bit embarrassing but at least he was no longer smashing the place up. 'He's gone now, ain't he? He ain't gonna be Cat Stevens now. His soul is stuck here, in limbo!'

'Yeah but *yours* ain't,' said Ted. 'You're nearly home! All we gotta do is the last two stages of the ritual. And they're a piece of piss! Well, more like a piece of shit, actually.'

'Oh yeah?' I said, scratching my shoulder. 'Why's that, then?'

Ted looked out at the darkness, then closed the blind and went back to his notes. We were in his kitchen. I was drinking tea and working out the wording for what I was about to propose. Martin was still trying to staunch the flow of blood from his nostrils, using a tea towel now. He also had a big plaster on his forehead.

'He's takin' his time,' he said.

Ted, not looking up from his notes, said: 'Well, these things take time.'

We went back to doing our own things, Ted now drumming his fingers. After a bit he looked towards the hall and shouted:

'Taking yer time, ain't you?' He let that hang for a bit then tacked on: 'Eh? Eggy?'

'Fuck off!' came the muffled response.

'We gotta get a move on, Egg! The ritual must be—'

'I told you to fuck off! *You* try doing this on cue. It don't work that way. Now leave me be. *Nnnnngggg...*'

'Look,' I said. I'd worked out the right words to use now, 'You don't really need me here no more, so I might as well—'

'What d'you mean, we don't need you here?' Ted was looking at me in a new way. It was probably the spare glasses he was wearing now but it felt like something else. Felt like I was seeing a different Ted. And I don't just mean one with mental troubles. I'd got used to that one now and even sort of missed him. No, this was a different type of Ted altogether. Somewhere inside, some time over the past evening, he'd gone to the next level. And I mean down, not up. If his life were a block of flats, he'd be in the cellar. 'Course we need you here. You're an integral part of this operation, Rik.'

'All right, well...that's nice and that. But if it's all the same to you I got stuff I need to be—'

'It ain't all the same to me,' he said, a bit too brusque for my taste. His big bifocal eyes went left and right and back to me without his head moving. 'You ain't going nowhere till I say so. And don't go getting no ideas about doing a flit. You flit, I go to the coppers. All right?'

'But Ted, I've done my—'

'All right?'

I sipped my tea. An owl hooted outside. 'Yeah.'

Eggy in the toilet went: '*Nnnnnnggg…*'

'Look, Rik,' Ted said after a bit, 'this is for yer own good. I told you – we're gonna return your soul to its rightful—'

'I ain't sure I want that, Ted.'

'You ain't got a choice. I got it all planned out for you. Tomorrow you start your training.'

'Training?'

'Yeah, training.' He got up and came over to me, not taking his eyes off me. 'Rik, this thing can't be done without training. Eggy worked on his boxing for weeks. Me and him took boxing training to a new level, incorporating all kinds of animal-based principles. Yusuf – God rest him – he tried to train his vocals for just as long. All right, nothing ever came of that but…Flamin' heck, Rik. Don't you lose faith now!'

'I been thinking about that,' said Martin, trying his nose for a moment without the tea towel. 'I don't reckon Yusuf wanted to go back. To being Cat Stevens, like. I mean, we already established that he never even liked his own songs, so—'

'He flamin' did! He loved 'Wild World' in particular, and used to—'

'Yeah but he liked the Maxi Priest version. I mean, fuckin' face it, Ted: Yusuf *topped* himself. He never wanted to go back to Cat Stevens and he never wanted to disappoint you, neither. So he—'

'Don't you say that!'

'But it's true, Ted. And do you know what else Yusuf told me? He told me he didn't reckon any of this would work like you say it will. He said it would put our souls into the bodies of old men, instead of going back through—'

'Shut up! I been studying this for months. *Months*. The reverse magic will take a soul back to the point in time when he was first filched. Of that I'm almost sure.'

'Almost?' Martin said, standing up and summoning some of the authority of a pissed-off giant. But his nose started pouring blood again at that moment and he sat down and went all meek. 'I mean, I thought…'

'Almost is as good as definite where I'm concerned.' Ted watched Martin for a few seconds, then got a wooden spoon out of a drawer and went over to him, saying: 'What, you don't trust me? After all this flamin' effort I put in on your behalf, you're sayin'…What? What are you sayin', Martin?'

'I'm just—'

'Hey Martin? What's Martin sayin', eh?'

'Ted, all I meant was that—'

Ted bopped him on the head with the spoon.

'Ooh! Ted, my head's fuckin'—'

Spoon again.

'I'm waitin', Martin. I'm waitin' for Martin to say what's on his mind. Cos I swear in the presence of the Devil himself that I don't know what it is.'

'The Devil?' I said.

I wished I hadn't.

He pointed the spoon at me and came over. Step by step, nice and gradual. 'Ricky-boy is makin' grunting sounds, is it?' he said. 'I didn't quite catch them grunts, Ricky-boy. You wanna grunt 'em again?'

Ted had his back to Martin. The big man could easily have stepped in here and put him down. Or even just bear-hugged him for a bit. But Martin wasn't much of a big man just then. His body was big but inside he was a little old lady.

This was nuts. Ted was a mate, my manager. 'Ted, you fuckin'

Charlie Williams

said "in the presence of the Devil himself", mate. And, quite frankly, I found that a bit—'

'Don't you flamin' lie to Martin, you dirty beggar!' The spoon was about half an inch from my nose. 'I said *God*, not the Devil. You tell him. Go on.'

'Ted…'

'Tell him!'

'Fuckin' hell, Ted…'

He lifted the spoon over his head…

Muffled sound of a toilet flushing, then Eggy strode in and dumped a Tesco bag on the table, saying: 'Right, there you go, you fuckin' impatient bastards. Mind you, I dunno how much of it you need.'

Ted already had the bag open and his face almost in it. 'Nah,' he said, nodding. 'This is fine.' A fly buzzed out of the bag and around his head, then back in again. 'There's some good shit in here.'

The smell hit my nose. 'For fuck's sake!' I said, moving to a neutral corner. 'Has he got what I think he's got in that bag?'

'Don't worry,' said Ted, going to the drawer and putting the wooden spoon back in it. He got something else out but I couldn't see what it was. 'It's only human faeces. Perfectly natural.'

'Natural? It fuckin' stinks!'

'I can't help it!' blurted Eggy. I could see him either hurting someone or bursting into tears. 'I bet your shit stinks as well, you…you fuckin'…' He punched a table leg, buckling it, and went and faced the wall in a strop.

Ted was watching him, stroking his chin. 'He's in a highly emotional state. His soul is on the cusp of transmigration. He's like a rocket, blasting up through the sky, about to burst out of our orbit and into a new atmosphere. Engine's on overdrive, all dials turned to—'

174

'I'm right here, you know!' Eggy shouted at the wall.

'Ted,' I said, 'just…just tell me why you've got him to do a shit in a Tesco bag. I mean, this is getting fuckin'—'

'Because it's part of the ritual. We've completed stage one: the performance. Stage two requires the shit of the host, upon which we must—'

'The host?'

'The host of the transmigrated soul. George Foreman's soul. Meanwhile, over in America somewhere, Mr Foreman is hosting Eggy's soul. In about fifteen minutes we're gonna switch 'em back! Ain't it flamin' excitin', Rik?'

'Yeah but—'

'Come on, we gotta do stage two in the cellar. It's all set up down there.'

He opened a door and beckoned everyone towards it. I noticed he was holding a big kitchen knife.

Martin went down first, holding a torch. I was next, Eggy coming behind me, poking me in the back of the legs. I could feel his nervous energy. And smell his shit, which he was carrying. I could smell something else down there, something even stronger. It wasn't the damp brick walls, which were pungent nonetheless. It wasn't Martin, who reeked like a bear at the best of times. I shuffled off the final step and stood on the floor of the cellar. Martin was shining the torch at his feet. Everyone was breathing hard. All I could hear was hard breathing.

'Like I was saying,' shouted Ted, still at the top of the stairs, 'stage two requires the shit of the host, upon which must be spilled the blood of the sacrifice. The *human* sacrifice!'

Eggy pushed me in the hip and I stumbled against the wall.

Martin shone the torch in my face.

'Switch the light on, Ted,' he shouted. 'We can't see to do it.'

I reached behind me and felt only cold, wet brick. I ducked

out of the beam and went sideways, treading on something soft and...

and...

Ted switched the light on.

I looked down and saw that I was standing on Gingernut, bound and gagged and staring up at me like all this was my fault.

Ted was down the stairs now. He passed the knife to Eggy. Everyone was still breathing hard, none more so than Gingernut. His nostrils were flaring like a horse's, a big stretch of black gaffer tape pulled over his mouth. Some of his moustache poked out of it. Blood was crusted around the nostril I'd plugged with the toothbrush. His bulging eyes were still on me and I now knew why.

He thought I was the only sane man in the room.

I was his only hope.

Eggy knelt down and pulled Gingernut's shirt up, showing his white belly. It had red hair all over it. Eggy's big yellow teeth were bared. He held the knife above his head, said some words I didn't recognise, then plunged it in Gingernut's chest.

I ran.

24.

I didn't know where I was going until I got there. My brain must have been working all right on some level because I didn't knock on the door. I knew she wouldn't let me in. Why should she let me in? I hadn't done right by her. I'd been obsessed with my own ambitions and neglected her needs. And if she knew what I'd got up to behind her back…If she knew what I'd seen and been involved in…

My eyes were closing. They had to. I couldn't keep them open any longer. The lids came down, soothing my eyeballs for all of a split-second. Then—

White belly. Yellow teeth. Flashing blade. Red—

The door opened.

Elvis frowned and said: 'Woss the fuckin' matter with you?'

I let go of my eyelids. 'I…'

'Hey, I thought you was dead?'

'Eh?'

'You chucked yerself off my balcony.' He was wearing a

Japanese dressing gown and I think I'd got him out of bed. But his quiff was up and shades on. 'That was the only reason I let you through my flat. You been trickin' me, Suntan?'

'No tricks. I jumped, but, er...a rubbish truck was passing below at that moment, and I landed in it.'

He squinted at me over the door chain. His glasses were black as the night sky outside, but I'm sure about the squinting. 'That right?'

'Yeah. So if you don't mind, I wanna try again.'

'I can't do that. After nine o'clock, I never let no one—'

'For fuck's sake, Elv! Look, if you don't let me jump off your balcony again, I'm going to the police.'

'You're what?'

'Assisted suicide, they call it. You let me jump off your balcony. And suicide's illegal, thereby making you an accomplice to...'

I stopped there because I noticed Shell's door was open and her standing in it, looking at me, jaws clamped shut. I should have kept my voice down.

'Ooh...' Elvis was saying, teasing out some of his quiff. 'That right? I never came at it from that angle. You won't go to the Neighbourhood Watch, will you? I'll lose me position if they finds out.'

'He ain't going nowhere,' said Shell. 'And he ain't committing no suicide. Get in here, you daft pillock.'

She grabbed my arm and yanked me inside. I thought she was going to give me a bollocking but she turned away and just stood there, arms folded. I didn't know what to say just then because none of it would have made sense to her. What I wanted was a big hug. That's why I'd come here. I'd seen too much of the world and I didn't know what to do. If she hugged me hard enough then maybe it'd be all right to close my eyes, and...

She turned around and hugged me. I wasn't sure if she'd

read my mind or done it off her own back or what. All I knew is that my eyes were closed now and I felt like I was home. We went to bed.

The lights went up. Spotlights shining down on my head. There was stage make-up all over my face and I knew I looked amazing, even though my moustache had been shaved off and everyone could see my lip. I looked like a beautiful alien. The crowd were going nuts, but in a silent way, mouths hanging open and eyes wide like humbugs in their heads. I tilted the microphone stand to the right, and they went even more nuts. It was a feeling more than a sound or anything you could see. We were as one, me and the audience. My fans. Some of them did look a bit weird, though. Like they were sick, or…

There was something wrong with one of the spotlights. It was too bright, making my forehead sweat and my make-up run. My hair was stuck up with a lot of lacquer and I was worrying about the fire hazard side of things. It had happened to Michael Jackson so it might happen to me. I looked offstage to get the attention of a roadie and noticed another version of me, identical and looking back at me. I must have been standing outside myself again, looking back at myself. I watched as the light went even brighter and started burning an actual hole in my head, the head of the man next to me, pushing aside his brain with fingers of molten metal and grabbing—

'—my hair, Rik! Rik, let go my hair!'

Something hit my face and I fell out of bed. The light came on and I saw that all was well. Sort of. I wasn't getting my head probed by a bright light, anyway. Just getting elbowed in the eye by Shell.

'Fuckin' hell, Shell,' I said, rubbing the damage.

My face was hot and dripping.

'You almost yanked half my hair out! What's the matter with you?'

'Your hair? Oh, sorry, Shell. I must have been…But it felt so…'

Shell was already out of the bedroom. It wasn't fair on her, all this. She'd helped me out, hugging me and calming my fears and bringing me back down to reality, and I'd repaid her by… what? I didn't know what the fuck I was doing. I was lying stark naked on the rug, looking up at that bright bulb hanging up there, reaching down into my—

'Shell.'

I was in the kitchen now. It's where Shell was, stood naked by the kettle, watching it boil. I didn't blame her for wanting away from me. I went up behind her and touched her shoulder. I was naked as well. She flinched away.

'I can't have this, Rik,' she said.

'I know. It was the dream…I thought I was—'

'Not that. I don't care about the hair pulling. It's all the other stuff, Rik. I…I don't even know if I can *look* at you now.'

Shit. She knew about Gingernut. I don't know how but she'd found out something, somehow.

'It wasn't like that,' I said. 'He was—'

'I mean,' she said, 'I just feel…ashamed. I'm so sorry, Rik.' She sounded like she was in pain, like she had a hand in a tub of boiling water. The words were getting wrenched out of her. 'You seemed like you didn't care about me no more, and he was…I met him at work and…'

She gave up and started crying.

This was a turn-up.

I watched her shoulders going up and down. I put my hands on them again and she didn't flinch this time.

'Shell,' I said, 'don't worry. I forgive you.'

She leaned back into me.

My arms went further around her, folding over her breasts. I felt myself stirring against her.

'I never stopped caring about you, you know,' I was saying into her ear. 'But…yeah, I do admit that I might have looked like I didn't care. It's just my dreams, Shell. I was following my dreams.'

'I know,' she said, sliding around in my arms and reaching around me. 'I'm sorry.'

'I'm sorry too, eh.'

She was kissing my neck, just below the ear. 'I love this,' she said.

'What?'

'Your birthmark. I love kissing it. If you look at it for a while it looks just like a—'

'Yeah, all right. Can I just ask you one thing, Shell?' I said, stroking her hair and sliding a hand down her back. 'Where is he? I mean, I thought you had him living in here?'

'I…I did, Rik.' She stopped the kissing. 'He's left. I should have known it, Rik. But…I just got it wrong. I was confused and I made a bad decision, but thankfully he's gone away. I'm sure he won't be back, Rik. Although he has left some things here. But if he does…'

'He'll have me to answer to.'

She hugged me hard. I hugged her back, but gentle. I was thinking The Righteous Brothers, 'Unchained Melody'. I was swaying to the music and humming it, and she was moving with me. We were two people in sync with a song, and it wasn't even playing in the everyday world. That is the power of music.

REAPING

LIKE any asset, a stored soul is of no use unless its value can be realised when required. I knew that this would not be necessary until the time came to do battle with the Devil, but I needed to be sure that it could be done quickly and efficiently. The Stairway would need all of my concentration if I was to successfully turn it against the Devil, and fiddling around with the reaping of souls would distract me from that.

To this end, I once again turned to canine experimentation. For the infant host, I acquired a mongrel puppy from the local dog's home, and for the High Denomination Soul, I attended a local dog show and collected the urine of the 'best in show' winner – a male Bichon Frisé. The soulshifting ritual was performed succesfully, and the mongrel puppy left to mature. After four years I decided he was as old in dog years as one of my human hosts would be on the summer solstice of 2009, and so the soul-reaping ritual was arranged.

For each of my High Denomination Souls I had kept a lock of infant hair, taken after the initial soulshift. This had been done with the puppy also, and I chopped the hairs as finely as possible and mixed them with pennyroyal, dragon's blood resin and goats' milk, depositing the compound in a small vial. The idea was to reap the soul on the move, so I went for a walk around the town, taking the mongrel with me on a leash (the location of the host is of no concern in the ritual, but I was mildly interested in the dog's fate from an academic standpoint). Walking along Bath Road, I recited the incantation and drank the compound.

At first nothing happened, and I began to wonder where I had gone wrong. Then I noticed that the mongrel was now walking unsteadily, unable to keep pace with me and showing signs of respiratory difficulty. I stopped to examine it. While I was looking under an eyelid a strange, electrical sound emanated from the chest area, and the entire body was briefly illuminated from the inside out, flashing the skeleton for a moment. Then the dog collapsed, dead.

I disposed of the body in a nearby rubbish skip and walked on. A pain in my head gave way to a lingering pressure, not unlike the precursor to sexual climax. My hands clenched and unclenched involuntarily. I felt superhuman, as if I could lift a bus. If the soul of a dog did that, what power would I gain from that of a human?

Two cars approached each other on opposite sides of the road. I willed them to collide, and they did. I walked away, smiling. Soon I was running. I ran for miles without breaking sweat, only stopping when hunger overcame me.

25.

'You want bacon, Shell?'

She'd just walked in, dressed for work and towelling her hair. She did look beautiful, I had to admit. I wanted to grab her but she wouldn't have it. The thing about Shell, she was no-nonsense. Dressed for work, she don't fuck about. Dressed not at all – that's for fucking about. I loved that about her. Both sides of it.

'Not for me, ta,' she said, draping the towel over a chair and sipping her tea. 'I need to lose some weight.'

'You? Lose weight? Don't make me laugh...You're perfect like you are. *Don't go changing*,' I started singing, '*to try to please me...*'

She was looking in the mirror now, brushing her hair.

I pictured it last night, hanging over my face.

'I ain't trying to please you,' she said. 'I mean, I am, but...Oh, I just don't want bacon.'

I smiled. She didn't smile. That didn't mean she wasn't happy, just thinking. About her hair. Her weight. Work.

'Hey,' she said, 'you got a call yesterday. From the Job Centre.'

'Yeah? Look, Shell,' I said, pushing bacon around in the pan, 'there's summat I got to tell you. It's about…Well, basically it's my dream, Shell…'

'Oh, don't worry about that. You didn't pull any out.'

'Eh?'

'My hair. The nightmare you had last night.'

'No, I don't mean…Look, you know I've had a *dream* for ages now. I'm talking about my music. It's the kind of stupid dream that never comes true, right? Only idiots believe they can make a living from music. Well…'

She was slowing with her hairbrush.

I had her attention.

'It's come true, Shell.'

'What?' She looked at me in the mirror.

'It's happening. You know the Miramar, in Burninghouse? They got branches all over the country actually, but the one in Burninghouse, I got a job there. The manager came down to see me at the Cairo and I got the fuckin' gig, Shell! And…and it ain't just a temp thing – it's a regular spot. Three nights a week! And you won't guess how much I'm getting paid for it, not in a million fuckin' years. Go on – guess.'

She thought about it for a bit, brush halfway down the back of her neck, and said: 'Burninghouse?'

'Yeah, you know—'

'I know where Burninghouse is. Three nights a week? How you gonna do that? You can't drive, and it's…what, two hours on the train? And I don't think you'll get one home that late.'

'No, we're gonna move there, Shell. Relocate, you know? The

boss there, he's gonna help me…I mean, *us*, out with a flat and everything. This is a chance for us, Shell! We can be moving up in the world. I'll be making a name for myself on a bigger stage, finally getting the—'

'I ain't moving to Burninghouse.'

'Hang on, just think—'

'I don't need to think. I ain't moving to Burninghouse. I got a job here, Rik. My life's—'

'Shell, I'm gonna be making *three* a *week*. And I don't mean three *quid*, I mean—'

'Three hundred, yeah. Look, it don't matter how much you make – it's in Burninghouse. And my life's here, Rik. If you wanna do it, if you wanna follow your dream, then go on and do it. I'm sorry, Rik, but I can't go with you. We've been through this before. You know how I feel.'

She finished with her hair and went back into the bedroom to do her make-up. She wouldn't do a good job of it today, the mood she was in.

I looked down at the frying pan. The rashers were shrivelled up to nothing. Some fat jumped out and hissed angrily on the hob. I didn't really feel that way myself. Shell was disagreeing with me yet again, but perhaps she was right. And not just about the relocation or commute or whatever. That job in Burninghouse…I didn't know if I really wanted it now. Not after last night, the knife and the black gaffer tape and the blood. I wanted to step back into a safe place from now on. I wanted to toe the line and be at home. I wanted to be with Shell.

I followed her into the bedroom and sat on the bed. The radio was on in there and the DJ was saying about today being the summer solstice, and that you should get out there and try and make your dreams come true because it's the longest day of the year.

'What did he say?' I said.

'Who?'

'The Job Centre.'

There was a pause and then: 'Rik, you just told me you—'

'Yeah, and you said you weren't interested. What'd he say?'

'Oh, come on, I ain't taking the blame for—'

'There's no blame, Shell,' I said, folding my fingers into each other. 'Look, I wasn't that interested anyway. It's…Well, there's no security in it. And I don't really like Burninghouse. I'm a small-town boy, eh.' I let out a very weak laugh. 'So, what did Mr Job Centre say?'

She gave me a nice look in the mirror then went on with her mascara, saying: 'He just said there was a job for you. You got to formally apply and stuff but he says it's a perfect match for your skills and interests. Not experience so much but he said you can make up for that with enthusiasm, in the interview.'

'Interview? Already?'

'Yeah. I'm sure it was noon today. I…I said you'd be there, Rik. You got to ring 'em back to get the details. I left the number out there.'

'Oh. Well…What is it, like? I mean, where—?'

'That record shop in town. HMV, or summat.'

'HGV?'

'That's the one. It's a sales assistant role.'

'Oh right?' I said, trying to sound chipper. I knew she was watching me.

'Yeah. They said the last bloke was sacked for being rude to customers and laughing at their selections, so they want someone who can come across positive and enthusiastic at all times. You can do that, can't you, Rik?'

'You know me.'

She came over and gave me a kiss on the head and a little

Charlie Williams

hug. It made it all worthwhile, that hug. I needed to never lose sight of that from now on. She went back into the kitchen while I examined my interlocked fingers. Things wouldn't be so bad. The phone rang and Shell answered it. I heard her talking for a bit in the kitchen, then she came through.

'It's for you,' she said, frowning. 'A Mr Marino?'

'Tell him I ain't in.' I didn't even think about it. I didn't have to. I couldn't let myself.

'You sure?'

'Yeah.'

'But who—?'

'The bloke from the Miramar.'

She gave me a concerned look. 'You definitely want me to tell him that?'

'Shell, just tell him.'

Ten minutes later she was gone and I was licking her lipstick off my face. After a cup of tea I showered and got myself ready for a busy day. Every day was going to be busy for me now. I was going to fill it with music and customers and enthusiasm...

And Shell.

She was what it was all about, I now saw. It's all very well singing songs but sometimes you've got to listen to them. Again and again they say the same thing: it's about your woman. You can do this and that in life and go for your dreams and fight for a cause, but it all comes back to the lady in your life. If you ain't got her, you're lost.

I could see that now.

I went to put some music on, and in the player I found the Bowie CD I'd put there a while back. Seemed like years ago. That life was behind me, with its struggles and violence and insane people all around. My life was going to be full of good things only now. And hard, honest graft. I took the CD out and put it in my jacket pocket. I wanted it out of the flat and gone from our lives.

In the hall I found the number that Shell had left. It was just gone nine so the Job Centre would be open now and I'd come across all keen. I picked up the phone and put it to my ear and Mr Marino went:

'Ah. Hello, Rik.'

26.

There was a dove outside on the edge of the balcony. I think it was a dove anyway. Either that or a pigeon. In Warchester pigeons and doves had interbred so much that they were pretty much the same species. He stepped from foot to foot and then settled down, cooing. I went to put the phone down.

But I couldn't.

What was the point? He'd only be there when I picked it up again. I didn't know how but I knew it was true.

'All right, Mr Marino?'

'I'm fine, thanks. Just a quick call to confirm your engagement tonight. Six o'clock, remember? For sound checks.'

'Ah, well…'

'Yes.'

'You see, I meant to ring you. I was going to, in the next hour or so. It's about the job, see. I can't do it after all.'

The dove was looking at something on the ground far below. One of his pals, perhaps. Or a female. I didn't know if doves got lonely but I had a feeling that this one was. The slant of his shoulders and the way he held his head, he seemed like a sad dove. In the white sky to his left, still far away, a dot was getting bigger. Another dove, I hoped, coming to perch next to him and make him all right.

'Sorry to have messed you around and all,' I went on, 'but I got personal reasons, Mr Marino. I can't relocate after all, and the commute would just be too—'

'I own your soul.'

'—much of a burden to…What?'

'You can't get away from me, Mr Suntan.'

'I…?'

I'd lost sight of the dot in the sky for a moment, but suddenly it was back in the frame, massive now and only a few yards away. But it was a buzzard, not a fellow dove. He swooped in, grabbed the dove and flew away with it, beating his huge wings once or twice before he was out of sight.

'That soul of yours, it's mine,' he said. 'It's my property and mine to do with as I see fit. So you come here tonight, as planned, or I'll snuff you out. I'll eat you alive, Mr Suntan. Just like I've eaten others. Do not cause me trouble, Mr Suntan.'

I saw Yusuf at his keyboard, plugging away at a tune while a truck came bombing towards him, huge buzzard at the wheel.

'Nothing to say in response, Mr Suntan? That's fine by me, but I must say, I thought better of—'

'Are you Jimmy Page?'

He was stumped for a moment. Only a moment though.

'That's an interesting question,' he said. 'A truly original one. I must say, no one has ever thought to pose that particular question before. At least, not to me. But the answer is no, Mr Suntan. No, I'm not Jimmy Page. Jimmy Page? Let's put it this way, if I *was* Jimmy Page you'd be in a much better position.

Jimmy Page is a crow, Mr Suntan. I am a buzzard. You are a pigeon.'

I blinked a few times and focused on a crow flapping away outside the window. You had all sorts of birds here.

'But…'

'Did you ever feel that something was missing, Rik?'

'What?'

'In your life. Did you ever feel that your life was…unfulfilled? And you can't quite put your finger on why?'

I heard a high-pitched sound from up above. You'd never believe that a big buzzard made such a poncy sound, but they do.

'I dunno what you mean, Mr Marino. I…erm…'

'You are only half a person, Rik. You think you are whole, but you're not. You are dislocated from the rest of yourself. And it was I who did it. Six o'clock. For sound checks.'

The line went dead. I got up and went on to the balcony. The crow gave up the struggle and spiralled down to the ground, cawing. I leaned out and looked up. There was another balcony above me but if I stretched out a bit I could see the roof. There was something moving there, sure enough. And possibly the talons of two feet gripping the lip of the roof. Then something came falling towards me.

I flinched and stepped in as a dove's wing fluttered past, bits of flesh trailing behind. It tumbled down to the road, where the crow noticed it and moved in.

'Fuck,' I said.

I picked up the phone again.

BRANDING

BRANDING the host organism is of vital importance, and the main reason I carried out all soulshifts in the presence of the new host. As a farmer brands his livestock to deter rustlers and avoid disputes with neighbouring farmers, so must a necromancer brand his hosts in order to readily identify them. The brand should take the form of a blemish on the skin, nondescript to the untrained eye but otherwise unmistakable. In my own operations I used a piece of bark from the rowan tree. Charged with the appropriate spell, the bark was used to render a tiny birthmark just below the right ear in the shape of an ejaculating penis and testicles. This show of potency was to ward off rustlers.

The brand, though cosmetic, was attached to the soul, and would follow it to a new host, should a rustler not be deterred.

27.

You got a decent view from this spot. On a good day you could see into the next county. On a perfect day you could see the county after that, so I'd heard. But today wasn't so good, and all I could see were grey clouds gathering on the horizon.

'Summat's different,' I said.

'It's the flies,' said Ted, sucking in the fresh air through his nose. 'They're gone.'

'Oh yeah. Too high for 'em up here, I should think.'

'No, they're gone from down there as well, in town.'

I mulled that one over for a bit, then said:

'Any particular reason you insisted on meeting here?'

'It's a very ceremonial place, here is. And we're here to enact a very ceremonial...erm, ceremony.'

'What ceremony? Look, can it wait? I just need a word about—'

'No it can't wait! He's waited his whole life for this and he ain't waiting no longer.'

'Waited for what? Who has?'

'Him,' he said, nodding in the direction of Eggy, who was a few yards away, examining a fern. 'We're releasing him back into the wild!'

Eggy looked up at us, such serenity on his face as to render him unrecognisable. 'Truly, 'tis the beauty of the Lord,' he was proclaiming. 'Nature's masterpiece, born of God's own soil. You can't beat it!'

Martin, stood behind Ted with the collars of his donkey jacket turned up, shook his head and said: 'I can't handle him like this. Can't we make him like he was before?'

'This is the true Eggy,' said Ted. 'This is the Eggy that he should have been from the start, if it hadn't been for that bloody Jimmy Page.'

'He was an aggressive little cunt before, sure enough, but at least he wasn't a fuckin' Bible basher. I quite liked that aggressive little—'

'Martin, it's George Foreman who you quite liked. The person we've known all along as Eggy was George Foreman, the surly boxer who got beat by Ali. He's back home now, in the big black body where he belongs. This here is Eggy. Get to know him.'

'I don't like him.'

'Ted,' I said, 'I need to have a word about—'

'Yeah, you said on the phone. Funny how you should change your tune so suddenly, I must say. One minute you want nothing to do with us – even though we had your best interests at heart, I might add – the next minute you want "a word".'

'The word of the Lord,' said Eggy, looking up at the sky. His little face was jolly and a bit simple-looking, nothing like the screwed-up clenched bum of a face I'd grown to know and hate. I saw what Martin meant, though. 'Ah yes, the Word. Of the Lord. 'Tis a thing most marvellous…and yet it can strike terror into the heart of any man who ignores it.'

'So, the ritual,' I said quietly. 'It worked, like?'

Ted glared at me. Then he called Eggy over, still glaring at me. 'Stand there, Egg. That's it, like so. Now look over yonder. See them hills over there? They're the Mountains of Ararat. Did you know that?'

'Verily, at the end of seven score and ten days the ark came to rest upon…'

'Look at his neck,' whispered Ted to me while Eggy prattled on. 'There. See?'

'What?'

'*There*, under his ear. See?'

'What am I seeing? I don't see nothing.'

'Precisely, my friend. It's gone, ennit? His little spunker.'

'Little sp—? Oh…'

He was right. There was no longer a birthmark beneath Eggy's right ear. I didn't know what that meant.

Just that it meant *something*.

'Jesus fuckin' H. Christ,' I said. Only quiet.

But Eggy heard it.

'Thou shalt not take the Lord's name in vain!' he screamed, pointing at me. 'The Lord will acquit *no one* who commits such a crime!'

'Yeah, all right, I'm sorry and all that. Look,' I said, turning to Ted, 'I believe it. Right? I have the utmost faith in the ritual, and all the magic stuff you've been learning about. I'm ready, Ted. I want you to get my soul out of here and back where it belongs – David Bowie's body.'

'Ah, so you've stopped questioning my sanity, then? I knew the missing spunker would change your mind.'

'No, it was…I just had a moment of clarity, Ted. That's why I came here. It all slotted together and I saw the truth.'

'The Truth,' said Eggy. 'Verily, the Truth lies within every—'

'Shut the fuck up!' Martin shouted.

'Judge not he who chastises his brother, even though his brother is actually innocent and only speaking the Word of the Lord, lest ye…'

'I'm happy for you,' said Ted. To me. 'Would have been nice having your proper support a bit earlier, but better late than never. Now, we got work to do.'

'I'll do it, Ted. I wanna get going on this *now*. So if you could possibly arrange my ritual for later today, say around five o'clock, I'm happy to—'

'What are you on about, Rik? We can't hurry this. There's plans to be made, training to be undergone.'

'I don't need no training, Ted. You said the ritual involves doing the thing that most defined him. That means doing a live gig. I'm already a singer! All I got to do is—'

'Ah, but you ain't a singer in the mould of Mr Bowie. We've got to study him, Rik…absorb his mannerisms, capture his essence…not to mention choose a suitable song to sing. Only then can the ritual be undergone. Plus we've got to find the best venue for your performance.'

'But I ain't got time to—'

'Besides, it's Martin's turn next.'

Hearing his name, Martin looked up and said: 'I'm a bit nervous.'

'Don't worry,' said Ted. 'Nerves are a part of it. Wayne Boyle, he used his nerves in the service of his craft.'

'Who's Wayne Boyle?' I said. 'And why's Martin got to go next? If he's nervous, shouldn't we give him time to—'

'He's had enough time! And besides, it's all planned for this afternoon. So you'd best make yourself available. Oi, Eggy! Get away from that sheep!'

'She is a creature of the Lord, a wondrous example of—'

'I don't give a toss who it's a creature of! You're frightening it! Oh, and Rik...Wayne Boyle was – is – an infamous local bank robber. He made away with millions of pounds worth of loot before—'

'Bank robber? I thought we were all famous singers? Er, and a boxer?'

'Yeah, well, we think Jimmy Page was just interested in bank robbing, or summat. Not that he actually intended on committing a robbery or nothing. I mean, we wouldn't want to defame—'

'Look, Ted, about this Jimmy Page business...Who told you?'

'Who told me what?'

'I mean, how'd you find out all about Jimmy Page, and his black magic and stuff?'

'Never mind that. A wise man can't reveal his sources, can he? You've either got faith or you ain't. I can't make you have faith.'

'I have got faith, Ted. In you, I mean, not necessarily in all the details of...Look, it's just that I been doing a bit of research of my own, and—'

'Oh yeah? You found out summat about him, have you? I'm always happy to add to my knowledge about Jimmy Page. Know thine enemy – that's what I say.'

'For fuck's sake, Ted. It wasn't Jimmy Page.'

'You what?'

'You heard. All this has got fuck all to do with Jimmy fuckin' Page or any other member of Led Zeppelin.'

Ted and Martin looked at each other.

'Then I saw another beast come up out of the earth,' said Eggy, chasing the sheep with a stick,. 'It had two horns like a lamb's, but spoke like a dragon.'

Ted said: 'What are you on about, Rik?'

But he didn't wait for an answer. He went off after Eggy, shouting at him to leave that poor young sheep alone. Martin wasn't interested either. And they wouldn't believe me anyway if I told them about Sam Marino. It was just too far-fetched.

Ted ran out of puff after about ten seconds and trudged back, sending Martin after the midget instead. 'You'll need to…meet up with us at one, round mine,' he said to me, panting. 'It's best you don't know too many of the details… don't want to cock it up. Martin knows what he's got to do anyway. We're just his support team.'

'I'll be there, Ted,' I said. 'But can we bring my one forward a bit? I mean, a lot?'

'Well, maybe. You'll need to do some of your own groundwork, though. Choose a song, watch some footage. It's the Ziggy Stardust period you want. After Martin's transmigration we'll see where we are. Eh? Can't say fairer than that.'

Martin was still after Eggy, who was after the lamb. It was like watching a cow chasing a chicken chasing a mouse. Which sounds a bit like one of Aesop's fables, although I can't pinpoint which one and what the moral might be.

Ted shouted at Martin to stop, saying: 'We gotta leave him to get by on his own devices now, Mart. Sink or swim, it's up to him now. We've done our bit.'

Martin came trudging back, dripping with sweat. We all had one last look at Eggy before he frolicked off out of sight, then we walked wordlessly back down the hill. I said goodbye at the bottom and they went to their car – a red Escort that I think was Martin's. As I carried on down the lane I looked back and saw Ted pop the boot, looking both ways before getting two spades out. Martin reached in and hauled out a couple of plastic sacks full of something heavy.

28.

'We ain't open yet.'

'When do you open?'

'Eleven on the dot.'

'What time is it now?'

'Ten fifty-eight.'

'Can I just ask you summat?'

'We ain't open yet.'

I had to do something. That's why I'd come here. I felt like I was up against it all, queuing up to fight a big nasty monster who I knew nothing about. I'd already been to the library and asked for books on magic rituals. They'd given me one on card tricks and a book about Paul Daniels and his wife Debbie McGee, which I might have been interested in another time, but not now. I needed more facts.

I needed less confusion.

'Are you open yet?'

'Not till eleven on the dot.'

'What time is it now, then?'

'Ten fifty-nine.'

'On the dot?'

'No, past the dot.'

'Come on, mate.'

'It's no use "come on mate"-ing – we ain't open yet.'

'I just need to ask a question.'

'We're a pub, not the Citizens Advice Bureau.'

'I'll buy a drink as well.'

'Not yet you won't – we ain't open.'

I looked behind me. Cars were going by on the Tything, people were going about their business. If they only knew, I thought. If they only knew the things I'd found out…the unholy practices that had taken place under their very noses. They were one side, ignorant and unquestioning and happy to just tootle along in a world they thought they understood. I was on the other, facing up to supernatural realities, forced into dealings with murderers, warlocks and famous celebrities. In a way I was more comfortable on this side, even though I was looking at a fate similar to Yusuf's if I didn't sort something out soon. But then I'd always known I was a bit different.

Bolts turned. A lot of bolts. Then the door opened.

'Security measures,' said a bald, broken-veined old face. 'A while back I got burgled, and the buggers had off with summat of great value.'

'That's a shame.'

'Oh, I got it back. But I been a lot more security-minded ever since, as you'll understand. And I'll tell you what – the first rule of security-mindedness is that you should never let on to people about what you've got hid.'

He went inside and I followed, feeling like I was on a training course. It was the first time I'd been in the Lamb and Flag and

I could see I hadn't been missing out in life. This was an old man's pub, devoid of glamour and style and mirrors and all the things a person like me needs around him when he goes out.

'I got some ideas about improvements,' he said, perhaps sensing what I was thinking. 'But you need resources, lots of resources. I'll be there soon, though. Very soon, aye. I been saving up over the years, making little investments. I got 'em all over town, mate. And soon I'll be cashing 'em in. I already cashed one in just yesterday, just to get things started. And once I got them all liquid, well…' He wagged a finger at me, smiling. 'Then everyone'll know about this place, oh yes.'

'Yeah, well,' I said, going along with it. I had to soften him up a bit somehow. 'You'll have to put an ad in the paper or summat. It's a competitive market out there, pubs and clubs and that.'

'I'll do better than an ad in the paper. I'm gonna do a light show. People'll see this place for miles around, and they'll know I've made me improvements.'

I doubted that. And I doubted that he stretched to Tequila Sunrises. I could see there was no point asking for any of the other drinks I called my favourites, so I just asked for a Coke.

'You came in here for a Coke?'

'No, I came here to ask a question.'

'You said you'd buy a drink as well.'

'I am. Can I have a Coke, please?'

He breathed deep, his big belly rising and falling, and said: 'The Lamb and Flag is not known for its Coke, but for its beer and very particular atmosphere.'

'I can see that, but I don't drink beer.'

'Why not?'

'It gives you a…' I looked down at his midriff, barely contained inside his horizontally striped polo shirt. 'I've just got to watch my weight. I'm a singer, see.'

'Singer, eh? We've had them in here. You wouldn't believe the ones we've had in here. It's the very particular atmosphere, you see. Here's the only place in Warchester that has it. Only place in the whole realm, far as most knows.'

'Actually, I was gonna ask you about—'

'Take a beer with me,' he said.

'No, ta, I don't—'

'Take a beer with me.'

I was wishing I hadn't come in here. I'd only remembered it after coming out of the library, Gaz's words to me in HGV yesterday. I knew it was Sam Marino who'd stolen our souls and not Jimmy Page, but there had to be something to find out here.

'There you go,' said the barman, setting down a tankard. 'That's a start in the right direction.'

I could feel my head getting muddled again, just when I'd started untangling it. And the brown stuff in front of me didn't look like it was going to help. I felt knackered and harassed and out of my depth, and I slumped down on the stool.

'Are you gonna let me ask this question?' I said. 'It's bloody important, I swear.'

'I can see that. Ask away, then.'

'Right, well…Did you ever have a bloke called Ted Regis in here?'

He looked up at the ceiling, squinting and shaking his head a bit.

'Never mind,' I said. 'I can see the answer's no.'

'Eh? No, I'm just looking at that spider up there on the beam. I could have sworn I tossed him out yesterday…Ted Regis, you say? Aye, he's been in here. Used to come in here regular, until not so long back. He was a fan of our very particular—'

'What did you tell him?'

'Eh? On what occasion?'

'What did you tell him…about Jimmy Page?'

'Oh…I must have told him the usual story, about black magic and stealing the souls of other famous individuals.'

Fucking hell.

'Course, it's all complete horse manure.'

Oh.

'Jimmy Page *has* been known to come here, though. He likes the very particular pork scratchings.'

'What did you tell Ted that for, though? He believed it, you know.'

'Hmm. Don't surprise me. I couldn't tell him the truth, though, could I? I mean, he's a bit mental, ain't he, your mate? You can see it a mile off. It's in the eyes. I'd watch him.'

'You couldn't tell him the truth?'

'No, I couldn't tell him that. I'm careful who I tell that to because, well, I don't want to be tagged as a nutter. I mean, it's a bit far-fetched, the truth is. So I just tell them the Jimmy Page version.'

'Oh yeah, like it's more believable. Look, can you tell *me* the truth?'

'Oh yeah, I can tell it to you.'

'What, because I don't seem mental?'

'No. I mean yeah, you do seem a bit odd, come to mention it. But that's by the by. I can tell you because, well, you plainly need to know it. Do you want to know it or not?'

'Hold up…I don't understand how you can tell me but not Ted, if we both seem—'

'It's simple: your mate Ted bears no distinguishing marks, other than a couple of scars and some random freckles. You, on the other hand, are branded.'

I angled the mirror to get more light.

'I can see you ain't enjoying that ale. Tell you what, how about one of them Tequila Sunrises?'

'Eh? Are you having me on?'

'You want a Sunrise or not?'

'Yeah, but how'd you know I wanted one? Can you...are you telepathic?'

'No, you just look like someone who drinks flouncy cocktails. I got some tequila round here somewhere...'

He was rummaging around in the bottles behind the bar. I wanted to ask him more about that branding business but he'd thrown me a bit, knowing about my birthmark.

'You know,' he said, 'I once had a bottle of urine amongst this lot for eight whole years. You wouldn't know it, would you? And all the while I thought it was crème de menthe.'

'Crème de...? But that's green, ennit?'

'Yeah. Says a lot, don't it? No one came in here and asked for crème de menthe in any of those eight years.' He looked over his shoulder at me. 'I'm proud of that record.'

'So you're saying...someone finally asked for crème de menthe, and that's how you discovered the...erm...?'

'Aye,' he said, shaking his head at the memory. 'Should have seen the poor feller. Only went and took him to hospital, didn't they? Nearly had the health and wossname people round here after that. Had to work some magic to get them off my back, let me tell you. Notice the shape of it, do you?'

'Eh?'

'The brand, on your neck.'

'Well, no, I hadn't really gave it much—'

'It's a cock and bollocks. An erect cock and—'

'Bollocks! It's just a fuckin' birthmark!'

'Oh aye? Birthmark it might well be, but it's also the brand.'

'But loads of people have got birthmarks! They can't all be—'

'Not in that shape, they ain't.'

'Well…For fuck's sake, it's just a coincidence.'

'Is it, now? Next person you see on the street, you have a look if they got a birthmark on that spot. I guarantee it won't look like nothing much.'

'That's bollocks! I mean, I don't mean—'

'And if perchance it should look exactly like a set of tackle, like yours, you have a look around their body for their affliction.'

'What?'

'Look at your face, Rik. What's that on your lip, there?'

'What the fuck are you on about?'

'I'm on about your harelip.'

'What? Me? I ain't got a hare—'

'Horse manure. No one your age would have a tash like that in this day and age unless it was to cover a harelip. And besides, you can see it.'

'You bloody cannot!'

'You can. It's glistened in the sunlight once or twice. And there you go – you just admitted it.'

'I never! Look, mate—'

'Don't you "look mate" me. You come here for answers and I'm giving you some.'

'But…' I was glowing red, I knew it. The bastard, putting me on the spot like that. 'It's only a little harelip. The doctors said it was hardly one at all. It only turns up a quarter inch or so on the one side. My social worker used to say it looked a bit like the Elvis sneer.'

'Yeah, whatever you say. The point being that you was chosen specific, as a newborn tot, because of that harelip. You say you're a singer? You ain't gonna get far in the world of singing with a tash like that. Eh? And if you shave it off you've got the harelip, so you're snookered. See what I mean?'

'Well, no…Plenty of famous singers have facial hair, and—'

'Horse manure. Look, do you want the truth or not? Because I ain't telling it to someone who don't even recognise it when he looks in the mirror each morning.'

'Yeah, I fuckin' do want the truth. And, well, maybe I have got a harelip. And maybe it does hold me back a bit, career-wise. Although there have been some precedents of—'

'The Gaumont,' he said, pulling himself another pint. 'On Foregate Street. Opposite the Odeon. It's a bingo hall now but it used to be a major venue. You wouldn't believe the acts who came there…We're talking The Beatles, The Stones, Jimi—'

'Hendrix, Cliff Richard, Engelbert—'

'You want me to say it or what? Cos it seems like you know it all already.'

'I don't. Soz.'

'Right, well…There was a doorman there, a proper military type, with the cap and epaulettes. It was him.'

I noticed that I had a glass in my hand, and that it used to have a Tequila Sunrise in it, and that it was now empty.

'What was him?'

'The villain of the piece. The one who's been buggering around with these souls.'

'A doorman?'

'Yeah. A doorman in the traditional mould, not one of these bouncer types. Ron Jonas, his name were. You'd never tag him as a black magic sort of feller, but that's just what he was. I don't know where he picked it up from. And he must have learned it well because word got around. See, it's down to him that all these big performers made the trip to Warchester. If you look at the records you'll see that they all came before they hit the big time. Do you see where I'm going here? Ron Jonas had a trick. And it was an old trick, because it had been done by the Devil himself going back years to the dawn of time. Sell him your soul, and in return you get worldly success in your chosen field.'

'Hang on,' I said. He'd put another Sunrise in front of me and I sipped it. 'How'd you know all this?'

'Because...' He looked left and right, although we were all alone in there. 'Because he used to bring 'em here. To do the ritual, like. Upstairs in a private room. That's how so many famous singers come here still. They keep coming back and they don't know why. They forget it all, you see, after the ritual. All they're aware of is the success they starts getting...they don't know that they ain't got their own souls no more. Nor did the little babes in the maternity ward down there. Like yourself. Do you know who you're meant to be, by the way? Someone from Mott the Hoople, perhaps? Or Cat Stevens? I've often wondered about him.'

'David Bowie.'

'Oh aye? That's not a bad one. That's quite impressive, I must say. Can I have your autograph?'

'Yeah, sure.'

He gave me a pen and a bit of paper, saying: 'Just put "To Randy, love from...etcetera..."'

I signed it and handed it back. I wasn't really able to enjoy it properly but this was a special moment for me: my first autograph signing. I'd often dreamed about it and now it was coming true.

'Who the fuck's this Rik Suntan?' he said.

'Look...' the tequila was working on me now. I don't know how much he'd dosed me with. It was working its way into my head like a tapeworm, eating information and cutting associations. I stood up, making a big effort. Straight away I reeled sideways and hit the wall with my shoulder, knocking the dartboard off.

'Seems to me you've had enough,' the man was saying, coming round the bar.

'Look...' I said again. Because I was trying so hard to hold it together. 'Do you know a Sam Marino?'

He stopped and looked up, squinting. Like when he'd been watching the spider earlier. I looked where he was looking and there was no spider, only dirty old plaster and cobwebs.

'Sam Marino?' he said, rubbing his chin now. 'Marino as in the anagram of 'I am Ron', you mean?'

'Yeah. I mean...Eh?'

'Nah, never heard of him.'

He grabbed my arm and dragged me to the door, saying:

'You know, he got it wrong about the stairway, your man Page did, in that song of his. It don't lead you to heaven. There ain't no heaven. There ain't no hell neither. There's just life, and after that there's nothing. So the idea is to keep yourself fit and healthy and living for as long as you can.'

'Yeah, well...I do try to stay healthy and—'

'Oh no, I don't mean you. I only cares about meself. You can get as unfit as you likes.'

He kicked me out on to the street, literally shoeing me up the arse into the path of an oncoming truck.

APPENDIX C: CASE STUDY 2
(9 MAY 1976)

SPECIMEN was a young English singer-songwriter of global renown, a sculptor of gorgeous melody and introspective lyric tinged with a folk sensibility. His urine had been acquired as part of the transaction detailed in Case Study 1, but while the American's urine had lain dormant for only three years, this sample sat for nine before it was used. This was because I was initially unsure that the donor was indeed in possession of a High Denomination Soul, but his creative development and rise to global fame over the intervening years had banished all such doubts from my mind. More than any other case, this one demonstrates the enduring cosmic properties of urine.

Despite the maturity of the urine, I had no serious reservations regarding its quality, since it had been sealed and kept refrigerated constantly. My confidence was to be borne out, but not before I had overcome a different problem: that of locating a suitable host organism. As a singer, songwriter and guitarist, it was difficult to know which disability would be best suited to suppressing his innate talents. I decided on lack of

Charlie Williams

speech, but with a further handicap in that the chosen infant was of Pakistani origin and from a Muslim family. Surely one of such race and background would be deterred from committing to a career in the performing arts, either from family pressure or societal prejudice? More likely both.

Having learned from Case Study 1 that the ritual must take place in close proximity to the infant, I piloted here my new technique of positioning a tea tray almost in contact with the infant's left flank and mixing the urine and blood on that. As predicted, the ritual took place smoothly and there were no apparent complications.

However, on investigation it was discovered that the donor had, at the moment of soulshift, suffered a spontaneous spiritual crisis from which he was never to recover. Hitherto uncommitted to any specific religion, he abruptly began a search for faith and meaning which led him ultimately and permanently to the Muslim faith. The soul of the infant host, despite his being only days old and oblivious of scripture, had overpowered the mature mind of the donor. Indeed, the donor even changed his forename to that of the host.

ADDENDUM
In effect, the donor and host were to switch faiths. While the donor took on the host's Islam, the host appeared to grow up at best casually spiritual, at worst atheist. Rejected by his devout family, he became something of a lost figure and a constant suicide threat.

29.

'You fuckin' twat! Get out of the road!'

I picked myself up and staggered to the pavement, waving at the truck driver. On the pavement I leaned against a Mondeo and caught my breath.

'Don't wave at me, you fuckin' twat!' the driver was still yelling. 'You wanna kill yerself, choose someone else's cab to do it under. I got work to do. Unlike some, you pissed-up fuckin' twat!'

The door of the Lamb and Flag was shut and didn't look like it had ever been open. There was a sign on it that said CLOSED FOR IMPROVEMENTS, with smaller letters under it saying WATCH OUT FOR MY LIGHT SHOW and I could have have sworn it hadn't been there when I'd gone in. Had I really been inside there, hearing all that strange stuff and drinking a strange Tequila Sunrise? I tried standing up, my legs feeling a bit more usable. It was half eleven and I didn't have much time. I wasn't even sure if I had *any* time. It might happen any second.

What might happen?

I started walking towards town, thinking about that. What was I worrying about here? There was a man in Burninghouse who reckoned he owned my soul, and said he could cash it in at any moment, like he had done with Yusuf's. But what if he hadn't taken Yusuf's soul? What if he was just shitting me up there so he could get me to do something, and Yusuf had just had a tragic road accident after all?

Or topped himself?

I was walking all right now and feeling better. The Sunrise had done its worst and my brain was sharp again. Or sharpish. I also felt lighter in other ways, like I was suddenly under less pressure. The more I thought about it, the more I realised that Marino was spinning me a line. And spinning that same line to that barman back there in the Lamb and Flag, by the sounds of it. Poor old Yusuf – not only had he been squashed, but his death was now being taken advantage of for nefarious purposes, by a very nefarious man.

I ducked into a paper shop and got the local news. It was on page five, under an article about an old lady having a heart attack in a city centre record shop. It had a picture of the truck and everything:

LOCAL MAN DIES UNDER LORRY

Local man Yusuf Habib was run over and killed by a 44-tonne articulated lorry yesterday. The tragic accident happened in Comer Road in the St Johns area of Warchester. Despite the efforts of ambulance and fire crews to revive him, Mr Habib was pronounced dead on the scene.

32-year-old Mr Habib of Igor Court, a deaf and dumb semi-professional keyboard player, left no dependants.

'It's such a shame,' said Doris Fairbanks, who had served Habib in a nearby newsagent only seconds before the accident. 'I remember chatting to him just before. He wasn't right, you know. He seemed to be complaining of chest pains.'

Lorry driver Roger Bunyan was unhurt. 'I couldn't believe it,' he said. 'I was just driving along and suddenly this bloke appears there in the road. I slammed my brakes on but it was too late. But do you know what? Just before I hit him I swear I could see his skeleton inside him, all lit up like on an X-ray.'

Mr Bunyan has been taken in for psychiatric evaluation.

'Well, where is he?'

'He don't work here no more.'

'What d'you mean, don't work here? He's worked here for years. Gaz was here even before it was HGV records, when it was still known as 'Your Price'. He can't just not work here no more.'

'He can if he's got the sack. Mr Whitchurch is interviewing candidates for the vacancy today. I think he was supposed to have one in now, although they haven't turned up yet.'

Sheryl was putting up a display for Zak Bremner's new CD, *Bremnology*. It was the first thing you saw when you came in and the last you saw when you went out. I wanted to kick it over, such was my frustration. But that wouldn't be fair on Sheryl, so I didn't. She wasn't such a bad sort, really. Even if she didn't know a thing about music from before her own generation.

'Look,' I said, 'I was just gonna ask Gaz a question. But it seems I can't, so I'm gonna ask you instead. All right? Just say the first thing that comes into your head. If nothing comes into your head, don't worry about it. All right?'

'Yeah. Whatever.'

'What song most defines David Bowie's "Ziggy Stardust" period?'

'Well, most would go for the track "Ziggy Stardust" itself but I'd say "Rock 'n' Roll Suicide". There's summat sad and tragic and yet defiant about the Ziggy character and I think this song sums it up perfectly. Bowie was a master of self-reinvention, you know. It's all about creating a new persona and then becoming it.' She put a handful of *Bremnology*s on the shelf and started whistling.

'That's a nice tune,' I said, still a bit shell-shocked. I'd have to reassess my opinion of Sheryl. 'That "Rock 'n' Roll Suicide", is it?'

'Course not. It's a new song from Zak Bremner. He was doing an interview on the radio this morning and he played it on his guitar. He's really good at guitar playing, you know. Especially on this song. It was called…"Toothache", or summat.'

'"Toothache"?'

'Summat like that. No…"Toothbrush". "Toothbrushes" – yeah, that's it.'

30.

They were in the kitchen, same as ever. I spied them through the kitchen window, sitting at the table with their mugs of tea and a big sheet of paper spread out before them. But there was only two of them now: Ted and Martin. I tried the back door: locked.

I knocked.

'It ain't one o'clock yet,' said Ted, opening the door. 'It's ten to. I said get here at one.'

'Well, I'm early.'

'I know. And I'm tellin' you you can't come in. See you in ten minutes.'

'Let him in, Ted,' said Martin behind him. 'We got it all sorted. Anything I don't know now, I never will know. I feel like my head's a balloon filled with baked beans.'

'We need every one of them beans.' Ted was addressing Martin but looking at me. 'That's why we can't even waste ten minutes. And it ain't just about beans – it's about the tomato sauce as well. That's your mood, Martin, your composure. You need to get yourself into the right frame of mind.'

'I just need a word, Ted,' I said. 'Beforehand, you know. I need to just talk to you a tiny bit about my turn.'

'We can't have distractions. From this moment until later on, after we've transmigrated Martin, there's—'

'But it's bothering me, Ted. It's affecting my brain, and I feel I won't be as effective in, er…assisting with Martin's transmigration. A quick word with you and I'll be all right.'

'Don't you hear me? The answer's no!' He started to close the door.

'Ted, come on,' I said, putting my foot in it. 'Are you my manager or what? Wasn't it you who got me singing in the first place? Haven't we been together all along, eh? Come on – one minute.'

Ted took his spare bifocals off and looked at me again, and he seemed more himself now. 'All right – one minute only.'

We went inside. The big sheet of paper was gone from the table. Martin nodded at me and smiled. He looked nervous. He was wearing a navy blue boiler suit that was so big it would have taken four or five normal boiler suits to make it. There was a brown leather holdall on the table beside him with a bit of paper sticking out of the top.

'Rock on,' he said, showing me his fist.

'Yeah,' I said. 'Rock on.'

I followed Martin into the hall. He shut the kitchen door behind us and said: 'What?'

'Can't we just do my trans…thingy straight after Martin's? I know what you said about training and that but I honestly believe I'm there. I'm prepared, Ted. I've got the perfect song and everything. "It's Rock 'n'—"'

'I told you: we need a venue. It's gotta be a proper performance, in front of a proper audience.'

'I got all that covered, Ted. The Feathers.'

'The what?'

'Feathers. Up Sledge Hill. They do karaoke there on Fridays, so we can do it tonight and—'

'Karaoke ain't good enough. It's got to be a proper performance, with backing musicians and the like.'

'This will be, Ted! Don't you remember when you first came to me and wanted to be my manager? Do you remember when that was?'

'Course I do. It was a turning point in my life, and from there I've got where I am today, arranging reverse-transmigration rituals for—'

'Yeah, and what was it that made you want to manage me? Was it the backing musicians?'

'No…as I recall, it was the fact that you've got the soul of David Bowie inside you.'

'But…What?'

'Look, I've no time to—'

'So you never saw commercial potential in me, as a singer in my own right? You never actually liked *me*?'

'Well, yeah…as it happens, I did quite like your pitch and tone, and I even thought it was enough to overcome your physical…you know, the lip thing you got going there. But that's by the by. You've got David Bowie inside, and—'

'Fuckin' hell, Ted…You fuckin' *tricked* me.'

'I never. I came to you with the intention of getting your soul back where he belongs. In other words: making you rich and famous. Because that's what Bowie is, Rik. And that's what you'll be, if you'll just hold your horses a bit and—'

'Go fuck yerself,' I said.

He reached out. I pushed his arm away and headed for the front door. There was a big mirror in the hall and I wanted to smash it with my bare fist, I was that fucking furious. I had my hand on the door.

'If you go now,' he said behind me, 'you'll forever be Rik Suntan: failed singer with a harelip and no good at nothing else. Because that's what Rik Suntan is, David. Rik Suntan is crap. He's flamin' hopeless, David, and there's not a chance in the world he'll ever come to anything at all.'

My fists were bunching.

But I knew I was going to throw no punches here.

In a strange way, I quite enjoyed what he was saying.

'But that ain't you, David. That's the whole flamin' *point*. Don't get angry at me. I ain't saying bad words about *you*...I'm saying 'em about Rik Suntan. You ain't him. You're David fuckin' Bowie. That's it – go on and look in the mirror. Look into them eyes. Who do you see there, deep down? Some feller called Rik Suntan? I don't. When I look into your eyes I see David Bowie. I see a flamin' *superstar*.'

After a bit he led me away from the mirror, saying: 'Come on, Dave. We'll get you back home soon, eh.'

31.

I was bursting for a piss.

And hungry. I hadn't ended up eating anything for breakfast and it was lunchtime now. Someone had just walked past the car eating a burger, and a waft of it had come through the inch or so of open window, setting my guts pining. It would be half an hour at least until I'd be free to get a burger of my own.

I looked down at the holdall, which was on the back seat next to me. The corner of a plastic lunchbox was poking out of it.

'You got sarnies in there?' I said.

But no one answered. And I forgot the question anyway because I could hear a siren, some way off but getting louder. We could all hear it, sitting like statues with our ears pricked. Ted was behind the wheel, swigging from a plastic bottle of lemonade. Martin was beside him, and I looked between them at the road ahead. It was the main artery through Warchester and a fair bit of traffic was about, although the cars were slowing up ahead and pulling over. Blue flashing lights appeared as a squad car picked through them. Ted gripped the wheel with one hand and touched the ignition key with the other.

'Shit,' I said.

The squad car came bombing towards us, another two behind it.

Too late to get out of this now.

'What are we...?' I started to say. But I stopped because the first squad car went past, tearing off in a southerly direction. The other two followed it. Up where they'd come from you could see a couple of fire engines approaching as well.

'Fuck me,' I said. 'Must be a fire in town.'

I was surprised to be the only one saying such things. Parked roadside opposite Warchester's main post office and heavily armed, surely anyone would get a bit tense when the coppers come blaring towards us. Then I felt the vibration, and traced it to Martin's entire body, trembling like a sober virgin outside a whore's door.

'Look,' Ted said to him, 'just relax, right?'

'I don't feel right, Ted. I got a pain. Here in me chest.'

'That's just the nerves. Remember the techniques I taught you. Use the *words*. Use them like a mantra. *Obolaye be kumbalaye...Obolaye be...* That's it, say it over and over until the sounds don't mean nothing.'

'They don't mean nothing *now*, do they?' I said. But there was something familiar about them. I'd heard them before, and recently.

'You shut up, Dave,' Ted said, winking at me to show that he wasn't being mean about it.

'*Obolaye ke bum...*' said Martin. 'I mean, *Obolum...*erm...'

'All right, leave it for now. But you know what to do, right? You're all straight on that now. And you too, Rik? I've planned this like a military operation, I have, and it's gonna run that way.

But you've got to put yourselves in a professional mindset. We're Wayne Boyle and his crew, right? We don't fuck about and we don't take prisoners. Saying that, we are only role-playing here, so don't get carried away.'

He downed the rest of his lemonade, belched and reached over for the holdall. Then he opened it and passed around the contents.

'I'm desperate for a piss, Ted,' I said.

'Not *now*. Remember: these is loaded. They've got to be loaded, I can't guarantee the quality of the magic otherwise. It's got to be authentic, see, and Wayne Boyle by all accounts used live rounds. It's like what I was saying to you earlier, Dave, about getting the performance right. You see where I'm coming from now, right? And where I'm going?'

'Yeah,' I said. Although I didn't know how true it was.

I was looking at the pistol he'd passed me. It was fucking heavy and smelt of oil. It was like some kind of tool you'd find in a drawer in a metal castings factory – functional and no-nonsense. And yet there was a glamour to it, too. A glamour that appealed to my artistic side. I was picturing a whole persona coming out of this one object here. The hand that held it…the sleeve of a shirt and suit…elsewhere around the suit there's a collar and tie and some nice smart shoes and up top would be some sort of hat. A trilby or something. I wasn't sure what you called them. I do now, though, because I've looked it up.

A fedora.

'Rik!' Ted barked. 'Stop daydreaming and get yourself ready.'

'I'm sorry, but I really do need a piss beforehand,' I said. 'Can't I just pop out and—?'

'No you fuckin'…Look, do it in here,' he said, passing back the empty lemonade bottle. 'And flamin' hurry up.'

'I can't do it in there!' I said. 'I ain't boasting, but my knob's way too big to—'

'You don't put it in, you just aim it at it.'

'Well…I just can't, Ted. For a start, I've never been able to piss while people are watching, and—'

'Martin – close yer eyes and look away. Rik wants some privacy.'

The two of them were heads down and eyes closed, like they were praying. I sat up and arranged myself into a viable position, then filled up the bottle. I could have filled another one but this would do. I felt all right.

'You done?' said Ted.

'Yep,' I said holding up the bottle. 'What d'you want me to do with this?'

'Just put it…' He stopped there. He was looking at the bottle and something was coming over his face. 'Just, erm…put it down there on the floor. That's it.'

'You all right, Ted?'

'Yeah, no worries. Just thought of summat, that's all. Look, I'm counting us in, right? Hold up…' He looked at his watch. 'Fourteen, thirteen, twelve…'

I planted the pistol in my pocket. Those boiler suits had big ones especially for the purpose. I knew mine didn't suit me but I'd be changing out of it soon enough. Later on I'd go looking around the charity shops for a fedora. This would be my new image, and I'd use it for my performance later on at The Feathers. I was a master of the new look, a chameleon, and nothing defined me better than a change of style. It didn't really matter what the look was, either – it was the way you wore it. It was all about becoming that persona.

'—two, one. Right, we're going in! And remember – loads of swearin'! And use the word "slag" a lot!'

We opened our doors and got out nice and calm. Martin was doing all right now, practising his deep breathing. I gave him a little nod. He looked the part: yellow hard hat topping off his boiler suit. I was dressed the same but I knew it didn't suit me as well. I knew what I wanted to wear and it would have to wait.

Not long now, though.

Only a few short hours, and then I'd be—

'Oi,' I said to Ted. He was still in the car, saying something quiet to Martin, who was leaning down to hear it. 'What you doing?'

'I'm doing my job, Rik. Playing my role.'

'Yeah but why are you still—?'

'Don't you listen? I'm the getaway driver. You can't do a job like this without a driver.'

'Yeah but...I mean, we ain't really doing a—'

'Rik, get a fuckin' move on! You'll fuck up the timing! You too, Martin. And trust me about what I just said, right?'

He wound up the window, glaring at me.

Martin was halfway across the road, holdall hanging low off his rigid arm. His other arm was planted in his pocket. He was using the pelican crossing as planned but the little man was on red. Cars were stopping for him anyway, and none of them beeping so far. In his boiler suit he looked like Odd Job from *Carry On Screaming*, so I wouldn't have beeped at him either.

I crossed the road. The little man was still on red but there was another squad car coming along and cars were pulling in. I reached the other side and made sure it went past, then went after Martin.

I reached him by the entrance of the Post Office. I don't think he was waiting for me but a woman was pushing her pram through the door in front of him and he had to wait. As we went through I started to pull down my mask from under my hard hat, but I noticed that Martin hadn't done his. I poked him in the side.

He jumped and yanked his arm out of his pocket. The fingers were gripped around his gun, finger on trigger, but it got snagged on the material and didn't come right out.

'Fuck's sake, Martin!' I hissed at him. 'Take it easy, mate. This is gonna be a piece of piss. This ain't real, remember? We're just going through the motions.'

'Yeah,' he said, letting his hand fall back inside the pocket. I knew he still had the finger on the trigger though. 'Yeah, this ain't real. Breathin' exercises.' His barrel chest started going in and out like a set of bellows.

It was a big place in here, not one of your little Post Offices. And full of people, many of them looking at us now, which was exactly what we didn't want. We were supposed to be invisible: two workmen popping in on their lunch-break to bank a cheque. Then the masks would go on, and people would finally notice us. It wouldn't matter by then, though: no one would have clocked us pre-mask so they didn't know what we looked like under them. Basic human nature, Ted had said.

But they'd clocked us.

And I didn't know what to do.

Pull the masks down now and everyone would remember the before and after.

Ted had also said to keep your eyes and ears open for changes in the conditions, so that's what I did. If you're on the lookout for them, you'll find them. I scanned around, looking casual, waiting for something, anything. And it came.

That young mother was over by the window, filling in a form on the ledge there. The baby in the pram beside her was looking right at me. I made a face.

The baby started screaming.

It was a strange, horrible sort of scream and it distracted everyone's attention away from me and Martin. I kicked him in the shin, nodded and pulled down my mask. He did the same, not quite so smoothly as myself and leaving it a bit lopsided with only one eye-hole lined up right, but he had it on. It was a Cliff Richard mask. Ted had got it for me but I didn't want it. I wasn't into Cliff Richard any more. 'Good lad,' he'd said at the time, handing me the one he'd chosen for Martin – Marilyn Monroe.

'I still don't see why I can't have the Marilyn one,' said Martin, back in the here and now. The baby was still making that horrible nails-on-a-blackboard noise and people were getting sick of it now, looking at each other in that disapproving way. Any second now we were going to be clocked in our masks.

'Everyone get on the fuckin' floor! Now!' shouted Martin. I was impressed. I never knew he had such a manly bellow in him.

I ran back to the doors and bolted them shut. That was my job over. It was all moral support now.

'Move it, you fuckin' wankers!' he was screaming. That bit was unscripted, but in the spirit of the plan. As long as he stuck to the plan we'd be all right.

They were going down all over and no screaming, not even from the baby. Mummy had stuck a dummy in his mouth and was kneeling next to him, sheltering him.

I walked back towards Martin, feeling quite powerful. He was by the cashiers now, pointing his gun at them. 'Get yer hands up where I can see 'em! And step away from the fuckin' counter!'

There were three of them and they were doing as requested, but we knew it was too late for that. One of them would have flicked a switch the moment Martin had started shouting. Ted had done his research and he knew how it worked.

Martin shouted at one of the cashiers to open up the glass partition, which she did. He got something out of the holdall and tossed it through empty, yelling: 'Used twenties and tens only, you fuckin' slag! And hurry up or I'll blow your fuckin' slag off!'

Slag off? I didn't like that. Not only was he veering from the script here but he was veering from sanity. And this was no time for that.

'You all right, Mart?' I said, going over.

'It's me chest. It ain't right. I can't breathe right.'

'Well...' I looked at my watch. 'We got half a minute and then we're out of here. And if we ain't, we're fucked.'

'It's all right, Rik. None of 'em's rung the bell.'

'They've got CCTV, you know.'

I spun around, looking at the punters on the deck, shouting: 'Who the fuck said that?'

'Me,' said a little man. He was lying on his belly, wrinkled face turned to me. 'They'll have got you on camera before you put them masks on. And by the way, you're a disgrace to the name of Marilyn Monroe. She'd have never—'

'Shut the fuck up!' I screamed.

He stopped there because his head exploded.

At the same time my ears went deaf.

'Fuckin' hell!' I was shouting, though I couldn't hear it. 'Fuckin' fuckin' hell!' My ears came back after a moment and straight away filled up with screams and shouting, and I wished I was deaf again. I got my gun out and waved it around at nothing, opening my mouth and not knowing what to say. I was in a bit of a daze. Martin shouted:

'Get down again, you fuckin' slags! Get *down!* Or I shoot some other slag!'

They did it, though still making a lot of noise. The old man was in a space on his own now, a pool of blood forming around him and spreading fast. Blood and bits of head had plumed out on the floor behind him like a red carpet. Martin ran through it towards the door. The holdall was slung over his shoulder. He started unbolting the doors and I snapped out of my daze. Time to go. I ran to him, skirting the gore and wishing Martin hadn't done that. Then again, the ritual was nothing without a blood sacrifice.

But didn't he need to spill some of the blood on his own shit, or something?

'*Obolaye be kumbalaye,*' he was saying as I got near him. We were still inside, the door shut and bolted. I could have sworn he'd opened it just then. 'Fuckin' hell, Rik. Me chest really is killing. *Obalaye be—*'

'Where's the holdall?' I said. Because he was holding only a lunchbox now. And the gun.

'*Obolaye be kumbalaye…*'

'Martin, where's the fuckin' holdall?'

'*Obolaye be kumbalaye.* I chucked it outside, as per plan. This is part of the plan as well. I'm sorry, Rik. *Obolaye be kumbalaye.*'

He pulled the lid off the lunchbox with his teeth and set it down on the floor between us. It had shit in it. A lot of shit. I couldn't smell it, though, because the air was filled with other smells and they were much worse.

I noticed that his gun was pointed at me.

He was no longer trembling.

'*Obolaye.* This is the way Ted said it had to be.' His voice was calmer than I'd ever heard it. 'I gotta do it. *Be kumbalaye. Obolaye be kumbalaye.*'

'Martin! Don't be a twat!'

'Orders is orders, Rik. You're the sacrifice.'

'What? When did Ted say that?'

'Just now, in the car. He said you ain't David Bowie after all, and you got to be the sacrifice. I'm gonna spill your blood on this shit here, then that's me done. I'm off to my real body.'

'What? You must have heard him wrong, Mart!'

He squinted and raised the gun.

I got mine out and shot him with it. But it didn't work. The safety catch was off and everything. It just didn't work, as if it wasn't loaded or—

'*Obolaye be…*'

I closed my eyes.

There was some sort of noise and I opened them. But it wasn't like a gunshot. More of an electric sound, like a short circuit. And Martin went all funny. It's the only way to describe it. He went all funny and turned into a skeleton for a moment, like an X-ray. After that he collapsed, falling sideways and hitting the floor so heavily that a cupboard full of passport application forms came off the wall.

'Martin?' I said. But his eyes were dead.

I prized his finger off the gun and unbolted the door.

APPENDIX G: CASE STUDY 4 (9 MAY 1979)

SPECIMEN was a local criminal of some national renown, nicknamed 'the snake' by the tabloid press for his enduring ability to slither around any obstacle. Clearly such a specimen was a departure for me. Each one of my other High Denomination Souls had been able to demonstrate a clear creative talent, either in the arts or (in one case) sports. It can be argued that a common bank robber and burglar possessed no such talent, and thrives on audacity and an absence of morality, which are more character trait than gift. It can also be argued that the bank robber is the highest denomination soul of them all.

In any case, the argument was taken out of my hands when the criminal in question burst in on me, wild-eyed, perspiring heavily and sporting a grisly bullet wound. He had heard of my burgeoning skills in the black arts and demanded, gun to my head, to be cured on the spot. I assented, handing him a bottle for his urine sample.

I left him 'holed up' in my 'gaff' (to borrow from his idiom), holding *The Skalanomicon* against my failure to return. The fact that he even knew of its existence – let alone its location – was proof in itself of the quality of his soul. It also meant that he would be engaged in the act of exploiting his talent (extortion by force) while I enacted the ritual. For I wanted his soul, and had no intention of curing him. I made an impromptu and, by nature, hazardous visit to the maternity ward. Time was of the essence, the criminal's injury being clearly life-threatening. My habit was to spend a long time reflecting on what kind of infant disability would best hamper the host's soul, but this time I had no such luxury. Guessing that the criminal's extravagant talent was built around his agile and diminutive frame, I selected the largest, most lumpen infant available. The ritual went ahead without mishap, a passing orderly being used as blood sacrifice.

I returned, excited and ill at ease. Never before had I been in a position to directly observe and question the donor post-soulshift. My professional interest followed the soul, and when it entered the body of the host organism the fate of the donor became irrelevant.

But the academic within me was curious.

I found him much as I had left him – sitting at an upstairs window, in possession of *The Skalanomicon*. But the nervous tension was replaced with confusion, the mistrust with mournfulness. On interrogation I found that he knew what he had hitherto done in his (ie: the donor organism's) life, but neither condoned it nor understood it. Indeed, he made a spontaneous vow to 'go straight', handing over *The Skalanomicon* and securing work as a caretaker at a local church.

The case had alerted me to the vulnerability of the most significant tome in the whole of creation, one which I was privileged to have in my possession. I devoted the following year to placing *The Skalanomicon* in a secure vault in a parallel dimension of its own, populated only by winged harpies whose sole motivation was to guard it. Later on I began writing this, *The New Skalanomicon*, and devising a curse with which to lace its sentences, thereby condemning to eternal damnation any soul who reads of it. Including you.

32.

I wanted to sit down now. And think about that. The thing that had happened to Martin there, with his skeleton and...

Something else.

Something brushing against me, just after the skeleton. A warm breeze with some texture to it.

It was Martin's soul. Wayne Boyle's soul, leaving that big hulking corpse and going home to...

No – getting dragged kicking and screaming from Martin and transported like a lorry-load of pigs to...

But I couldn't worry about that now. This was not a time to reflect. People had been trying to kill me. A person who I'd *trusted* had set me up as a human sacrifice. And another one wanted my soul for his supper. I had to protect myself here. I had to stand up for what's mine, fight for who I was. Because I was someone worth fighting for, even if others didn't know it. Or perhaps they did?

Perhaps they were jealous?

I mean, who would the average punter be?

1. A boxer who's famous for getting beat
2. A bank robber
3. A world famous superstar of pop.

Who would you rather be?

I snapped out of it and looked over the road. The driver's door of Ted's car slammed shut and the engine wheezed, smoke billowing out of the exhaust like brain matter from the back of that old man's head. It jerked forward and tore off up the road. I shouted something as it went past, catching sight of Ted and exchanging a quick look. There was a world of meaning in that look. It meant *I'm here. You're fucked.* It meant *Everything I've told you is bollocks.* It meant *Fuck off,* and *You ain't David Bowie really, you fucking twat. You're a failed singer with a harelip.* It meant a few other things as well, none of them nice, all of them adding up to one big, cold fuck off from Ted.

Part of me wanted to write a sad song about betrayal.

The other part wanted to stand in the road and point Martin's gun at the back window of the Escort, and that's the part that won. I didn't know how to aim but I knew how to close my eyes, make a wish and say fuck it. I fired.

It almost broke my wrist, I tell you.

The car went sideways and into a lamp post. It seemed almost silent on impact but then everything was silent just then, my eardrums suffering once again from the gun report. I ran to the car, my hearing coming back already. People were standing around and running out of shops and estate agents and offices, shouting and squealing and pointing at the unfolding drama. It was like I was in a film.

I was a man without a plan, operating on instinct and

adrenalin not really knowing what he was doing but knowing what he had to do. I was aware how much I was fucking things up for myself, firing shots at cars in the main street through town. I knew that it would have been wiser, perhaps, to scoot off down a side street and hide for a bit. But that option was not open to me. Not after he'd said them things to me as he was driving past.

You ain't David Bowie really, you fucking twat, he'd said. Or had he? I wasn't sure now. I wasn't sure of much. There was only one thing I knew.

That I was David Bowie.

And I had to defend that at all costs. Which meant shutting down any man who tried to take it away.

I neared the crashed Escort, holding my gun high. The Marilyn Monroe mask was still on and I felt all right within myself. It was all about image, you see. It always had been. Marilyn mask, boiler suit and handgun. For what I was doing here there could be no better look.

The car was making hissing sounds and there was a lot of dripping. I looked through the shattered passenger window. Ted was slumped over the wheel, face turned to me and eyes open but not seeing. There was blood all over his head, and a crack across the top like it was a broken egg. I thought he was dead. Then his lips started moving.

'What?' I said.

I put half my body right in, leaning on the holdall and feeling the money inside under one hand. The other still held the gun. 'Fuckin' spit it out, you…you…For fuck's sake, Ted. Why'd you have to go and…and…'

'You're…' he was saying, picking up a bit of strength now. I could see it in his eye, full of blood though it was. 'You're…'

'What? I'm what?'

'You're…'

I could hear a siren.

'Your piss,' he said finally. 'It ain't green.'

The eye burned bright for a moment, like he was making a massive physical effort. Then the lid slid down and his whole body started to slump.

I looked down at the holdall.

The siren was closer.

I turned and saw all the people looking at me, smoking fags and folding their arms under their businesslike tits, grinning and gawping. I waved my gun at them.

They screamed.

I screamed as well: 'Good evening, you fuckin' cunts! I got a confession to make!'

I was Marilyn Monroe in a boiler suit. Half sex goddess from yesteryear, half psycho killer from the horror films. It's all about creating a new persona and then becoming it.

I called this one Marilyn Myers.

I strutted the front of the stage, working them. All eyes were on me. Ears strained for my next word.

'I ain't who you think I am!'

I moved towards them, laying my look on face after face. I was putting a lot of heart into it, baring my soul for the audience to have its way with. I believe that this is the only way to deliver material.

'I ain't Rik Suntan, you fuckin' twats! I'm—'

But the siren was too close now.

I ran.

I knew who I was.

Inside, I always had known.

And no one was going to tell me different. I knew.

I know.

*

I'd been running for some time. It was a miracle that I hadn't been found yet. A stroke of luck in the extreme, the kind I didn't ever remember having before. But back then I was Rik Suntan, a twat with a harelip who didn't know whose soul he carried.

Now I knew it and accepted it.

And good things were happening for me.

I was in an alley, facing down a locked door at the end of it that looked like the classic tradesman's entrance. A couple of kicks and I had it open. I closed it behind me as best I could and crashed around in darkness for a while. I should have glanced inside while the sunlight was shining in, but I'd had things on my mind at that moment.

Priorities ordering themselves.

A plan forming.

After a couple of minutes of stumbling around I located a door handle and turned it, coming out into the rear of a car repair shop. A radio was on somewhere but no sign of life. I got down low behind an old Jag and took my boiler suit off, turning it inside out and putting it back on. It looked like a totally different boiler suit. I looked quite good in it, actually. Especially when I found a leather biker jacket hanging up and put that on. It had pointy shoulders that seemed to go with the look. On the way out I got a bit of engine grease on my hands and restyled my hair a bit. Looking at myself in the office window, I didn't think I looked different enough. You could tell it was me a mile off. The moustache was a giveaway.

I needed to do something drastic.

On a worktop I found a Stanley knife, and in the bathroom there was some Swarfega. Not the best shaving tools but they'd have to do. I set to work, and within a couple of minutes I didn't recognise myself. It's amazing what having no eyebrows does to your face.

33.

There were police everywhere. I didn't see many but I could hear them and feel them. I skirted around the back streets and down to the river, buying an ice cream in a shop down there. A man walking along with an ice cream is probably not a man who's just been involved in a bank robbery and indirectly killed someone, my thinking went. It was a bit desperate but I didn't know what else to do. I had to get to the train station. I had to get to Burninghouse for six o'clock, otherwise it was skeleton time.

Kiss your soul goodbye time.

This was the plan I'd been formulating, the priority that had singled itself out. Not such an ingenious plan, you might be thinking, but you ain't heard it yet. Let's look at the background first, the things I'd found out about myself:

1. I was David Bowie
2. I had a really good disguise

3. Looking at myself in a couple of windows, I could see that I looked a bit like Limahl out of Kajagoogoo
4. But without eyebrows
5. And with a moustache
6. Without your eyebrows, your tash looks about twice as big
7. When someone crosses me, and I've got a gun in my hand, I'm capable of pulling the trigger
8. Leading indirectly to his death
9. I could get away with stuff

That all being the case, why was I letting Mr Marino fuck me around? I felt empowered now, full of...erm, power and stuff. What was to stop me from pointing this here gun at Marino's head and ordering him to...to...?

Or just shooting him?

If he was dead then he couldn't eat my soul. Could he? And I could return it back to its rightful body at leisure, now I knew how the ritual was done. And that's if I even wanted to go back. Maybe I'd stay as Rik Suntan, now I'd worked out how to use him properly. Wasn't Rik Suntan just another persona, like Marilyn Myers and Limahl with no eyebrows? Wasn't he just another one of David Bowie's characters? I mean, *my* characters? He had a harelip but I could learn to live with it. I could *use* it... make it fashionable even. People would start having harelips cut in instead of sewn up.

Maybe I'd tinker with the details a bit, but it's that sort of thing.

It wasn't so hard to get to the train station. Most of the coppers were clustered around Ted's crashed Escort and the Post Office, and they didn't know who to look for anyway. They had two robbers deceased and accounted for. Witnesses might tell them about Marilyn in a boiler suit but they'd have a job finding him. Especially with me on the train already and pulling away towards Burninghouse.

I gazed out the window, feeling like this was the last time I'd ever see the place. Maybe it was. Seemed like the town was too small for me now. I needed the big city, a large canvas upon which to paint my new personas. I'd miss Shell, true enough. But now I wasn't in her presence I could see the wider picture. I could see that she held me back, made me yearn for home comforts and emotional support when I didn't need them. So, no.

Fuck her.

'Excuse me...can we have your autograph?'

It was two schoolgirls, about fourteen years old and trying not to giggle. I smiled, although it was a bit rude of them really. If you're going to ask for an autograph you should be respectful, not snorting through your fingers.

'Look,' I said, still smiling, 'if you're gonna be all disresp—'

'Oh, please don't get angry! We're just...Well, Simone's just...'

'Lucy fancies you.'

'Shut *up*, Simone! Erm, we just saw you and thought you wouldn't mind if...It's a good disguise and everything, the moustache. It's just that, well, we're big fans. And fans *know*. Don't we, Mone?'

'Yeah. We *know*.'

'Yeah.'

I became aware that there were quite a few people on the carriage. It was good that these two had come up to me. They were bringing me out of myself, back into the real world. I had to be more cautious, watch how I looked and came across. Up until then I'd been in a bit of a bubble.

'All right,' I said, still smiling that lopsided grin but also keeping my eye moving all around. I had to watch for dangers. 'Where you want me to sign?'

'Well...' Lucy took a deep smiling breath and lifted her shirt. Not all the way, just a few inches above her belly button, which had a ring in it. 'If you could write "To Lucy", or whatever, on top of the ring, and sign it under, I'd be—'

'And can you sign my arse after?'

'Simone!'

'I just mean the cheeks. He could fit it on the cheeks.'

'Yeah, but we're on a train!'

'Yeah, but...' She looked at me, face screwed up like a little kid who wants a biscuit. 'Could you? Could you sign my arse *please*?'

Who was I to turn away a fan? 'No probs,' I said, taking a marker pen off the belly button one. I wrote a little dedication – slightly more risqué than she'd asked for but I was feeling generous – and scrawled the name under it. She had a tight little tummy and the pen moved over it like oil paint on canvas. The signature looked great, lopsided like my grin.

'There,' I said, turning to the arse one. She was starting to hitch her skirt up. People were harrumphing and rustling newspapers all around. Maybe the girl was going a bit overboard here but you couldn't knock her. She was excited to meet her idol. I held the marker out, thinking up an even saucier dedication.

'What's this?' the belly button one was saying. 'Lemon someone? What's he writ, Mone?'

She stopped hitching, skirt half-mast, and read out: 'To Juicy Lucy...Love from Limahl from Kaja...he's run out of space on the last bit.'

'Limahl? What have you signed it "Limahl" for?'

The other one was sniggering, saying: 'It's a joke, Luce. I think it's funny.'

'Oh…Well, I'm not sure if I…'

'Lighten up, Luce.'

'Will you sign your proper name underneath? Please?'

There wasn't much room left but I had a go.

They stared at it for a while, making sure they were reading it right. Then Simone said: 'Rik who? Sultan?'

It was getting embarrassing now, but I wasn't worried. I had other thoughts in my head. Like, who did they think I was? If I wasn't Limahl or Rik, there was only one other person I could be.

'David Bowie?' I said. There wasn't much conviction in my voice because I couldn't understand how it could be so, since I hadn't done the transmigration ritual yet. But maybe they could see something I couldn't?

Maybe my soul was coming through?

They were both frowning, shirts and skirts pulled down now. One of them said: 'Who?'

'He said David Bowie.'

'Who's he?'

'That old singer. My grandad's got some of his records. They're shit.'

I stood up. My hand was in the pocket of my leather, holding the gun. But I didn't pull it out. I ain't stupid.

'Go on, fuck off,' I said. They yelped and ran off down the carriage, waiting by the door until the train stopped at the next station, and they got off.

They had asked for it, though. Hadn't they?

I mean, you don't just stand in front of a man and tell him he's shit.

'You're a fuckin' weirdo!' one of them shouted from the

platform as the train pulled away. The other was yakking into her mobile phone. 'And we're callin' the papers on you. We're gonna ruin your career!' She held her own phone up and it flashed in my face.

I blinked.

A lot of people had got on the train at that stop and I was working my way past them, trying to be gentle and polite but not having the patience to do it properly. I had to get to the toilet quick, so I could look in the mirror and see what was going on here. I felt like I was in a state of limbo, not knowing who I was and how people saw me. I had to get it straight. Until then, I felt strange and itchy, like I was wearing someone else's dirty underpants. Or like I could feel something crawling under my clothes.

There was someone in there when I found the toilet, so I knocked and waited. I knocked a few more times, then the door opened and a very fat and pissed-off man came staggering out, looking for an argument by the looks of him. But when he saw my face it seemed to strike him with awe, and he relaxed and let me past.

'Soz about the stink,' he was saying as I shut the door on him. 'If I'd've known it was you, I wouldn't of done a shit.'

He was right about the stink. But never mind that – there was no mirror. You could see where it had been but someone had smashed it, judging by the shiny fragments on the floor. I picked up the biggest one and tried to get a look at myself, but it was too small and all I could see was my eye. I stared at it for a while anyway, looking into my pupil and sensing things turning over behind it. But I couldn't feel them in my own head.

A middle-aged woman was waiting outside the toilet and she bustled past me when I opened the door, saying: 'Pooh… Uurgh…' and waving her hand. I put my foot in the door before she could close it and said:

'Can I just ask you one thing, miss?'

'Well, I can hardly breathe for the stench, but I suppose I can hear. If you hurry.'

'Do you recognise me?'

'Recognise you?' she said, peering over her glasses. 'Well, you do seem somewhat familiar. Are you famous, then?'

'Yeah, I think I am.'

'Then you shouldn't defecate in public lavatories. A member of the public will follow you in there and forever associate that smell with your face. Goodbye.'

I went into the next carriage. A short way along I saw a bloke sitting on his own and recognised him. 'Gaz,' I said. Because that's who it was.

You know, from HGV records.

'Gaz?'

APPENDIX H: CASE STUDY 5 (18 JANUARY 1981)

SPECIMEN was a singer of burgeoning world renown and obvious talent, whose modus operandi seemed to be periodically to create a new image for himself. This was an interesting case, and it demonstrates the enduring cosmic properties of urine. His sample came to me via my usual urine handler, and was in fact one of the earliest of his many procurements. However, although the urine was delivered on the night of 4 June 1973, the soulshift was not done until many years later.

The reason for this was a prosaic one. One of the refrigerators I normally stored urine in to preserve its fresh state was broken at this time, and so I temporarily stored the contents in the cellar, it being the coolest place. The bottle then became lost amongst other bottles down there and later mistaken for crème de menthe. It was eight years before the error was uncovered.

The donor still being alive and having increased his renown by then, there was no reason not to proceed with the soulshift. Since the singer's creativity was based on image as much as musicianship, an infant host was sought with some facial disfigurement that would make it impossible for him to exploit that creativity. I located such a specimen with a severe harelip. Even with surgical reconstruction, his face would never survive the camera's glare. He was one of a pair of foundling twins, and would be easy to monitor as he grew up in the local children's home. The ritual went ahead without mishap.

No outward change was observed in the host's behaviour post-soulshift. This was normal and not a cause for worry. The behaviour of infant organisms is by and large uniform, so two wildly disparate souls might exhibit exactly the same behaviour when the organisms are at larval stage. This was not the case in the example of the soulshifted boxer, where the infant immediately began behaving aggressively post-soulshift, but that was patently a case of two hugely disparate souls being exchanged. Donor and host seemed to be more compatible in this instance.

This was born out by the subsequent behaviour of the donor, who appeared to continue his music career without interruption. However, upon release of his next long player in 1983, it was clear to the world that he had taken a more mainstream approach to his music. Gone were the ideas and wild creativity, replaced by crowd-pleasing, funk-influenced pop.

This was to be my thirty-seventh and final soulshift. After several years of effort – and many years ahead of schedule – I was in possession of the number of High Denomination Souls required to reach my goal. I now had twenty-six years in which to prepare for my ascent up The Stairway in pursuit of enough power to fight the Devil.

34.

I knew who I looked like now. The woman sitting in front had got her make-up mirror out for a moment and I'd had a peak. It was obvious really, when you compared my reflection with the CD case I'd found in my pocket. I was the spitting image of David Bowie in his Ziggy Stardust persona. But with a massive moustache.

Things were falling into place.

Gaz was sat next to me, staring straight ahead and clutching some sort of leather satchel to his chest with his good arm. There was definitely something wrong with him. He smelt of smoke and petrol.

'What's the matter, Gaz?'

'Bastards.'

'Who?'

'Cunts.'

This was the last thing I needed, getting caught up in

someone else's drama. But in a way it was a good thing. If I was on my own I'd only worry about my own problems, and there was nothing I could do about them while I was on the train. Plus I owed Gaz one, in a way. He'd put me on to Randy at the Lamb and Flag, who had pointed the finger conclusively at Sam Marino.

'Ah, shit,' I said, remembering something else. 'You got the sack, didn't yer?'

'Wankers,' he said, clutching the satchel tighter. 'Wankers wankers wankers. And fuckers.'

I looked at him. He was swaying back and forth slightly, humming a very quiet tune.

'You feeling all right, Gaz?'

'Burninghouse,' he said, surprising me with a straight answer. 'Gonna fix it. Gonna fix them.'

'Oh yeah? Look, I heard about your job. You know what? I reckon you could get it back. But you've got to make some changes. It's your approach to people, Gaz. You got to—'

'Gonna fix the world. It's fucked, see. We lost the rhythm, back there somewhere. We ain't got the rhythm and so we're lost in the woods…can't see round the trees. I'm gonna set that right, Rik. I'm gonna get the rhythm back for people, and they'll be able to see round the trees and get out of the woods again.'

'Trees, eh?'

'Yeah. I'm gonna cut 'em down.'

'What with?'

He clutched his bag. I don't know what he had in there but if it was a saw it wasn't a big one. A small hacksaw, perhaps. Gaz was on drugs, I was sure of it. He'd got sacked, gone on a bender and worked his way into a psychotic episode. Which gave me an idea.

But I had to test him first.

'You got the time, Gaz?'

'Yeah,' he said, looking at his watch, 'half three.'

He'd passed. 'Cheers,' I said.

'You're welcome. I'm gonna cut the big one down first, Rik. That one goes and the rest'll be easy.'

'Oh right? You need a hand with that, Gaz? Cos I do think you're right. I reckon we're lost in the woods.'

'You do?'

'Yeah. I ain't lost personally, but I can see how others are. And they didn't used to be, Gaz.' I was saying all the right things, lighting all his candles for him so he could see enough. Just enough to walk down my path. 'We've got to set them straight.'

'We have, Rik. You and me.'

'That's right. But will you help me with summat first?'

'What? I mean, yeah…But—'

'We've just got to go see someone.'

'I can't, Rik. I'm sorry but…but I'm on a mission. I can't be diverted from it. This is it for me, now. I can't afford to get—'

'But Gaz, this is a part of it. This man we're gonna see, he's one of them trees. A big one.'

'Who is he?'

'Well…' I didn't want to tell him. Seemed foolish to supply information to one so unstable of mind just then. But I couldn't see what harm it would do, either. 'He works in the music business, Gaz. He's a svengali.'

Gaz was looking at me with new-found interest.

There were police at Burninghouse Old Street Station. Lots of them, some with firearms. I didn't know who they were looking for but it was probably me, so I swapped jackets with Gaz as soon as I saw them. The biker jacket changed his look completely, turned him into a different person almost. Even more so when I took his glasses off him and made him wear a baseball cap he found in the pocket.

'I can't see without my glasses,' he said.

'And I can't see *with* your glasses. But, you know, we got to be careful. There's a lot of police here. I think they might have heard about our plan to chop the trees down. Our deforestation mission, if you like.'

'What are you on about, Rik? I was talking in metaphor back there. I don't really intend to chop down trees.'

'No, I was just…Never mind. Just look relaxed.'

Gaz's old army jacket was a bit crap and smelled of mildew, but it worked on me as much as the biker jacket did on him. But whereas mine made him look better, his turned me into a dickhead. I wasn't complaining, though. It got us out of the station and into the shopping centre.

HGV Megastore was up ahead and I saw it just in time, diverting Gaz through Boots. The emotional state he was in, he didn't need his nose rubbed in it.

'You didn't need to do that,' he was saying as we went through the make-up section. 'I don't have a beef with my ex-employers. It's the whole music industry in general. The record outlets, they're just at the end of the chain. It's the links further up that I'm after. The big links at the other end.'

I wasn't sure what he was on about, but him mentioning beef had made me peckish, so I bought a ham sandwich.

'You want one?' I asked him.

'Yeah, why not?'

He chose a ploughman's and we went outside to eat them. Took us about five minutes to find an exit but it was sunny when we got there, and we swapped our togs back and sat on a wall. While I ate I went over the details with him one last time.

'You just hold the gun on him, right? We're gonna have a strange old conversation and he'll do some weird things, possibly involving some…well, faeces. But I don't know about that. It's probably going to be different with him doing it, because he's the…ah, don't matter. You just need to remember that you don't have to shoot him. Only shoot him if I give you the sign, which will be like this.'

I did a cut-throat gesture. To be honest, I knew I wouldn't be needing it. Things were simple now, because they always are when you point a gun at someone. Meeting Gaz on the train had been the final piece in the jigsaw. I knew how to get my soul back now, and Gaz was the perfect person to help me do it, him being a bit weird himself.

'And then,' I said, 'the phone will ring and you answer it. It'll be David…Well, a very famous man on the line will say "Rock 'n' Roll Suicide", and that's the password. That's your cue that it's all worked, and you just turn and leave. Right? Don't wait for me to come with you. If I seem like I want to come with you, well, you can let me. But keep your eye on me, because I can't vouch for myself.'

'You said you was gonna help me with the trees.'

'I will, Gaz. And this is a tree we're dealing with here.'

'But you said—'

'Yeah, all right. I did say I'd help you and I stand by it. All right. Wait outside for me afterwards, OK? I'll be down in, say, five minutes. All right?'

'Promise?'

'I swear on my soul.'

It took a lot longer than I thought to get there. But I'd been in a limousine last time and had wandered back afterwards in a daze. I wasn't in a daze now. My mind felt like it was made of crystal. My thoughts were clear like diamonds, and just as unbreakable. I wasn't so sure about Gaz, though.

He kept stopping.

'Gaz,' I said after the third time, 'there is a certain amount of urgency involved here.'

He was looking at a poster in a window advertising the Burninghouse leg of the *X Factor* auditions. Which were today, if I had the date right. There was a grinning mugshot of that nasty bloke on it, the one who slags off all the contestants.

'I know,' he said, giving it one last look. He seemed to be trying to burn the image on to his brain, 'there is.'

'It's just up this hill here.'

We walked on.

I panicked a little bit when we got to the top of the hill. I was sure the turn-off for his underground car park was back there on the left, but I couldn't see it. It was as if it had never been there, and I was just starting to wonder if there wasn't some black magic going on here when a wall went up and a silver Porsche turned off the road and bombed through where it had been. Then the wall went down again.

Maybe that was Marino.

Up close I could see it wasn't a wall, but one of those garage doors that look a bit like walls and go up and down via remote control. Next to it was a short set of stone steps leading up to a big door and a set of buzzers, the one at the top with a gold embossed 'SM' next to it. I took a deep breath. I took a massive breath. I pressed the buzzer.

The intercom said: 'Who there?'

'David Bowie. Oh, I mean—'

'David Bowie? The fame superstar?'

I don't know why I said that. Really I don't. Well, I do. Because it's true, isn't it? I was David Bowie. But I don't know why I said it there. It was about the worst thing I could say at this point. Talk about putting him on his guard, letting Marino know I was on to his game. Mind you, I was only talking to the foreign driver, and not Marino himself.

'Heh heh,' I said, making it sound convincing. 'Just having a laugh there. No, it's Rik Suntan.'

'I see. You come, Mr Suntan. You take the stair, however. Lift kaput.'

The door buzzed and I pushed it open.

'That was him?' said Gaz, coming in behind me.

'No, that was Mick.'

'Mick who?'

'Oh, never mind that.' I gave him the gun. 'Now, remember what we said – all you got to do is point…Er, Gaz.'

I didn't like the way he was fondling the gun. 'He's a fuckin' bastard,' he said. 'A dirty fuckin'—'

'No, he ain't like that.'

'You said he was a svengali. You said he was a tree.'

'Yeah, but he's polite with it, you know? He does things civil. He'll listen to reason.'

He pressed the lift button. 'Then why are we resorting to—'

'Don't use the lift,' I said. 'It's bust. We got to use the stairs.'

'The lift ain't bust. I can hear it coming.'

'He said use the stairs. Come on. I think I need to go over the details with you one more—'

'He's fucking you around, Rik. He's playing power games. They're all the same, these cunts.'

'No, he's…Look, just because the lift's coming don't mean it ain't bust. It probably won't open, or…'

There was a ping and the lift door opened. Gaz went in and said:

'Mind games, Rik.' The doors started closing. 'They're all the same, the trees are.'

I ran to the lift, trying to get my fingers in there before it closed, but failing. Just before I lost sight of him I saw him get his satchel off his shoulder.

I stood there listening to the lift going up. Then I started running up the stairs. My heart was beating like a drummer drumming full tilt on a snare drum, and my ears were filled with the resulting racket. Why the fuck had I roped Gaz into this? I should have known something like this would happen. All he had to do was hold the gun, and...

Ah, fuck.

I was making an effort to tread soft as I neared the top floor. My legs were like lead but I had to be quiet. I was listening out for gunshots. Not that I'd know what to do if I heard them. If they were Gaz topping Marino, I might be in the clear. A dead warlock can't hurt me. Can he? I didn't know, but it seemed like he couldn't. What was that the bloke had said in the Lamb and Flag? *There's just life, and after that there's fuck all.* Yeah, that was a good one. So maybe this was the best way after all. If Gaz was psycho enough to murder Marino, that'd be just fine. I'd just skip on out and leave him to take the rap.

I mean, I hadn't *asked* him to, had I?

So yeah, I was walking slow up the final flight. I was dragging it out, giving Gaz a nice long chunk of time to pull the trigger. 'Go on, Gaz...' I found myself saying. But no shots were heard. I put my ear to what must be Marino's door, it being the last one and made of something looking like gold. I couldn't hear a sound in there. Not even distant voices.

The door opened.

'Mr Marino wait you,' said Mick the driver. But instead of standing aside to let me pass, he grabbed my arm and yanked me in, locking the door after and leading the way down a wide corridor with a fluffy, cream-coloured carpet. It didn't seem in keeping with a warlock, somehow.

'Mr Marino in mood,' Mick was saying. 'He has visitor. One he not expect.'

'Yeah? Who?'

'Is not matter.'

But I knew who.

The question was why didn't Gaz just pull the trigger?

Mick went into a room and closed the door after, telling me to stay put. I thought it a bit rude, asking me to wait in a corridor, but it was a nice corridor so I didn't mind. I was fascinated by the carpet, which was really fluffy. I was quite drawn to a couple of lovely paintings on the wall as well. Behind it all I was waiting for the sound of a gunshot, and planning my exit.

'You go in,' said Mick, here again.

'Really?'

'Yes, really. Now move.'

'Hold up,' I said. 'How come the frostiness? I mean, you're talking to me like I'm a slave, when yesterday you was more—'

'Mr Marino say you under contract. That mean you *are* fucking slave. Like me. But I slave longer than you, so I give you the frost. Now shut the fucking cakehole.'

I couldn't believe the treatment I was getting. But he was right: I was a slave. Unless I could pull this off. And for that I needed Gaz.

Just don't let me down, Gaz.

I went through the door, scanning for his eyes.

And finding those of Zak Bremner instead.

35.

I could have sworn Marino went a bit white when he saw me. Such was the power of disguise. He actually thought I was the real David Bowie. Not that I wasn't, of course. You know what I mean.

'Ooh, that's a nice look you've got there, Rik,' he said, when he'd recovered. 'I like it, I do like it. Ziggy with a moustache – a nice variation. And a necessary one, in your case, eh?'

He tapped his nose and winked at me.

'But tell me something – you're not trying to make some sort of comment on Zak's style, are you? Because if you're insinuating that he borrows from Mr Bowie, you're wide of the mark. It's more subtle than that. But you'll learn it.'

'Yeah,' I said to him, but looking at Bremner. 'Can I just ask you summat, Mr Marino? Why is *he*—?'

'I'm so...emotional,' Zak Bremner was saying, grinning like a twat. 'Really I am. This is...I've waited for this moment for so fucking long. But I always knew it would come. Not only did I always know you existed, I always knew we'd have this moment. And now we have! We're here!'

'Look,' I said to Marino, 'I don't quite like this. Why's he here? And what the fuck is he on about?'

'Can't you see what's going on, Rik? I have dropped enough hints for you. I've had to play this one carefully. Lord only knows what kind of shit would come our way if the press found out about this. No offence, Rik. But you must admit – I did give you the hints.'

'What fuckin' hints? What the fuck—?'

'Calm down, Rik. No one is trying to hurt you here. Don't you recall me saying that you're only half a person? Remember that? I said you're dislocated from yourself, or something. You remember? Well, here you are. There's your other half.'

'Eh? What the...? Are you sayin' I'm bent or summat?'

He went silent for a moment, making me think I'd put my finger on what was going on here. Then he started laughing.

Loud.

Throwing his head back and clutching his round belly. And Bremner was laughing too, though not in such a hearty manner. There wasn't anything hearty about Bremner. He did look a bit gay, actually.

'Fuckin' pack it in!' I roared, slamming my fist on a table. Something fell off on the far side and thudded on the carpet. I didn't care. I wanted more things to thud on the carpet. I wished it was Marino I'd slammed my fist into, watching as his head fell off the far side.

I was *that* fucking angry.

I'd forgot all about why I'd come here and who he was. You'd get no begging for mercy from me, not with him taking the piss like that. If I'd had the gun on me I'd have pulled it on him right here and plugged him in the guts.

'Now come on, Rik,' he was saying, no longer laughing. 'There's no need for—'

'Are you laughin' at my harelip? Are you? Is that what you're takin' the piss out of?'

'Rik, for pete's sake—'

'Fuck Pete – I want the truth. Are you or are you not laughin' at—'

'You've just had the truth!' Marino shouted. 'Really, I'm not in the habit of stating the obvious. But if that's what you're asking for then I will. Rik, meet your brother. Your long-lost, identical twin brother, Zachary Richard Bremner.'

'Eh? What kind of shit is this?'

'Rik,' Zak Bremner was saying, 'don't do this. You *knew*, right? How could you not know? My face has been everywhere. And we're practically identical, even now. And—'

'We ain't identical! We don't look nothin' like each other. I got way better bone structure. And…the hair, and…And there's no fuckin' way you could grow a tash like my one.'

'But you've done your hair like me. Sort of. I mean, you did that on purpose, right? To show that you…I mean, I thought you—'

'My hair? I fuckin'…Do you know what? I done it like this cos the fuckin' *coppers* was after me and I had to disguise myself. It's fuckin' *motor oil*.'

'Oh. Well, I use TruGel. But…What about the song? You gave me your song! When you did that, Rik, it was like…oh, I've never felt such…'

'Yeah, I gave you the song. I was doing you a fuckin' favour! Your songs are shit, mate. I was giving you a proper song.'

'But…OK, fine, if you wanna…Shit.'

No one spoke for a bit. What could anyone say?

I couldn't believe how much I was being fucked around here.

Marino must have seen me coming a mile off, and he'd set this one up to throw me. I was starting to get my thinking head back on now, getting wise to his ways. Strange that he happened to know Zak Bremner, though. Maybe he'd conjured him up on the spot? This was probably the sort of thing they do, warlocks. And I hadn't fallen for it. He'd thrown a big one at me and I'd shrugged it off. He was no match for me. Look at him over there, huffing and puffing by the fireplace. He was trying to work out a new angle.

Let him try.

'Mikhail tells…' He cleared his throat. I had him on the ropes here. 'Mikhail tells me you announced yourself as a Mr Bowie. Most interesting. A joke, Rik? Or some sort of cryptic—?'

'Right,' I said. Because I'd had enough. 'Let's get down to fuckin' cases, shall we? I came here to—'

'I've met him, you know!' that twat Bremner was saying. 'David Bowie. I know him quite well, Rik. You should meet him some time. He's an incredible fella. We really sort of…clicked. Do you know what I mean? It's like we'd known each other in a previous life, like…like he was my long-lost bro, and not you. Only jokin' there, bro. I'm really glad it's you and not him. I mean, I know you're not quite used to…erm…'

He gave a nervous smile and looked away.

I could feel Marino glaring at me. Like a buzzard glares at a pigeon. Well, I wasn't a pigeon. I was at least a crow. A very powerful crow, feeling more powerful by the minute. And as buzzards went, he was a ropey one.

He went over to Bremner and whispered something to him, then Bremner sloped out, shooting me one last look with those big, pathetic brown eyes.

He was lucky I didn't black them for him.

When the door was shut, me and Marino made eye contact

and held it. This was it, I felt. We were engaging in battle and I was up for it.

'You heartless, ungrateful little...' he said, striking the first blow, '...turd.'

'Yeah, all right,' I said. 'Whatever.'

Let him wear himself down, then I'd wade in and...I wasn't sure yet. I'd do something though.

'Do you realise how much effort I put into tracking you down? Orphanage kids like you, there's no proper records. And Zak's adoptive parents were hardly accommodating. You see, Rik, they remembered all about you. They saw the two of you as newborns. They saw your affliction and decided to just take Zak. And I don't blame them. It's like that Johnny Cash song, "A Boy Named Sue". They knew you didn't need looking after. With your curse, you needed the opposite. You needed the roughest upbringing imaginable. And look at you now. It worked! I've rarely seen such confidence onstage as I saw when I came to your club. Only once or twice before have I ever seen it, and we're talking big, famous names. But you're never going to make it big, Rik. You're strong inside but weak on the surface. And that's where it counts. No one wants to hear a song come out of a face like yours. But you don't need me to tell you that, do you?'

'I...'

That's all I had to say. I was wrong about him. He wasn't a ropey old buzzard at all. He was a fucking vulture. And a strong one. He'd sensed my weakness and gone straight for it.

'Look, Rik,' he said, pouring some Scotch into two glasses, 'I'm not getting at you here. Despite your spectacularly rude outbursts I do have some sympathy for you. And possibly I've handled it the wrong way, dropping a bombshell on you like this. But I'm a businessman, not a social worker. I got you here tonight on business. That's the only reason I tracked you down to that one-horse town of yours. Zak asked me to, but I wouldn't have done it if I hadn't seen commercial potential. I want to offer you work, Rik. You're Zak's secret identical twin brother. And not only can you sing, but you can sing exactly like Zak. Do you realise what possibilities that opens up? It means...'

Still holding the two glasses, he went to the door and made sure it was shut and no one was listening.

'Zak is not the man he was, Rik. Too much powder has passed through those sculpted nostrils. This last album...production costs went through the roof. He just can't sing the same way any more. And performing onstage? Forget it. All that is gone. But you could do it.'

I was on a chair at the table. I don't remember sitting down. He put a glass in front of me.

'Not only could you do it, but you could do it *better*. With you performing and recording, the Zak Bremner brand would go *stratospheric*. And don't worry about your face. What the best surgeons can't fix, make-up artists can. You should see the effort that goes into making Zak presentable. Did you realise he has a plastic septum? Just think, Rik – the fame you always craved, the adulation you knew you deserved. I'm offering you all of that. And money.'

There was a sound somewhere else in the flat and I heard voices. I wanted to run to them, just to see what was going on. Not that I gave a shit. I just had to get away.

I couldn't handle this.

'You'll be a team: Rik doing the performing and recording, Zak doing the appearances and photo shoots. A real family team. What are your initial thoughts, Rik?'

'I...Well, I'd have to talk it over with, erm...' I found my mouth saying.

I didn't want it to.

It just went ahead and said these things.

'I'd have to think about it, yeah. I mean, there's all kinds of details, and...'

'Forget details for now. Do you want to sing on the biggest stage imaginable? Or go back to Warchester and carry on with your glorified karaoke?'

I sipped some of the Scotch.

It burned my mouth a bit but not too much. I could get used to it. You could tell it was expensive stuff and that made a difference to me.

'I...'

I stopped there because there was a knock at the door. Three knocks, actually, followed by the limo driver coming in and saying:

'Is visitor, Mr Marino. Another not expect visitor. He say he with Mr Sunburn.'

'What? You had someone with you, Rik?'

The driver said: 'He have cripple arm, sir. And he a bit...He give me the frost, sir.'

APPENDIX J: AN UPDATE TO APPENDIX H

AS stated elsewhere, it is vitally important that your urine handler is trustworthy. I learned this lesson the hard way.

In Appendix H I described the soulshift of a famous musician whose urine I had mislaid for several years. The harelipped infant host was one of a pair of twins whose cots were side by side in the maternity ward. The ritual went well, the host branded and the donor's subsequent actions left me in no doubt that souls had been exchanged.

It was only after several years that I noticed anomalies in the growing host. Everything seemed normal at first. Like the other hosts, the harelipped child grew into a frustrated and depressed young man, showing an urge to exercise his talent within a public arena but unable to overcome the inhibitions derived from his disfigurement. But this host was resourceful, and worked out a crude way of disguising his harelip by way of a large moustache, thereby allowing him to break through and begin showing his talent to the world.

This in itself was not a problem. Had the host continued to gain fulfilment from his talent (thereby diluting the value of his soul to me), a further physical disfigurement could have been arranged. The problem was the nature of the material he chose to perform. Whereas he hosted a zeitgeist-riding soul full of imagination and innovation, his musical output was at best bland and derivative, at worst execrable. Rarely did he perform self-penned material, and when he did he exposed himself as a borderline halfwit. The bulk of the songs he sang were cover versions of the most clichéd, cheese-laden songs known to mankind. Something was wrong.

Being in possession of a High Denomination Soul, each host has a further source of self-consciousness other than their physical impairment, and this is green urine. The host in question, when I connived to stand next to him at the urinal after one typically empty performance, discharged urine that was a pale yellow. In short, his soul was normal. Which led me to one conclusion:

My urine handler had supplied me with a sample from a different infant. And the only other infant within soulshifting range when I performed the ritual was his twin brother.

A little research made it all clear. After my thirty-seventh and final soulshift I lost touch with my urine handler. It seems he adopted a young child around that time, and over subsequent years nurtured him into something of a musical prodigy. Quickly he gained fame and fortune, based around an act that emphasised his image as much as his musical talent.

(Interestingly, the host's image did not periodically change, as had that of his soul's donor before the soulshift. Rather it seemed frozen on one that evoked the donor's at the time when the urine sample was taken: June, 1973.*) He was clearly born to be a star.

Or, rather, soulshifted into being one.

And in the background was his adoptive parent and manager, my former urine handler, orchestrating his career and reaping the gains.

I had been cheated. For all those years I had been guarding over my flock of thirty-seven sheep, unaware that one of them was a goat and would bear no wool.

But I had found my stray lamb now.

And I took my revenge on the disloyal urine handler, cursing him with an affliction that would forever remind him of his dishonest dealings.

---

* This suggests that a shifted soul is, in effect, on hold, frozen in time at the point of the ritual. It would be an interesting (if fruitless) experiment to attempt to return a shifted soul to its donor. Would it return to 1973 and resume as if nothing had happened? Possibly, but I suspect that it would return to the donor as he is now, in this case a much older man, and the resulting disruption would appear to the outside world as the onset of senile dementia.

36.

'Well, anyone would be confrontational if they'd been stuck in a lift. Did you not tell him that it was broken, Mikhail?'

The driver was looking my way. They both were.

I had to do something here.

The stakes had changed and Gaz didn't know about it.

'Yeah,' I said, getting up. 'That'll be, er…my mate Gaz, yeah. I think he's got a bit confused. I told him to wait downstairs in the foyer for me. He's obviously, erm…'

I went past the driver and into the corridor. I was dreading what I'd find there. Gaz with the gun out, waiting to blow Marino away. Or pissing on that lovely fluffy carpet. Maybe he'd found Zak and started pistol whipping him.

But Gaz wasn't there. I looked around the corner by the aquarium. He wasn't there either. The squid was, though, waving at me. I didn't wave back.

'Where is he?' I asked the driver, who was coming up behind me.

'I leave him here,' he said, nodding at the big leather sofa down there by the window. 'He seem odd. You get rid him, OK? If not, I get rid him.'

A toilet flushed nearby.

'Oh, very nice,' he said, 'he make himself a shit without ask. Is rude, your man.'

'Psst! Rik.' I turned and Zak was stood in the kitchen doorway behind me, holding a slice of white bread. 'I'm making a sandwich for your buddy. You want one? We've got peanut butter, Marmite, jam...anything you want.'

The driver was stood next to the bathroom door, arms folded. I found myself going into the kitchen. The radio was on. '*In other news,*' said the newsreader, '*former World Champion boxer and celebrity entrepreneur George Foreman has run amok at a fund-raising gala in Chicago, throwing plates at guests and attacking Muhammad Ali. Fifteen armed police were required to—*'

'You like Marmite?' he said, flicking off the radio and going to the fridge. 'I like Bovril myself. But I am a vegetarian so I shouldn't eat Bovril, really. Or is it Marmite? Anyway, I like them. I like jam too. What's your favourite sandwich, Rik?'

I thought of the most disgusting type of sandwich I could imagine. 'Corned beef, peanut butter and tomato ketchup.'

'Really?'

'Yeah.'

'Well...well, that's amazing, Rik! That's my favourite as well!'

He was at the table now, buttering some peanut butter. The smell was making me sick. I noticed him shoot a glance at my face.

'You ain't got a birthmark, have you?' I said, showing him mine. 'Just here.'

'Birthmark? Fuck, is that a...? Well, no, I guess I don't have one of those. And, you know, the make-up girls can cover up things like birthmarks. And you can even have them removed. Surgeons can do anything these—'

'Did you have a birthmark removed? Like mine, I mean?'

'What? Er, no…I never had anything removed, Rik. But it doesn't mean we're not identical. I don't think so, anyway. Does it?'

'I dunno.'

'No, nor me.'

There was a bit of silence. It wasn't comfortable.

After a while he said: 'You know, I don't feel so well.' But I think he was just filling up the quiet.

'Look,' I said, 'I never meant what I said, about your bone structure. And your songs. Your songs ain't shit. I was just a bit, you know…'

'Yeah, that's fine, Rik.'

He finished making his sandwich and lifted it to his face. Ketchup was dripping out the sides and a slice of corned beef hanging out. 'Mmm-mm,' he said, and took a big chomp of it. He smiled at me, chewing. After five or six chews he stopped and gagged. 'I'm feeling like shit, Rik,' he said, leaning on the table. 'Here, in my chest. It hurts to breathe.'

'Is about time,' I heard the driver saying out in the corridor. 'Poo, it stink! You make shit here, yes? Is disgust. You no make shit here without ask.'

I was out there sharpish, ready to grab Gaz's arm before he pulled the gun. He saw me and I shook my head at him, mouthing the words: *It's off. It's off…*

And I'm sure he understood it because he nodded once at me and winked. Then he reached into his pocket anyway.

And pulled out a coin.

'There's twenty pence,' he said, giving it to the driver. 'That's the going rate for commode use at mainline rail stations.'

Charlie Williams

'Is joke?'

'Gaz,' I said, 'we got to—'

'Ah, there you are.' Marino came out holding both glasses of whisky. 'Your drink was starting to evaporate.'

'Look, Mr Marino, I gotta go. Me and Gaz here have. But—'

'No worries, Rik. You go away and think about what we've discussed. It's an exciting situation, isn't it, Rik? And I'm only thinking about the commercial side. Your head must be spinning with all the other aspects. Mikhail will give you my card. Call me, OK? Don't make me come looking for you.'

'Yeah, all right, Mr Marino.'

I had Gaz by the arm, leading him back down the corridor with the fluffy carpet. He didn't speak or struggle, and I was surprised by that. The radio in the kitchen was playing 'Purple Haze' by Jimi Hendrix. Mick was behind us. I remembered about Zak and looked back.

He was in the kitchen doorway, clutching his chest with one hand and waving with the other.

I waved back.

Mick had Gaz out the door already. When I caught up he gave me a card, saying: 'Next time, not bring your man here. He nasty boy.'

'He ain't nasty. He's all right,' I said. 'But maybe I won't bring him next time.'

We were going down the stairs. It was good to be out. I'd come such a long way since I'd walked up them, and now I wanted to think about that. Gaz was happily humming to himself anyway so I could ignore him and have a minute's quiet reflection. I couldn't begin to grasp what had happened here. And so quickly as well. Everything had been turned around. Baddies had becomes goodies, hopeless ambitions had been made possible. One minute the world had been full of bad magic, then it was normal and predictable and I had a place in it. I was an only child. Now I had a twin brother.

That was the sticking point, right there.

Because it just didn't seem right.

I mean, fair play, we looked a bit like each other. But you heard us together back there. I'd given it a go, you saw that. I'd gone into that kitchen and attempted a bit of bonding with him. But there was fuck all there. He was one type of person and I was another. He was a bit of a twat, to be honest. And I was the opposite of that.

Weren't twins meant to be peas in a pod?

Mind you, I could live with it. If Sam Marino wanted to make all my dreams come true on the back of it, fuck it, I was in. They'd think I was Zak Bremner, but who cares? I didn't give a shit as long as they gave me the love while I was up there. I had a life of superstardom stretching out before me. Stadium gigs, private jets, groupies, state of the art recording studios...I stopped.

I wanted to go back up there right now.

If there was a contract, I wanted it signed.

Right now.

Why fuck about? I'd spent my whole life fucking about. Marino was right – all I'd achieved so far was glorified karaoke. What a marvellous phrase, coming from a man who knew the business inside out and knew a star when he saw one. All that time I'd spent with Ted as my manager...what a fucking waste. And look how it had turned out:

All of them dead.

His madness had spread like poison, infecting everyone around him and dragging them into a hell that should have been for him alone. I was the only one who had got out of that. And it was no coincidence. I'd been spared. Fate had me down for higher things.

And now they were happening.

And the madness was behind me.

'...*tomorrow, or just the end of time...*'

'You what?' I said.

We were back on the street now. Gaz's humming had grown into full-on singing, as you've just heard.

'Oh, just that song,' he said. 'It's a sentimental song for me, "Purple Haze" is.'

'Yeah? I don't like heavy metal myself.'

'Metal? Oh, I see…No, it was written and recorded in a time before metal existed. Metal came out of it, yeah, but it weren't metal.'

'Oh yeah? I didn't know that. Look, I was just thinking about popping back up—'

'That's right. And do you know what, Rik? Some days…some mornings when I wake up, and I'm in and out of sleep still, I can remember it. I can remember writing that song. I feel the words as they first came to me, my fingers playing over the fretboard of my Strat.'

'Gaz,' I said, already halfway back up the ten or so steps leading to the main door, 'what the fuck are you on about?'

'I'm on about me writing that song. I'm Jimi Hendrix, Rik. Inside of this body is the soul of Hendrix, shifted here a long time ago by a very bad man who knew magic. Who *knows* magic, Rik. Didn't you know that?'

He came and stood on the step below the one I was on. He turned up his face and looked into my eyes.

'I mean, you must've known it. You've got it, just like me. Right there under your ear.'

'Got what, for fuck's sake?'

But I knew what. I could see it on him as well.

It was all true.

'The brand.'

We looked into each other's eyes for a moment, searching for the soul that was buried deep inside. I looked at his withered arm, and I knew he could see my lip. Then he looked at his watch.

'But...'

'But what?' he said.

'But...Marino.'

'Who's Marino?'

'Him up there. It was him who—'

'I got him covered, Rik. Come on,' he said, jogging on to the pavement. 'Not that my life's worth much, but we've got exactly one minute and...five seconds to...'

I couldn't hear what he was saying. He was off down the road.

I went after him.

'What?' I was shouting. 'What d'you mean, your life ain't worth much?'

'It ain't. And nor's yours. We're fucked, Rik. Our hours are numbered. Our souls are gonna get reaped, this very night. Any last ambitions you've got, it's time to drop your fears and go for it.'

'What are you on about? Can we just slow—'

'Forty seconds!'

'What is!'

'The cancer that eats at the heart of popular music – I'm curing it, Rik! I'm curing that cancer! That's my ambition. That is my final gift to the world.'

'Wait!'

'You said he was a tree, Rik...A pop svengali. And you're right. I couldn't believe it when I saw whatsisface in there... Cack Bremner. I left them a present, Rik. I dropped a little

273

calling card for them in the bathroom. I'm curing the cancer, Rik! Twenty seconds!'

'Twenty seconds till what? What calling card?'

I couldn't keep up with him. You'd never imagine that a stooped little weed like him could cover such ground. He went round the corner and peeked back around it, looking over my shoulder.

'Ten seconds!'

'Till what? *What*, Gaz? What are you lookin' at?'

'You'll see. And there's more, Rik. After this we've got the big one. It'll send out a message to the music industry, a big V-sign to the fat money men who want to fill our souls with crap! Or, should I say, a big "X" sign.'

I tried to see what he was seeing, looking back up the street. But there was nothing. Only a couple of cars and a group of lads walking past Marino's building back there. They all had the Bremner haircut.

'The message will spread like benign antibodies, wiping out the cancer and—'

The lads hit the deck as the top of Marino's building exploded, sending smoke, fire and bits of his luxury penthouse into the blackening sky.

I looked at Gaz, flames reflected in his mad eyes. His spots were glowing red, black hair billowing out behind him. He put a fist in the air and went: 'Yesss!'

'What? We got him?' I said.

'Too fuckin' right we got him!'

'So...What? Our souls are all right, now? They ain't gonna get stole away from us?'

'Eh? Course they fuckin' are! We're gonna die, Rik!'

'But...how can he get us now? You blew him up!'

'What the fuck are you on about? That bloke up there ain't

nothing to do with it, you twat! He's just a pop svengali. It's *Randy* who's reaping our souls!'

'Eh? Randy? You mean...do you mean that one from the Lamb and Flag?'

But he was off.

I went after him. It was hard because everyone else was going the other way, wanting to get a bit of warmth by the bonfire. I caught up with Gaz and grabbed his satchel as he went round the next corner.

'Get off it!' he screamed in my face, finally stopping. 'I still got one left in there and it's bloody fragile! And we need it, Rik. We got the big one to do yet! We're gonna lay down a marker – "X" marks the spot!'

He was off again already, me staggering behind him. I was flagging.

My soul was weak.

THE HUMAN SOUL: AN AFTERTHOUGHT

THE human soul is an obdurate thing. For years I have guarded my flock of hosts, and not once has one of them succumbed to the depression and despair to which I sentenced them upon replacing their common or garden souls with a high denomination version. I have learned much about the human spirit from observing these rare specimens, and gained a lot of assurance for when the time comes to cash them in and fight Beelzebub.

But I have learned more from observing the harelipped one, the goat disguised as a sheep. Despite having a vastly inferior soul to his stable-mates, he achieved more in his time that any of them. While they all buried their heads in the sand of thwarted ambition, he pressed ahead with his dreams.

In short, he got on with it.

Sometimes I have wondered if it is not *his* soul which is of greater value, though his urine runs yellow and his taste in music disgusts me. I have wondered if thirty-seven such average souls from the common herd might better serve me in my coming bid to ascend The Stairway. But it is irrelevant. I do not own his soul.

He is a free man.

37.

A shaft of light was beaming into the sky across town. It had been there since dusk, and seemed to be getting brighter. It was like a searchlight pointing up from the earth. Or down from space. And there was something else funny about it.

The doorbell went, and she went in off the balcony.

'Oh,' she said, peering over the chain at Elvis from next door, 'it's you.'

'Yeah. You all right, Shell? I was just wondering...are you scared, or anything? I mean, this malarkey in town and that. I thought you might be scared.'

'Malarkey?'

'Yeah...It's just that, well, I'm the Neighbourhood Watch repres—'

'You mean that armed robbery at the Post Office?'

'Eh? Oh, yeah. That and the blaze at the record shop. I thought you might want someone to—'

'Why would I be scared by that? I weren't in either of those places. And I'm safe at home anyhow.'

'I can see that. But I just thought…you know…'

He looked at the floor, shaking his head. There was a sound down the hall and he flinched, then pressed his fat body against the door.

'Fuckin' hell, Shell,' he whispered over the chain. 'I'm scared. I'm fuckin' scared, Shell! Can I sit with you? Can I just sit with you for a bit? *Please*?'

She did nothing for a while. Rarely had she ever even spoken to Elvis, so why should she let him in now? What did he want?

Then she caught the smell, coming over the waves of Blue Stratos aftershave. Sweat dripped from the end of his nose. Even through his dark glasses she could see the hunted look in his eyes.

'I'll let you in,' she said, unchaining the door, 'but only because I feel sorry for you. And my Rik's coming home any minute, all right? Just so you know.'

Elvis was inside before she'd finished speaking.

'I'll just go to your bog, if you don't mind. I can't seem to stop…erm…'

She went out on to the balcony and watched the light. It was a bit brighter, and seemed to be reaching towards some sort of dark mass above it in the sky, like an airship. But it was no airship.

'It ain't straight,' she said, when Elvis came out. 'That light out there ain't straight. Have you looked at it close? There's like a zigzag in it. Like…I dunno, like…'

'Stairs.'

'Yeah, that's it.'

She looked at him. He was sitting in Rik's armchair, rubbing his jowly face. She said: 'Do you know what it is, then?'

'Yeah, I do. It's the Lamb and Flag, up on the Tything.'

'Oh yeah? They said on the radio they don't know what it is. No one can get close, they're saying, because the whole area is—'

'Look, can we just watch a bit of telly? I'm sorry but...I'd just really like to watch a bit of telly with someone. Just for a bit. Come on, eh?'

'Well...' She came in and shut the door and curtains. 'For a bit, yeah. All right.' She turned on the telly and waited for the picture to come, which always took about four seconds. 'This all right for you?' she said when it came.

'Yeah. I like music.'

'I'll just make some tea. All right?'

From the kitchen door she examined the back of his head as he watched *The X Factor*. The kettle boiled behind her. When Rik came home, she decided, she would talk Elvis into getting some help.

'It's the live auditions, Shell!' he shouted, without turning. 'You're missing 'em.'

'Ooh, can't miss the live auditions, can I? I'll be with you in a sec, Elvis.'

There were so many people like him these days, depressed and afraid of the world outside. All they needed was a little medication.

'I've got some biscuits,' she said, putting the tray on the coffee table and sitting on the sofa. 'They're choccy ones.'

But he didn't hear. He was absorbed in the show. At least it would take his mind off his troubles. 'I didn't think it'd be on, Shell,' he said, eyes on the screen. 'They said earlier they'd caught someone trying to smuggle a bomb in.'

'A bomb? Where?'

'There, the telly studio where they're doing *The X Factor*.

Heard it on the radio, saying it was a lone terrorist or summat. It's barmy tonight, Shell. Kickin' off everywhere. But do you know what? The show must go on. It's the live auditions!'

She watched him, trying to think about mental health issues but actually thinking about loneliness and living alone. His face was still and exhausted, like someone who has stopped crying after a long time. But suddenly it came alive.

'Blinkin' heck,' he said, leaning close to the TV. 'Look who's here!'

She glanced at the screen, only half interested, then picked up a magazine. *The X Factor* wasn't a favourite show of hers – she preferred the soaps – but she'd seen enough of it to know that this was the audition stage. One clown after another was wheeled out for ritual sacrifice in front of the smug judges, with the occasional decent singer thrown in to make it all seem worthy. Rik hated this show and refused to apply for an audition. It cheapened the efforts of proper singers like himself, he always said, or something. Of course, the real reason was his harelip. Everyone knew that. It was one thing singing in front of your home town with a disfigurement like that, but it would take some guts to do it on national TV.

Rik didn't have that.

'Would you put *down* that fuckin' magazine and look at this, woman?' Elvis was shouting, pointing at the screen. 'It's your blinkin' bloke, that is!'

The magazine fell to the floor.

'*And you are...?*' the main judge was asking.

'*Rik Suntan.*'

'*Rik Suntan?*' one of the female judges was saying, sniggering. '*Niiice name. Were you born with it?*'

'*No, I was born David fuckin' Bowie. And tonight, Matthew, I'm gonna sing "Rock 'n' Roll Suicide".*'

'Matthew? Er, I think you've got the wrong show, erm, what was his name? And can we bleep that bit out?'

'Get down here!'

'Fuck! He's got a gun!'

'You – get down here! Not her, you. The fuckin' nasty bloke, whatsisname.'

'Listen, mister...Just put down the gun, and we'll—'

'Don't fuck me about! Get down here in front of me! Fuckin' shift!'

'Oh Jesus...'

'Move it! That's it, get down on yer knees there. Obolaye be kumbalay...Obolaye be.... Keep still, you cunt! Time takes a cigarette...Obolaye be kumbalaye...Puts it in your mouth... Obolaye be...'

Elvis grabbed the plate of biscuits and started cramming them into his mouth, saying: 'What's he doing, Shell? Why's he got that gun?'

'I...I dunno what's...'

'And why's he takin' his pants down and squatting, Shell? And he's...Is he doing a...?'

'Obolaye be kumbalaye...Oh no no no...Obolaye be kumb... nnnnnnnggggg...'

'Fuckin' hell, Shell! He's pulled the trigger! He's just fuckin' shot Simon—'

But Elvis's skeleton briefly flashed under his flesh, like an X-ray, and he fell back, unconscious. Outside, the stairway grew another step into the sky. The dark mass above it shimmered as a billion flies swarmed.

'Kumba...You're a rock 'n' roll suicide...Obalaye...nnnn nnnnnnnggggggg...'